THE FEMALE HEART
AND OTHER PLAYS

The Female Heart

Woman From the Other Side of the World

God, Sex and Blue Water

State Without Grace

by

Linda Faigao - Hall

Preface by Luis H. Francia

Afterword by Ian Morgan

Edited by Randy Gener

NoPassport Press

Dreaming the Americas Series

The Female Heart And Other Plays: The Female Heart;
Woman From the Other Side of the World; God, Sex and Blue
Water, State Without Grace by Linda Faigao-Hall, copyright
2013, 2012.

This publication is made possible in collaboration with NoPassport Press.

Book Cover Design: David Derr. Cover image photo credit: Holly
Laws. Interior Design: Randy Gener and Caridad Svich

ISBN: 978-1-300-66055-2

NoPassport Press: Dreaming the Americas Series. First edition 2013,
2012 by NoPassport Press, PO Box 1786, South Gate, CA 90280 USA;
NoPassportPress@aol.com, www.nopassport.org

The author dedicates this anthology to the two men in her life

Terence and Justin

without whom this would not exist.

PREFACE

BOATING ON TWO RIVERS

In Tagalog, there is a wonderful saying, *Namamangka sa dalawang ilog*: Boating on two rivers (at the same time, it is implied). An impossible task, it would seem. Yet, because of circumstances, people do the impossible all the time. This is certainly true of immigrants who move to these shores and, not necessarily cognizant of the Judeo-Christian tradition, must continually adjust their way of being in the United States to create some space for it while at the same time keeping alive (or attempting to keep alive) their own traditions. And it is certainly true of the Filipino expatriate, who *is* conversant with the Judeo-Christian context and partly for that very reason, and partly for reasons of a complex, colonialist history, can navigate the rivers of Malay, Hispanic, and American cultures.

Various cross-cultural currents have coursed through Philippine history, forming part of the modern-day Filipino's cultural DNA. Many elements of those cultures, and the changes that ensued, were forcibly introduced by strangers from different shores who had seen in the inhabitants of this Southeast Asian archipelago putative subjects of colonial kingdoms. This might be the only advantage of the colonial experience, one that is extremely useful in this age of globalization: the ability to be in several places at the same time, while holding still; to speak more than one language; to be able to consider several, even contradictory, trains of thought simultaneously, without being fazed. In this ever-shifting landscape, ambiguity looms as a permanent feature, where hybridity reduces nationalisms to pieces of paper, and borders exist so that we may cross them.

In his fiercely lyrical *America Is in the Heart*, a classic of Asian-American literature, Carlos Bulosan charts the travels—and travails—of his alter ego, Allos, who escapes drowning in the sea of troubles that this country was to brown men in the era before World War II, when racism, blatant exploitation, and emasculation constituted their lot. An intrepid navigator of troubled waters, Allos not only survives—he is after all used to boating on two rivers at the same time—he also participates actively in the shaping of the American Dream.

In like fashion, a strikingly similar voyage is what the playwright Linda Faigao charts as well. She is a keen and, often unsettlingly so, accurate observer of the Filipino/a boating on two rivers. She zeroes in, not on the physical voyage, which, while essential, is much less interesting than the interior voyage, one that never fails to astonish, terrify, humble, frustrate and exhilarate. It is a voyage that never ends.

This interiority, that mirrors and at the same time eclipses the physical one, is what Faigao explores. Not that the external world fades into irrelevance. On the contrary, the classic impetus for the immigrant voyage, the desire for a vast improvement over a demeaning life due to poverty and oppression (economic as well as social and political), provides the setting and catalyst for the dramatic action. But it is a journey that is preamble to the real one, one that isn't necessarily seen by the naked eye, or that people often turn their backs on.

Faigao works within the solid tradition of the emigré artist who comes from elsewhere, who *is* in the United States but not always *of* it. Which makes her an acute and imaginative chronicler of what ensues when the past that is never quite the past and the utilitarian present come up, like geological plates, against each other, upending smooth narrative arcs. This threat of perpetual derailment, much as the monsoon or fierce tropical heat in the Philippines, is a constant element in the lives Faigao-Hall cares very much about, particularly those of women of color.

This voyage of interiority might appear to be familiar territory and much of it is. But lurking always in the wings, as it were, are the specters of the amorphous, the different, the other, the weird configurations that each journey takes, shaped very much by the unique cultural currents that flow in and through that particular journey, that make the journey possible at the same time that they work against it. No two journeys are alike: every journey that is worthwhile is worthwhile in its own way.

No longer is it enough, if it ever was, to presume that the classic voyage limned in mainstream U.S. theater—that of Willy Loman, say, in Arthur Miller's *Death of a Salesman,* or of the Tyrones in Eugene O'Neill's *Long Day's Journey into Night*—will do for all the various partners in the American enterprise, who now come in all colors and creeds, all these varied voices remaking American theater (and the other arts as well), aspiring to a Whitmanesque vision of a multitudinous, noisy democracy that is equally true in the arena of theater as it is in politics. Cultural contexts once viewed as exotic are now routinely invoked and evoked, confronted, examined, and questioned, as part of what defines not just American characters but the very character of America itself.

Part of the difficulty that confronts artists of color, whether in the theater or in literature, is the presumption that mainstream models should suffice to speak universally. It is a familiar argument that astonishingly in the twenty-first century continues to hold some currency. The postcolonial Asian-American has her own multilayered existence, where such ambivalences do not provoke suspicion, and resistance to a homogenizing assimilation is a given, but not always successful. Faigao's characters break out of the straitjacket that is monoculturalism; if there is to be a unity it has to be one born of diversity.

Thus, in *God, Sex & Blue Water*, Clarita Kintanar's stigmata, acquired in a Philippine island now buried beneath the waves, erupts at inopportune moments in her Brooklyn life, a tangible reminder of what she remains even in a setting that would argue against such manifestations. Adelfa Ocon in *The Female Heart* experiences a feminist epiphany about her origins and her condition, in a land where the only constant seems to be capital with its ravenous appetite for consumption, and where even humanity has a dollar sticker.

They are brave, adventurous souls and encapsulate perfectly Linda Faigao's own brave voyage into the no-longer-new world, bearing the precious gift of navigating two rivers at the same time—a transformative force she so wisely uses for her art.

LUIS H. FRANCIA

THE FEMALE HEART

By

Linda Faigao-Hall

THE FEMALE HEART
Premiered in 2006 at Diverse City Theater Company &
Ensemble Studio Theater in New York City.

Cast of Characters:

Anghel, a Filipino, late 20's

Adelfa, his sister, early 20's

Rosario, their mother, 50's

Roger, Caucasian-American, early to mid-30's

Time: 1992 - 2001

Place: The action shifts between Manila, Philippines and
Park Slope, Brooklyn, New York, 1992 to 2001.

> (There are two spaces: one is set in the present, in
> Park Slope, Brooklyn, New York, a well-appointed
> bedroom with two sidetables, a television set, a
> telephone.
>
> The other is the landscape of ADELFA's
> memory where distant and recent past
> events come to life.
>
> This play's text will indicate whenever
> action occurs in the present.
>
> AT RISE: Spring 2001 in Park Slope. A TV
> dance program is on, music spilling into the
> space. ADELFA is picking up letters strewn
> on the bed, sorting them in date order. As

she nears the end of this sorting, she finds a red envelope still unopened. She picks it up and stares at it. It reminds her of something. Dance music goes up. A few beats.)

ADELFA (VOICEOVER): "Reverend Mother Superior Natividad, Reverend Father Kintanar, my mother and my brother Kuya Anghel, my dearest sisters and brothers in the parish of the Risen Christ –

(Lights go up on ANGHEL in Smokey Mountain: he's seated on a bench, eating purple yam ice cream, watching ADELFA who's standing in front of him, reading from a sheet of paper. ANGEL's face has been half-covered by a handkerchief but now it's slipped and it is now draped around his neck. He is wearing plastic gloves and boots and next to him is a hook-shaped metal rod. Once in awhile, popping sounds can be heard coming from the trash.)

ADELFA: "… and our honored funders and benefactors at our sister parish in Sydney, Australia. Today, June 15, 1992, I graduate from the parish of the Risen Christ High School in Smokey Mountain in the Philippines."

ANGHEL: (Clapping his hands.) Spriketek! 'tang ina! Ang galing mo!

ADELFA: That's just the introduction,Kuya.

(ANGHEL gives her the rest of his ice cream.)

ANGHEL: Lola Epang's ube. Today's special.

ADELFA: Salamat, po.

ANGHEL: Sikat mo talaga. Making speeches. Just like those politicians on TV!

ADELFA: Father Kintanar said he's taping it and sending it to Sydney.

ANGEL: Sydney? Talaga ba? You mean everyone in Australia will know you're a baldictatorian! First high school graduate in all of Smokey.

ADELFA: Valedictorian. Hindi naman. Lola Epang finished high school. Her diploma's hanging outside her window, di ba.

ANGHEL: Uy, she found that one in the trash.

ADELFA: Tutuo ba?

ANGHEL: She wrote her name on it! Sigi na. What else are you going to say?

ADELFA: I have to thank everybody. My teacher Mr. Paredes... Mother Superior. God. But I told Father K, I only want to thank my mother and my brother. I only want to thank you, Kuya, and Inay.

ANGHEL: That's a short speech.

ADELFA: Then I'll tell the parents of Smokey to get out of here. Leave this place. So let your children stay in school.

ANGHEL: Aba, not everyone is a baledictorian like you, Adelfa. Their parents pull them out because they need help working the garbage.

ADELFA: Then there's no escape.

ANGHEL: Hindi naman. If they work hard, they'll do well. Look at us. We own the biggest junk shop in all of Smokey. Seventeen jumpers work for us. And I'm the boss. And besides, it's not garbage. It's recyling. Waste management, di ba? Your own words.

ADELFA: It's still garbage. Basora.

ANGHEL: High school graduate lang, ang yabang mo. It takes a man to do this job. And it's honest work. It's better than begging. And it's always here. Nobody loses his job. Even Marcos lost his job, di ba? And here, in the bottom of the world, there's nowhere to go but up.

ADELFA: I'm sorry, Kuya. I didn't mean -

ANGHEL: The best part of Smokey. Basora from Hyatt. From tourists. And it's ours.

ADELFA: I promise, Kuya, as soon as I get that high school diploma, I'll go find work at the mall. A salesgirl. I'll be wearing a nice clean dress, selling shoes, handbags, RTW's. And the only people who'll take away basora will be the janitors. Then I'll get you and Inay out of Smokey into a rooming house in Baclaran.

ANGHEL: A rooming house in Baclaran. And what will I be doing?

ADELFA: I'll find something for you at the mall.

13

ANGHEL: And what will I show them? Lola Epang's diploma? The nearest I ever been to school was picking up trash from La Salle Boys High.

ADELFA: You went to school.

ANGHEL: Until fifth grade only. That won't even get me a job at Shakey's Pizza.

ADELFA: Nobody human should live like this!

> (Lights change. A slide show of ADELFA giving her speech, and clips of Smokey Mountain.)

ADELFA: "... June 15, 1992, I graduate from the parish of the Risen Christ High School in a community called Smokey Mountain in the Philippines, my home. I was born here. And just like any community in millions of places in my beloved country, it has clinics. Schools. A church. Junk shops, food stalls. Even ice cream.

Except that underneath my feet, is a cement footpath that winds its way through 18 hectares of trash, 750 feet high. To our honored donors at our sister parish in Sydney, Australia, this is equivalent to a mountain of garbage as big as 45 football fields and as high as an eight-story building. Yet it is home to twenty thousand people who live and work here, searching for scrap metal and other recyclables, enduring the stench, the flies, the toxic waste, and the smoke that gives the mountain its name, the fog and haze that come from the spontaneous combustion of sewage – Smokey Mountain... "

> (Lights change.

ANGHEL is scavenging. ADELFA enters;
she looks exhausted, dispirited. She's
carrying a cup of coffee. She sits on a stool.
ANGHEL joins her. She gives him the
coffee. ANGHEL takes it.)

ADELFA: Cuppa Java. Coffee. Eighty-five pesos.

(ANGHEL almost drops it.)

ANGHEL: 'Tang ina! Eighty-five pesos? What's in it?
Imelda's pee?

ADELFA: Café latte. Coffee from America. The manager
is a friend of mine.

ANGHEL: What's wrong with Nestle?

ADELFA: Mas masarap ito, Kuya.

ANGHEL: O sigi nga. (Taking a sip, expecting
something different. A beat.) It's still coffee!

ADELFA: (Disconsolate.) And I'm still jobless. Dunkin'
Donuts. Kentucky Fried Chicken. Cuppa Java. Zero.

ANGHEL: I know. I know. You come home every day,
looking so sad. Don't be discouraged. One of these days,
it will happen. I guarantee it.

ADELFA: It's been a month! There's just too many of us.
And so few jobs. Saleslady. Waitress. Barrista. Nothing.

ANGHEL: Barrista?

ADELFA: They make this coffee. Four thousand pesos a
month, Kuya.

ANGHEL: Four thousand a month? Just for making coffee?

ADELFA: I told you. It's not just coffee. Café latte. Cappuccino, espresso. But I'm only a high school grad!

ANGHEL: (Peers into his sack and takes out a tight ball of black debris. He peels it with a knife. Underneath is a bar of soap.) Cheer up.

ADELFA: (Smelling it.) Palmolive?

ANGHEL: Ivory.

ADELFA: Thank you, Kuya.

ANGHEL: What do you think of Cebu Teacher's College?

ADELFA: Mr Paredes. He went to Cebu Teacher's.

ANGHEL: So you wanna go there?

ADELFA: What?

ANGHEL: Do. You. Want. To. Go. There.

ADELFA: I heard you the first time, Kuya. It's not funny.

ANGHEL: Uy, am I laughing? Don't you have dreams, Adelfa?

ADELFA: I used to.

ANGHEL: You stop dreaming, you die. You'll find a job at the mall, then we'll rent a room in Baclaran. You'll have a nice clean job making kape latti. And then what? Didn't you say you wanted to be a teacher once?

ADELFA: That was a long time ago, Kuya.

ANGHEL: So how about now?

ADELFA: Stop playing with me. It's cruel. And I'm tired.

ANGHEL: They don't call me Anghel for nothing. Something miraculous has happened!

ADELFA: What are you talking about?

> (ROSARIO enters, from behind a mound, carrying a sack.)

ROSARIO: Adelfa, jackpot! Jackpot! Did you tell her? To even dream of a way out… Stinky Mountain. Hopeless Mountain. If your Itay could see us now…

ANGHEL: I'd spit in his face, 'tang ina.

ROSARIO: Remember when you wanted to go back to Bicol. But I told you to stay. Stay in Smokey. There's hope here. Where there's garbage, there's life.

ADELFA: Did we win the sweepstakes?

ANGHEL: I sold the junk shop. Lola Epang met our terms. An hour ago.

ADELFA: But she's been trying to buy it for years!

ROSARIO: She's no fool, Lola Epang. She thinks there's a future here. All these foreigners sending money.

ANGHEL: The money from the shop will pay for your first year of school. We'll figure out the rest.

> (ANGHEL picks up a piece of debris,
> flinging it over his shoulder.)

ADELFA: But what will you and Inay live on?

ANGHEL: I'm selling everything. Our lots, too. The
Hyatt. (Jumping to another mound, gesturing, like a
king.) This one. Tio Berto had this lot since the 50's. Itay
inherited it in 1974 –

ROSARIO: No. 1970.

ANGHEL: 1974, Inay.

ROSARIO: No. Your Itay split in '70.

ADELFA: Stop arguing. I don't understand!

ANGHEL: Adelfa, who's the best dancer in the barrio?

ADELFA: You. Except maybe for Ronald Reagan
Rampatanta. But he's getting old. What has this got to do
with anything?

> (ANGHEL picks up the cassette tape
> recorder from DL.)

ANGHEL: Spare parts from the dump. I put it together
myself. A 'demo tape.' Last week I went to see someone
in Quiapo who's got a dancing school there. I'm going to
be a DI!

ADELFA: A DI? A dance instructor!

ANGHEL: Remember the Mother Teresa Hip Hop Jam?

ADELFA: When you won first prize?

ANGHEL: He saw me dance. He said if I ever needed a job to look him up. So I did.

ADELFA: (Breathlessly.)And?

ANGHEL: (Shaking her hand.) Good evening, Ma'am. I'm your D.I. for the evening, Ma'am. My boss taught me how to say it. Okay, ba?

ADELFA: Okay? It's perfect!

ROSARIO: I will never sell another piece of junk in my life. This time tomorrow everyone will be envious of us.

ANGHEL: The boss is giving me an attaché case, so people will think I'm a lawyer. You'll have to call me attorney. That's me, Adelfa. Attorney Anghel Ocon

ROSARIO: And lonely rich ladies from Green Hills will pay you to dance with them at the Marriott.

ANGHEL: Sabi nang boss, he said the best D.I.'s make one thousand five a night. But if I get the American tourists, I'll get paid in dollars. One hundred dollars a night, daw! How much is that, Adelfa.

ADELFA: One US dollar is 40 pesos... four thousand pesos. That's how much barristas make a month! One hundred dollars a month. You can make that in one night?

ANGHEL: Spriketek! I'll work overtime. Hit all the hotels. I have connections. I know all the garbage people there.

ROSARIO: Then one day you'll meet someone young and beautiful and rich who'll fall in love with you.

ANGHEL: And I'll be honest with her. I'll tell her I used to live in Smokey -

ROSARIO: Punieta. Why?

ANGHEL: If she holds it against me that's how I'll know she's not the one, di ba?

ADELFA: Cebu Teacher's College...Me. It's never been done before. Nobody from Smokey ever went to college. I can't believe it. I'm dreaming. Is it a dream?

> (ROSARIO sits down and opens her sack, peering inside.)

ROSARIO: My last pick! (She spots something, takes it out.) No label? (Opens it, smelling it.) Jackpot! Oil of Olay. Tourists. They throw everything away too soon. (Takes out a baby food glass jar) Baby food. You know Father Kintanar gives me ten pesos for fifty of these? Sabi candle holders. But Lola Epang said she'll sell them for twenty. Pambihira. (Throwing it back to the lot.) Americans. Food just for babies...

ADELFA: They have food just for dogs.

ROSARIO: What?

ADELFA: For cats, too.

ROSARIO: (To ANGHEL.) Tutuo, ba?

ANGHEL: This used to be trash from the PX years ago. (Spots a printer cartridge from the ground.) Punieta.

Look at this. I got a bunch of assholes working for me! They missed this! A printer cartrid.

ROSARIO: Susmariosep. Hayteek.

ADELFA: 'High tech.' It means high technology. 'High tech.'

ROSARIO: 'High tekology .' They missed it.

ANGHEL: They have no motivation. 'High tik' is the best thing that ever happened to garbage. See? A Canon. One hundred and fifty pesos…easy.

ROSARIO: Lola Epang will probably sell it for three hundred. (Beat.) The hours I spent on my knees praying for this day to come… (To ADELFA.) I was right. I knew you'd be the one.

ADELFA: I promise you, Inay. This mountain will never cast its shadow on us again. (To ANGHEL.) What changed your mind, Kuya?

ANGHEL: Graduation day. On the stage. When they called your name - Maria Adelfa Ocon – Baledictorian! And that speech. Proudest moment of my life. I knew then without a doubt - how you're made for bigger things, Adelfa. (Touching her face.) You're not going to be a salesgirl. You're going to be a teacher. Inay is right. You're the ticket.

> (ADELFA watches wide-eyed as ANGHEL jumps from his perch and turns the tape deck on.

Dance music roars into the space. Some parts of the music is reminiscent of the music heard when the play began.)

ANGHEL: (To ADELFA, in English.) Good evening, Ma'am. I'm your DI for the evening.

(ADELFA and ANGHEL dance. ROSARIO joins them.)

ROSARIO/ADELFA/ANGHEL: O. Cha cha! … aba...salsa! … tango! … disco! Disco!

(They dance, their bodies moving in perfect harmony as Smokey Mountain casts its long shadow on their happy hopeful faces. The music segues into rap music.)

ROSARIO: (Freezing in her tracks.) Ano yan?

ADELFA: Rap, Inay. Rap!

ROSARIO: Rap? (She's a quick study. She resumes dancing.) Wow! Super star, o. Super star.

(Lights change. Two years later.

Strobe lights go up in the memoryscape, the throb of harsh, deafening dance music. Air is thick with the smell of sweat, heat, bodies undulating in the dark.

ROSARIO, carrying a small bag, and ADELFA enter.

A male in a g-string enters, dancing. A piercing wave of sound, cheers and catcalls collide with the music. The man is graceful, erotic, sensual. Water from somewhere above him cascades down his body; he caresses himself, his hands leaving swirls of white foam where they slip and glide. This is macho dancing. A spotlight hits the dancer. It is ANGHEL.

The music rises, the dance becoming more sexually suggestive. ANGHEL begins to strip; the music gets louder and more abrasive. ADELFA watches in horror and then flees from the scene followed by ROSARIO.)

ADELFA: The Angel of Desire? He's the Angel of Desire?

ROSARIO: He's the club's biggest dancer, Adelfa. They say he's bigger than Spartacus, the star he replaced.

ADELFA: Spartacus. I don't know what you're talking about? How long has he been doing this?

ROSARIO: Right after you left for college.

ADELFA: That was two years ago! Two years ago he was a D.I.

ROSARIO: He was never a D.I.

ADELFA: What?

ROSARIO: Soon after you left, Peaches spotted him outside the club —

ADELFA: Peaches Bodoy? She's a prostitute, Inay. What does she have to do with this?

ROSARIO: You know her mother, Cherry Pie. She used to live in Smokey years ago. Peaches saw him outside the club and she told Lola Epang –

ADELFA: You listen to gossip, Inay?

ROSARIO: And Lola Epang told me. One night I followed him to work – I saw it all. He asked me to keep it from you.

ADELFA: And you agreed? All this time, you knew and you didn't tell me? Is he bakla? Is he gay?

ROSARIO: Don't you know your own brother?

ADELFA: Some people say if you do this work long enough, a man will turn gay.

ROSARIO: He's more of a man than your Itay ever was. How do you think we could pay for your school and the rent?

ADELFA: But a macho dancer. A macho dancer!

ROSARIO: Half of those dancers are married. Their wives wait outside the club with food. During the break they have supper together. I wait with them. I bring Angel his change of clothes.

> (ANGHEL enters. At first he doesn't see
> ADELFA. He opens ROSARIO's small
> overnight bag and takes out a T-shirt. Then
> he sees ADELFA. A few beats.)

ANGHEL: What are you doing here? (To ROSARIO) What's she doing here, Inay?

ROSARIO: I'm tired of keeping secrets!

ADELFA: You lied to me.

ANGHEL: Yes, I did.

ADELFA: Why?

ANGHEL: From Smokey Mountain to the Hyatt? Did you really believe that? I can't get past the security guard!

ADELFA: I don't get it!

ANGHEL: Packaged sex tours for gay men. What is it you don't get?

ADELFA: You're not even gay!

ANGHEL: It's a business. I'm a professional. Spartacus - it took him a year before they'd let him do the soap and water number. It took me three months. I'm a star, Adelfa. I have repeat customers from all over the world, paying me in dollars, marks, yen. I'm still king of the goddamn mountain.

ADELFA: That day at Smokey. I told you I was going to get us out of there.

ANGHEL: Serving coffee to the rich and stupid? We'd be back in Smokey sooner than you think. Didn't you tell me nobody human should live there?

ADELFA: They closed Smokey down.

ANGHEL: And many more dumps take its place. Same mountain. Same people. There are dogs in Makati that live better. I can't go back, Adelfa. It's too late. I've seen the world.

(He is seized by a spasm of coughs.)

ANGHEL: I have another show in ten minutes. (Pause.) You were ashamed of Smokey. Are you ashamed of this one, too?

(He exits.)

ADELFA: Two years you kept it to yourself!

ROSARIO: He wanted you to finish college.

ADELFA: (Impetuously.) So why am I here? There's a boat going back to Cebu in an hour. I have papers to write. Exams next week!

ROSARIO: (Fiercely.) Adelfa! Sasampalin kita. I'm making dresses for the office girls in the apartment building next door. But they're going to the mall and buying them off the rack. RTW's. Ready to Wears! Punieta. I'm losing my customers. I can't make enough for him to quit and for you to continue with school.

ADELFA: Quit? Does he want to quit?

ROSARIO: Didn't you see how thin he is?

ADELFA: I'm not blind!

ROSARIO: He's tired all the time. There are days he can't get out of bed; nights, he wakes up sweating; he's cough's gotten worse. Last week, he began complaining of chest pains.

ADELFA: Has he been to the clinic?

ROSARIO: He takes pills. They don't help. That's why I asked you to come. To see for yourself.

ADELFA: Maybe he needs a break. Maybe that's all he needs.

ROSARIO: Then we will continue to be blessed. But what if he's really sick?

(ADELFA falls quiet.)

ROSARIO: I've borne this shame in silence. I don't pray anymore. All my prayers come up hard as stones. I could even bear the thought of going to hell. But I will not watch my own child die.

ADELFA: Die? Why are you saying that? He's not going to die!

ROSARIO: Spartacus was complaining of chest pains. Now he's dead. I'm afraid to think!

ADELFA: Inay. Inay. Let's not jump to conclusions.

ROSARIO: They're building a new mall. Lola Epang said it's the biggest mall in Asia. Maybe you can get a job there.

ADELFA: You need a college diploma, Inay. And only the very rich go there. I'm not even sure if they'll let me in the door. Salvatore Ferragamo… Versace…

ROSARIO: You can do it. I know it. I feel it in my bones. You're young and strong --

ADELFA: And hopeful. All I had was hope. And you put it there.

ROSARIO: I'm so sorry, anak. But that dream is over.

> (Silence, like a heavy blanket, falls on both of them, muffling all sound.)

ROSARIO: You understand, don't you?

ADELFA: Wait. Wait. Please.

> (ADELFA begins to weep.)

ROSARIO: Are you crying for yourself or for him?

ADELFA: I don't know where I end and he begins.

ROSARIO: We survived Smokey. We will survive this one.

> (Lights change. A year later.)

ADELFA: It's Roger's. As he promised, Inay. An airline ticket. And a check.

ROSARIO: Jackpot! How quickly God answers all my prayers. No. Better than the jackpot. A miracle. Angel is safe.

> (ANGHEL walks in on them. Something has gone out of him. He looks sick and frail. During this scene, ANGHEL coughs into a handkerchief occasionally.)

ANGHEL: Safe from what?

(ADELFA shows him the airline ticket.)

ANGHEL: What's that?

ADELFA: An airplane ticket to America. And a check.

ANGHEL: Five hundred dollars. Where did you get it?
Who gave it to you?

ADELFA: I went to the library - there's hundreds -
maybe, thousands of American men who want Filipino
wives.

ANGHEL: What are you talking about?

(ROSARIO brings out a catalogue and
places it on the table. ANGHEL peers down
at it.)

ANGHEL: (Trying to read it.) Ke—kerry – blossoms?

ADELFA: 'Cherry Blossoms.' They bloom in Japan.

ANGHEL: So what's that to us?

(ROSARIO opens it to a page. ANGHEL
looks at it and takes a step back. He looks at
ADELFA.)

ANGHEL: What's your picture doing in it?

ADELFA: It's a business, Kuya. A mail order bride
catalogue business. A woman sends her picture to this
catalogue, and it's published. A man who's looking for a

wife buys the book for fifty dollars, and if he likes her picture he writes to her.

ANGHEL: Pen pals?

ADELFA: No. Cherry Blossoms is only for men looking for wives. Six thousand women, Kuya, in this book alone. Half of them from the Philippines.

ANGHEL: (He sweeps the book off the table.) Whose idea was this?

ROSARIO: Mine.

ANGHEL: Inay?

ADELFA: I received ten letters – from Germany, Australia, Canada, the US –

ANGHEL: From all over the world. Just like the men I dance for. So we're two of a kind, Adelfa? There's nothing special about you either?

ADELFA: I was honest. I was ready to be any man's wife for three hundred dollars a month. Only one wrote back. An American. Roger Flynn. He's got a real estate business in a place called Brooklyn.

ANGHEL: How do you know he's not black? Or an old man?

(ADELFA gives him a photograph.)

ANGHEL: (Looks at it.) But he's very handsome. What's wrong with him? And how do you know it's him?

ADELFA: He fits what they say in the book. (Opening to a page, reading.) "Demographic profiles of men –"

ANGHEL: What?

ADELFA: " ... seeking mail-order brides... 94% white... in their thirties... incomes higher than average..."

ANGHEL: So what?

ADELFA: They need to have money, Kuya. They have to pay for travel. And they're educated. "Only 5% never finished high school, 42% are in professional and managerial positions" -

ROSARIO: And tall! Very tall! Average height, five feet seven!

(ANGHEL and ADELFA look at ROSARIO. A beat.)

ADELFA: And if it doesn't work, the agency will send me home. For the man, there's a money back guarantee.

(ANGHEL grabs the ticket to rip it up but ADELFA and ROSARIO struggle with him. ROSARIO manages to pull the ticket away from ANGHEL.)

ANGHEL: How long has this been going on? And behind my back? Don't you have any respect?

ADELFA: Since I quit school.

ANGHEL: Quit? You said you're just taking the year off!

ADELFA: You're sick.

ANGHEL: I feel better everyday. I'm going back to work and you're going back to school! I'm taking the pills they're giving me at the clinic.

ADELFA: St. Joseph's aspirin? Who are they? Volunteers. Socialites from Makati. I've tried the mall. But the money would only pay for the rooming house. Inay's laundry – the food. But nothing for a doctor. A real doctor. In a hospital. Three hundred dollars a month will take care of it all.

ANGHEL: I'd rather you sold shoes. Marrying a man you've never met - how did that happen? It doesn't make sense!

ADELFA: At first I thought of being an OFW. An overseas worker. So I took a test.

ANGHEL: What test?

ADELFA: A government test. It was very easy. Cooking, sewing, baby-sitting. Entertainment skills. They give you a certificate that says you're an artist. They send you overseas. Even arrange the visas.

ROSARIO: At first, they wanted to send her to Saudi.

ANGHEL: Do you know how many women come back in body bags from the fucking Middle East?

ADELFA: I know that! So I thought of Japan.

ANGHEL: Japayukis! (To ROSARIO.) I thought you didn't want her to be a whore!

ROSARIO: Watch your mouth! That's why she's going as a mail-order bride. Adelfa will be a wife in the eyes of the law and of God. Married to an American, living in America. How many women in the country would go through hell to get the same chance?

ADELFA: Some marriages turn out right. Here. (Taking out sheets of paper.) Copies of letters from women who found husbands. Good husbands. The office clerk gave them to me. It's a risk I'm willing to take.

ANGHEL: Why?

ADELFA: You're sick. And we're poor. We'll always be poor. But I can get you well. It's something I can do. Be someone's wife.

ANGHEL: Aren't you afraid for yourself?

ADELFA: We're more afraid for you.

ANGHEL: Don't you want to fall in love someday? You're giving away your life.

ADELFA: And why not? You've given yours.

ANGHEL: But not my heart.

>   (ANGHEL is seized by a spasm of deep, racking coughs. He exits.)

ROSARIO: He's been spitting blood. Take the check and cash it. Marry this man Mr. Flynn. And save your brother's life. God will bless you.

>   (Lights change. Four months later.)

ANGHEL (V.O.): "My dear Adelfa, You said snow looked like dust dancing in the wind. I thought it came down all at once, like a blanket. Splat. And there it is. So did you eat it. Father K says that's how the Chinese invented ice cream. They put sugar in snow. Guy named Marco Polo loved it and gave it to the world. Never heard of him. Is it true? Your loving brother, Kuya Angel...

ROSARIO (V.O): "That photo in the Prospect Park. When I saw it, I cried. As if you were inside a Christmas card. Then you said snow has many shades of white? White is white. Then you said Roger had to use a pick axe to break up the frozen black mud. What black mud? So what happened to the white snow? Next time, explain everything, ok? Love, Inay "

> (Lights on ROGER in the memoryscape.
> ADELFA is wearing a white cotton dress.)

ROGER: Your pictures didn't do you justice. We've been married a month, and I still can't keep my eyes off you.

> (He gives her an elegantly-wrapped gift. He puts it on the bed.)

ROGER: Open it.

ADELFA: Another one?

> (ADELFA unwraps it. It is a beautiful piece of batik sarong.)

ADELFA: It's beautiful.

ROGER: Only the best. Because you're precious. Go ahead. Try it on. Take down your hair, please?

> (ADELFA exits. ROGER sits on the bed, waiting in anticipation.)

ROGER: I've always loved Oriental women. Now I'm married to one... am I lucky or what?

> (ADELFA comes back in, wearing the sarong. She has taken down her hair, and has transformed herself into what looks like a 'fantasy' of the 'exotic Oriental'. ROGER is stunned by her transformation.)

ROGER: You must never wear anything else.

> (She starts to take off the batik.)

ROGER: No. Keep it on. This one fits all my pictures.

> (He kisses her. There is something harsh and insistent about his kiss. ROGER gets carried away and whacks her behind, sharply. ADELFA instinctively pulls back.)

ADELFA: What's wrong? You're angry with me? I won't wear anything else, I promise!

ROGER: I've been very gentle with you. All this time. Patient.

ADELFA: Yes. You are gentle. Very gentle. So why are you angry now?

ROGER: I'm not angry. (Laughing sheepishly.) I'm just playing.

ADELFA: Playing?

ROGER: (He holds out his arms to her.) You know you can hit me back.

ADELFA: What?

ROGER: Hit me back. I'm a bad boy... go on. Hit me. I won't get angry. Promise...

> (ADELFA gives him a light slap, playfully, unsure of herself. ROGER laughs. ADELFA begins to laugh, too. He pulls her tenderly in his arms.)

ROGER: See? Don't look so scared. I'm harmless. Really. (Pause.) Don't hate me, please.

ADELFA: Hate you? I don't know you. How can I hate you?

ROGER: We're married now. You're my wife.

ADELFA: Did I do something wrong?

ROGER: No, no, no. I fell in love with you just from reading your letters. But seeing you the first time – bringing you here – this past Christmas has been the best I've ever had... I'm the luckiest man in the world. (Kissing her tenderly.) I'm gonna take care of you... you and your family. I promised you that.

ADELFA: That was the agreement.

ROGER: Best deal I ever made. Hey, don't cook tonight. You like Italian? Let's go to Cucina.

ADELFA: Pizza? (Pronouncing it 'pi-cha')

ROGER: No. Not pizza. How about fettuccini Alfredo.

(ADELFA tries to take off her sarong.)

ROGER: I really like you in it. Always look like that, please? It fits all my pictures.

(Lights change. The telephone rings. ADELFA picks it up.)

ADELFA: Hello?... Yes. I accept.

ROSARIO: Adelfa? Did I wake you? What time is it there?

ADELFA: It's seven in the evening, Inay. Where are you calling from?

ROSARIO: I'm at the mall. I'm using a phone card.

ADELFA: Is Kuya Angel with you? May I speak with him?

ROSARIO: He's at home, resting. Where's Roger?

ADELFA: He's at work. He should be home soon.

ROSARIO: Send us more pictures, okay, anak?

ADELFA: I just sent –

ROSARIO: And the food? Are you finally getting used to the food?

ADELFA: The food? Last night we had --

ROSARIO: You know what we did last night? Angel, Ronald Reagan Rampatanta and I went to Lola Epang's carenderia for dinner. We ordered the Special Beefstik. I wore a white dress. It was so clean.

ADELFA: That's nice, Inay.

ROSARIO: We couldn't finish the beefstik. We had it for breakfast the next day and lunch and dinner.   Why are you so quiet?

ADELFA: You talk, Inay. I'll listen.

ROSARIO: Anak, I'm so ashamed to bring this up.

ADELFA: Ano yan, Inay.

ROSARIO: Adelfa, anak, has he started giving you the three hundred?

ADELFA: Bakit, Inay?

ROSARIO: We went to PG Hospital for a check-up. But they asked him to stay overnight – the next day, I was short 2,500 pesos. So the hospital didn't release him.

ADELFA: What do you mean, Inay?

ROSARIO: Sabi daw, they'll hold him until I can pay in full. Ang galit ko. I was so angry. I wanted him to just walk out. But I didn't know where they put him. Sabi daw he's in a special room. I tried looking for him but it's like an open market - like Divisoria – it was so crowded and big - so many sick people.

ADELFA: So what did you do? Where's Roger's five hundred dollars?

ROSARIO: That's what happened. I gave it all to a Dr. Valdes, a private specialist. He was able to get him out of there. Okay ba, anak?

ADELFA: (Relieved.) Opo, Inay. Get the best. Do you understand? Get the best.

ROSARIO: Thank you, Adelfa. I'm so confused. Even in Smokey, working twenty years, he's never been sick like this. What did you want to say to Angel?

ADELFA: I just wanted to hear his voice. (Pause.) Inay, I'm so – confused.

ROSARIO: About what?

ADELFA: Being married.

ROSARIO: (Laughing.) Ay, naku. Just be patient. You'll figure it out soon enough.

ADELFA: I hope so.

ROSARIO: Men are easy, Adelfa. Just do what they say. I have to go, anak.

ADELFA: Please call me again tomorrow. I miss you and Kuya Angel! I love you!

(Lights change. Three months later.

ANGHEL (V.O.): What's that you're wearing, a malong? Is that the fashion there? Half a year into your marriage and you already look like an American!

ROSARIO: Dr. Valdes wants to do more tests. They're very expensive. I'd put away fifty dollars for a telephone but perhaps next time. So that $300 is almost gone. That picture of you cooking lasagna. Without the meat. Just cheese… how pretty you look… you must be happy…

(Lights change. Three months later. ROGER is in the memoryscape.)

ROGER: That brownstone on St. John's? Sold! (He sweeps her off her feet.) There's nothing I can't sell these days! (Giving her a playful slap in her rear) I feel like fun and games tonight.

ADELFA: Fun and games?

ROGER: Yeah. Something really special. (Beat.) Ever heard of role-playing?

ADELFA: No.

ROGER: It's like - acting. I'll go to Lemon Grass around the corner. Sit at the bar. Then you follow a few minutes later. You see me. You pretend you don't know me. Then you pick me up.

ADELFA: Pick you up?

ROGER: You're from out of town. You feel lonely. Then you see me. You find me -- you know, attractive. (Flustered.) This is so embarrassing.

ADELFA: A let's pretend.

ROGER: Yes! You're a quick study! That's good. And then we come back here to play some more.

ADELFA: Like those movies… Bomba. Sexy movies.

ROGER: Kind of. But it's – consensual. Harmless, you know.

ADELFA: Like an actress... like this... (Taking on a sexual pose but not successfully.) "Hi, Mister... you wanna good time?" Like that? "Twenty-five bucks..."

ROGER: What?

ADELFA: I'm playing... "Twenty-five bucks, Joe..." Joking only, Roger...

ROGER: Wait. Hold on. Would you be more into it if you got something for it?

ADELFA: (Beat.) Maybe.

ROGER: Twenty-five... that's not bad.

ADELFA: No?

ROGER: No.

ADELFA: Really. (Pause.) Another twenty-five and I'll do anything you want.

ROGER: Hello...

(Lights change.)

ROSARIO (V.O.): An extra fifty dollars! God bless you, anak! You have no idea how much we need it - especially now. Dr. Valdes said he called you yesterday. HIV. Anghel has HIV. He said you asked him not to tell Anghel because it might upset him. So he told Anghel he's got TB. He's also ordering drugs from Hong Kong. They're more effective. I told him, get the best, di ba?

(And another.)

ANGHEL: There's something I'm missing. All you do is talk about your chores. You must keep the cleanest house in Brooklyn. What else do you do, Adelfa? You don't mention any friends. It sounds like Kuya Roger keeps you close to home. Thank you for the leather wallet you sent for my birthday. It's so soft. Dr. Valdes said I have TB. When I was in Smokey, almost everybody had that. Why is it I'm getting it only now?

(Lights change. ROGER is unpacking grocery bags.)

ROGER: (Shaking his head.) Adelfa? Honey! I said paper not plastic.

(ADELFA enters.)

ADELFA: What?

ROGER: You keep forgetting, Hon. Don't you want to save the planet?

ADELFA: (Without irony.) Save the planet? You want me to save the planet?

ROGER: I said "toilet bowl cleaner", not "shower and tub." And "window" cleaner. Not glass.

ADELFA: Dirt is dirt.

(ADELFA exits, and once in awhile peeks into the room.)

ROGER: No, it's not. In this country, it's a science. And look at all these garbage bags! There must be a dozen boxes in here.

ADELFA: It's for Inay.

ROGER: Rosario?

ADELFA: Nay Rosario. Nay Rosario. Back home, we never address anyone older by their first names. Kuya Angel calls you Kuya Roger.

ROGER: But we're in America. Here everybody's equal. (Pause.) Okay. So why are you sending Nay Rosario garbage bags?

ADELFA: Smell it.

ROGER: I'm smelling.

ADELFA: Lemon! I wrote her about them. She wouldn't believe me so I sent her a pack. Now she won't use anything else. I even told her about our bathroom.

ROGER: What about the bathroom?

ADELFA: Even our toilet paper smells like potpourri. And I told her about the spray that makes ca-ca smell like vanilla ice cream!

(Lights change. Three months later.)

ROSARIO: The medications are working! Anghel is getting better! I go to mass everyday now. Adelfa, I love it where we are. The air is so fresh, the sky is blue. And the stars. When I was in Smokey, I never noticed them before. But here at Baclaran , they look big and bright. Was I dead and now I'm alive?

> (All of a sudden, the sound of glass breaking is heard coming from offstage.

ROGER: (Alarmed.) Jesus Christ! What's that? Adelfa?

ADELFA: (Walking into the scene, Down Center.) An accident. I'm sorry.

> (ROGER seats her on a chair. He kneels in front of her.)

ROGER: You hurt?

ADELFA: Please don't be angry.

ROGER: I'm not. But what broke?

ADELFA: A flower vase.

ROGER: We have one?

ADELFA: Mrs. Santorini was selling it on her stoop.

ROGER: You're buying Mrs. Santorini's junk now?

ADELFA: It was only 50 cents.

ROGER: You want a flower vase, I'll buy you one from Macy's. Are you sure you're not hurt?

ADELFA: It broke in two pieces. That's all. (Pause.) Are you so protective of me, Roger?

ROGER: Of course, I am.

ADELFA: Then why -- I don't understand -- last night --

ROGER: I know. I'm sorry I got carried away.

ADELFA: You are carrying away all the time! Why can't we make love without the playing.

ROGER: I enjoy our games, don't you?

ADELFA: But you always end up getting mad at me. If you didn't, we can play all you like.

ROGER: But I told you I'm not mad at you. It's not about you. I can't – I need to play. It's a paradox. You understand what that means?

ADELFA: You love and hurt?

ROGER: Sometimes you surprise me. I'm under so much pressure. I can't find listings as fast as I can sell. I need another broker. The one I've got can't keep up!

ADELFA: So it's work that makes you angry?

ROGER: I have rage issues.

ADELFA: What?

ROGER: Sometimes things come up for me. Then I get mad and I lose control. But at least I'm aware of it. That's half the problem licked.

ADELFA: I don't understand!

ROGER: I used to see someone. Sometimes talking helps. You gain some insight about why you do what you do, who you are, where you've been in life.

ADELFA: A girlfriend?

ROGER: (Laughing.) That's precious. No. It's called therapy. I paid her a hundred thirty-five bucks an hour. You're not gonna understand it, Adelfa. It's very American.

ADELFA: How many hours, Roger?

ROGER: Let's see... one a week. Five years, give or take.

ADELFA: Five years?

ROGER: Exactly my feeling. All that money and she said squat. My life still sucked. So I quit and thought of doing Anger Management instead.

ADELFA: Anger what?

ROGER: Anger Management. They have an intensive four-week program at the Wellness Institute.

ADELFA: There's a school for this?

ROGER: No. It's just another form of therapy. But then the business took off. I couldn't find the time. So I dropped out. And then I found you. I realized I didn't need Anger Management.

ADELFA: So I am angry manager.

ROGER: No. I told you. I'm not angry with you. Please don't take it personally. I have so much garbage in my life!

ADELFA: What garbage?

ROGER: The remains of my past.

ADELFA: That's garbage?

ROGER: Don't you have things in your life you want to get rid of but can't? And every time you think about them you get angry? But I don't want to burden you with them, Adelfa.

ADELFA: Roger, we have a good life. Don't you think it's a good life?

ROGER: There's always something.

ADELFA: No, there isn't always something.

ROGER: That's because you expect so little.

ADELFA: But this is not so little. A beautiful house. A booming business. I'm sending money home every month. Inay's moved out of Baclaran to a bigger apartment. My brother's getting the best care. Life is good.

ROGER: I've had such a hard life, Adelfa.

ADELFA: But you don't have a hard life now.

ROGER: Look, you don't get it. To you, life is simple. Food, clothing and shelter.

ADELFA: You need health. And family. Family is essential.

ROGER: I'm not ready to have a family.

ADELFA: I'm talking about mine.

ROGER: Yours. I envy you and your family. You have no idea how lucky you are. (Pause.) But you never talk about your father.

ADELFA: Kuya Anghel said one day he went to buy some salt and never came back.

ROGER: Salt? Salt… How interesting… I wonder what that means. Salt…

ADELFA: Salt. You know, salt… what you put in your food… or tears. Tears taste of salt.

ROGER: How old were you?

ADELFA: I was just born.

ROGER: You never get over things like that. It doesn't matter how old you are.

ADELFA: But if I don't remember, what would I need to get over?

ROGER: Your soul remembers everything.

ADELFA: If that's true, then there's no escape.

ROGER: I used to think so. But that's before I met you. You've never felt despair, have you, Adelfa.

ADELFA: How can you say that?

ROGER: Do you know despair has a sound? The sound of breaking glass… I grew up wearing shoes all the time in the house. Or, else I'd step on shards of glass or china my parents threw at each other in their rages. No matter how hard she tried cleaning up, she could never find them all. Don't you wonder why we only have acrylic? Thank god for acrylic.

ADELFA: I'm sorry, Roger. Maybe you should go back to that woman. The therapy. Or be an Angry Manager. I'll help you. I went to the library yesterday - I'm sure they have books on Anger --

ROGER: You did what?

ADELFA: I saw this book. In the library. Around the corner.

ROGER: You went to the library? Keyfood. St. Francis. Duane Reade. That's it. I told you. I forbid you to go anywhere else.

ADELFA: Roger, why can't I work? I'm not afraid of work.

ROGER: Being my wife. That's your work. And you're doing a great job. I can finally look forward to coming home everyday now.

ADELFA: I have two years of college! Make me your secretary. I'll go to computer class. Learn Word processing. You said you're busy.

ROGER: I've a friend Tony. His wife's from Romania. He sends her to Excel training and next thing you know, she's run off with a classmate from the Ukraine. So he says next time he gets a new wife, he's gonna keep her home and her passport under lock and key.

ADELFA: Don't you trust me?

ROGER: Of course, I trust you. I trust you more than my ex-wife.

ADELFA: (Pause.) Ex-wife? Ex-wife! Like me?

ROGER: No way. Nothing like you. You're one in a million, Adelfa.

ADELFA: Six months we write each other. You never told me!

ROGER: What's there to say? That Joanne couldn't put up with my crap? She was so impatient. American women. You have to get it together right here right now. Well, some things take time. They don't know how to suffer.

ADELFA: American women are splendid! We envy them in the Philippines.

ROGER: That's the only place to do it. From half-way around the world. Get close enough, and they're all the same - spoiled, ungrateful, too damned independent. Do you know there's a huge market just on Filipino women, Adelfa? Tony says they make the best wives. And he's right. You're understanding. Hard-working. You don't talk too much. And when you do talk, you speak English. You're - perfect! (Pause.) Please don't let this change anything between us.

ADELFA: What you're doing for Angel. And Inay. I could never pay you back.

ROGER: Let me make it up to you.

ADELFA: What are you going to do, Roger? Buy me something again? Don't buy me anything, please.

ROGER: I never in my life heard a woman say, "Don't buy me anything." (Taking a few bills from his billfold.) A raise. Fifty more a month. You deserve it. And that's another thing. Joanne. She was so fuckin' high maintenance. When she asked for money, it was always for something - a car - the latest model Miata. When you ask, it's so your brother can live another day. You're so grateful. Because you've been poor. Poor people never take anything for granted. There's something to be said for poverty.

ADELFA: There's nothing to be said for poverty.

(Lights change.)

ROSARIO: Fifty dollars more a month? You must be making Roger very happy. I'm so proud of you, anak. You must tell Roger how grateful we are. Here's a picture of us in front of Kentucky Fried Chicken. Do you like my white dress?

(Lights change. Three months later.)

ROGER: So what's with the dress?

ADELFA: It's a Donna Karan. I thought you liked it!

ROGER: No, I don't. It's too short. Too tight. What are you trying to prove?

ADELFA: You bought this for me.

ROGER: Hon, I'm playing?

ADELFA: Oh, okay. (Pause.The pushes him back) Fuck you!

> (They laugh. ADELFA hits him hard. He hits her back.)

ROGER: Oh, yeah? So let's do it. (Aroused, he pins her down. She struggles.) Oh, she's feisty tonight! Say the words, Adelfa. Say the words... ADELFA: No!

ROGER: No?

ADELFA: Make me!

ROGER: Oh, yeah?

> (ROGER pulls her hands and she grabs the headboard as if she were being bound and tied to it. They are breathless with laughter. ROGER exits.)

ROGER: (Offstage.) Okay, Hon? Ready? You're gonna do it this time?

ADELFA: Yes.

ROGER: Okay...

ADELFA: (Overcome by giggling.) Save me.

ROGER: I can't hear you!

ADELFA: SAVE ME, WHITE MAN!

> (ROGER runs into the room and mimes rescuing her, a damsel in distress. They erupt into paroxysms of laughter. A few

beats. Then the laughter recedes. They begin kissing each other. A few beats.

Then ROGER pulls out a cord from his back pocket. He pulls ADELFA's hands and begins tying them together to the headboard.)

ADELFA: What's that? What are you doing, Hon?

ROGER: It's you who need to trust me… will you trust me?

ADELFA: Yes, yes. I trust you. What are you doing?

(He tugs at her, tightly. She winces.)

ROGER: Please?

ADELFA: Honey, This isn't fun.

ROGER: I'm sorry… (But he tugs at them some more.)

ADELFA: No!

ROGER: Please? (On top of her.)

ADELFA: (Ferociously.) I said NO! GET THE FUCK OFF ME!

(ROGER steps back.)

ANGHEL: Your letters don't sound like you. Remember the snow? Your first Christmas? I can't hear your voice in my head. And then there are my dreams. Last night you wanted to tell me something but I couldn't make out the words, your face, hidden. What do you want to tell me? Why do I dream such dreams?

ROGER: What I do to you – this is not who I am. I wish I was someone else. I'm so aware of what's wrong with me. But it doesn't keep me from hurting you. I could go back to therapy and talk until I'm blue in the face, but it's still like turning over mud. I have so much love for you. I can feel it – this sweet solid thing that sits in my heart, waiting to be free. Someday… soon… I promise. It's gonna happen. I feel it. But you've got to believe me.

ADELFA: You know what I want? This. This moment now. When I'm crying and you're sorry and I believe you… I feel hopeful. Hope is a wonderful thing. You can see the stars.

ROGER: That's why I love you. Everything amazes you. Stars. Garbage bags. Oprah Winfrey.

ADELFA: Oprah Winfrey is splendid.

ROGER: No. You. You're splendid.

ANGHEL: You say you keep seeing me in your dreams. I don't see you in mine. But I know you're there, shrouded in darkness and silence. What does it all mean? You look so different in these pictures. Your clothes are very stylish. But you look thin. And you never smile. Why is that? I must be crying in my sleep. I wake up always, my heart pounding, your face, an after image, and the taste of salt in my mouth. Here's a picture of me. Inay took it the day I left for the sanatorium.

(Lights change. Three months later.

ROGER has a piece of paper in her hand.)

ROGER: They need more? We're already sending them three hundred fifty bucks a month!

ADELFA: It's drug resistant TB.

ROGER: Drug resistant TB? How the hell did he get that?

ADELFA: I don't know! (Pause.) The drugs from Hong Kong have stopped working. Dr. Valdes says he's going to try new ones from Australia, but Kuya Angel needs to be monitored closely. He needs to stay in the sanatorium indefinitely.

ROGER: Indefinitely. I don't like the sound of that. Are you sure this doctor's legit?

ADELFA: Inay chose him. I trust her.

ROGER: And Rosario needs an extra 50 for a cell phone?

ADELFA: It's for Kuya Angel.

ROGER: We pay close to 200 bucks a month in long distance calls already.

ADELFA: There's a sign at the pharmacy on Seventh Avenue for a part-time cashier -

ROGER: Out of the question. We've had this talk before. (Pause.) Drug-resistant TB. Are you sure Anghel's not faking it? So he doesn't have to work? Don't you think it's suspicious?

ADELFA: Don't you ever say that about Kuya Angel.

ROGER: What do they do? Sit around all day and wait for the check? It's like welfare except that I'm the fucking government.

ADELFA: That's unfair!

ROGER: But it's true!

ADELFA: How dare you judge my family.

ROGER: You're too kind. They're taking advantage of you.

ADELFA: How can my own family take advantage of me? Everything I have is theirs!

ROGER: I'm your family now. I'm looking out for you. You have nothing of your own. It's fucked up.

ADELFA: It's not fucked up! Stop saying that!

ROGER: It's called denial.

ADELFA: And in my country it's called the truth.

ROGER: The truth? Okay. So what's the truth?

ADELFA: (Pause.) Never mind.

ROGER: (Pulling her back, roughly.) Not never mind. Come on. Tell me. What the fuck is going on?

ADELFA: (Letting go of his hold.) Anghel was sick before you and I wrote to each other and he's still sick. That's why I married you. So we could pay his medical bills. That's why I stay. And wait on you hand and foot.

And sometimes - sometimes I hate you so much I stop breathing!

>(She turns to run but ROGER catches her, cupping his hand over her mouth, while with his other hand he rips her dress off. He heaves himself on to her and kisses her as she thrashes wildly at him. He drags her to bed. She struggles in vain. He pushes her down, on her stomach.)

ADELFA: (Wincing in pain.)I don't want to play, Roger.

ROGER: (He climbs on her back and begins entering her from behind.) Yes, you do.

ADELFA: No, please, Roger.

ROGER: Yes, please Adelfa.

ADELFA: I said I don't want to play!

>(ROGER pulls out a bill from his pants pocket.)

ROGER: A fifty.

ADELFA: Keep your money!

ROGER: Oh, the bitch wants more! (Pulling out another bill.) Twenty.

ADELFA: I said let me go!

ROGER: Easy does it…come, Adelfa… come, baby… I like it… it's good… oh, yes…oh, baby…oh, baby…

(ADELFA screams. The sound rips the air in two.)

ANGHEL: You're sending us so much money. The 350 a month. Then there's the fifties – twenties. Are you working outside the home now? Are you keeping some of it for yourself? You seemed so distant last night on the phone. And your letters are short with nothing to say. Even my life seems more interesting than yours and Adelfa, I live in a sanatorium.

ROGER: (With extreme tenderness) I'm so sorry...

ADELFA: I told you to stop.

ROGER: (Inconsolable.) I don't mean it... I didn't mean it... please...

ADELFA: You've never done anything like that before.

ROGER: I'm not worthy of you... it's so damned hopeless... I'm hopeless... Please don't hate me. Do you really hate me?

ADELFA: No, Roger. I don't hate you. I told you. This you. Now. This I love. I'm in love with this you.

(Lights out.)

ROSARIO: "Did I tell you Dr. Valdes is moving Angel to another sanatorium? Dr. Valdes says it's better than the one he's at now. He's got his own room and twenty-four hour care. I'm looking for a house near there, so I can visit him everyday. But they're expensive in this part of the city. But don't worry. I think we can afford it. Happy birthday, anak. I'm sending a heart-shaped pouch filled with adelfas I grow in the garden. Dr. Valdes says I've made a "potpourri." It's French, daw. Imagine that?

>(Lights up on ROGER and ADELFA in the memoryscape. A month later.
>
>ROGER has a piece of paper in his hand; he's reading it.)

ROGER: Do you know what this is? It's a bank statement. A private checking account!

ADELFA: Give me that!

ROGER: Why do you have your own checking account, Adelfa?

ADELFA: How did you get hold of that?

ROGER: I went to high school with the mailman. We have an arrangement.

ADELFA: An arrangement?

ROGER: Let's just say I make sure I know what goes in and out of this house.

ADELFA: Roger, you yourself told me to have something of mine.

ROGER: Without telling me? I'm hurt! Don't I give you everything you want? What are you planning to do with it?

ADELFA: Save money. Go back to school. I thought if I saved enough of my own, you'd change your mind.

ROGER: You're lying.

ADELFA: I'm not.

ROGER: Dangerous combination, Adelfa. Money and women. A woman gets hold of a little cash and she's out the door. Joanne was smart as a whip. She even went to NYU. I used to like smart women. Until I found out how exhausting they are. They never shut the fuck up! You're not going anywhere. I bought you. I bought your family. I bought your house. And everything in it. Your brother is still alive. Every fuckin' breath he takes, he takes because of me.

ADELFA: You can't pay me enough for what I do for you.

ROGER: What are you gonna do about it?

ADELFA: I quit!

ROGER: Quit? Quit. And go where?

ADELFA: Do you think I care? You'll never see me again. Who'll put up with you then? I'm one in a million, remember? I'll find work. I have skills. I have two years of college.

ROGER: From the Philippines? We eat people like you.

ADELFA: I was wrong. There's something to be said for poverty. Once you survive it, you can survive anything. And besides, it's the easiest country in the world. I've seen the stuff that's thrown away.

ROGER: I've got your papers. Your passport.

ADELFA: I'll get a lawyer.

ROGER: Lawyers cost money.

ADELFA: I'll get a woman. An American woman.

ROGER: You don't know Americans. We like our victims blameless.

ADELFA: It's a big country. I'll find someone who'll understand.

ROGER: Your brother will die.

ADELFA: And you'll be wishing you were dead. Everyday - all alone and lonely in this sad, empty house where nothing ever breaks.

ROGER: Stop it! You're scaring me!

ADELFA: Three thousand. A month.

ROGER: What?

ADELFA: A raise. Three thousand a month. Not one penny less! I mean it.

ROGER: You're crazy! You're nuts! (A beat.) A thousand.

ADELFA: Twenty-five hundred.

ROGER: Fifteen hundred.

ADELFA: Twenty-two hundred.

ROGER: Two thousand.

ADELFA: I'll take it.

ROGER: But on my own terms.

ADELFA: What are they?

ROGER: Only one phone call a month. And I have to be there. No letters.

> (ADELFA sits down.)

ROGER: Adelfa –

ADELFA: No. Wait. Wait.

> (A heavy silence descends on them both as if she's listening to something finally break inside her.)

ADELFA: How did I get here?

ROGER: Do you accept my terms or not?

ADELFA: Yes.

ROGER: And one more thing.

ADELFA: It doesn't matter now.

ROGER: Find it in your heart to love me exactly the way I am.

ADELFA: Give me the money, and I love you already.

> (ADELFA moves Down Left and puts on a new sarong. She takes down her hair. Lights change. A year passes.
>
> During the following Voice-overs, ADELFA enters and exits carrying

shopping bags, trying on different shoes,
clothes, handbags, each change of
accessory, costume, as expensive as the
next. She is transformed into an
expensively groomed woman, perhaps the
kind of woman ROGER has referred to as
'high maintenance.")

ROSARIO: What's the IBM computer for? I don't even
want to turn it on. I'm scared it would explode. And I
can't sleep on that new mattress. It's like sleeping on air.
So I'm still sleeping on the floor.

ANGHEL: Dr. Valdes told me you sent him a shopping
list. Adelfa, Inay doesn't need a 25-inch Sony TV. Or the
AT & T phone. What kind of a telephone is it we have to
read a book to call someone? The fridge. She goes to the
market everyday. She gets everything fresh.

ROSARIO: Mondays, the whole neighborhood comes for
the Bay Watch. Tuesday, all the women in the baranggay
watch Oprah. Wednesday nobody comes because it's
only the Seinfeld. We don't understand that show.
What's so funny? Last night, Ronnie, Lola and I watched
The Exorcist on the Toshiba. We all fell asleep.

ANGHEL: My dear Adelfa, don't send any more things.
It just confuses Inay. They're just things, Adelfa. Stuff.
And it always comes down to this. Someday they'll be
garbage.

ROSARIO: The landowner is going to write you a letter .
Something about the building. About a condo. What's a
condo?

ANGHEL: You've done it, Adelfa. Congratulations. You should be proud of yourself. Roger's check comes regularly every month now straight from the bank.

ROSARIO: Did you hear about Lola Epang? When they closed Smokey Mountain, the government built another garbage dump at Payatas. So she moved there. There was a trash slide on July 20. The garbage fell on the squatters. They all died. Look how this letter is smudged with tears. We are so blessed, Adelfa. God has been so good to us. He's given us Roger.

ANGHEL: Your letters are few and far between. You don't call anymore. I'd rather hear you lie than not hear from you at all. My nightmares remain silent, shadows without sound. Something is wrong.

ROSARIO: Ronald Reagan Rampatanta asked me to marry him. Ronnie has been a great comfort to me. And he's still a good dancer. He's teaching me the hip hop!

ANGHEL: Your cell phone has been disconnected. I call your home but it's always Kuya Roger who answers. I can't share my fears with Inay. I don't want her to worry... So this is what it means losing you – sorrow in my bones, and in my heart, the burden of its weight...

ROSARIO: I catch myself singing all the time. As if I've always lived here in this place... Smokey Mountain... was it all a nightmare?

ANGHEL: I sat up all night waiting for your call. It never came. You didn't even send a card. You've never missed my birthday, Adelfa. How can I say this? That day we danced at Smokey. That was the happiest day of my life...

ROSARIO: Who would have thought we'd own a condo... or I'd fall in love again? At my age? A miracle. My life is full of miracles.

ANGHEL: Last night, you appeared in my dreams again. Your face remained in shadow, but this time, I finally heard you, clear as a bell. "Save me..." You said , "Save me." I woke up, screaming. I'm way past the sadness. Now I'm simply afraid. Something has gone terribly wrong. I know that now. And you've chosen not to tell me.

(A telephone rings. No one picks it up.)

ROGER: Go head. I'm here.

(ADELFA doesn't move. A few beats.)

ADELFA: Why, Roger. You and I have finally one thing in common.

(The phone stops ringing.)

ADELFA: The sound of my despair.

(Fragments of letters flood the air, overlapping each other as lights go down gradually.)

ROSARIO: I can't get hold of you. I keep leaving you messages. Have you changed your number? Why don't you call me? Angel's condition changed all of a sudden. Even Dr. Valdes doesn't understand...

ANGHEL IS VERY SICK STOP CALL US STOP

ANGHEL IS IN A COMA STOP

ANGHEL DIED LAST NIGHT STOP I HAVE NOT
HEARD FROM YOU STOP WHY STOP FUNERAL
TOMORROW STOP

>   (Blackout. In the darkness, a heart-rending
>   wail. A few beats.

>   Lights go up in the memoryscape. ADELFA
>   is holding a telegram in her hand. ROGER
>   places a batch of letters on the bed.)

ADELFA: Dead? Kuya Anghel is dead? No! NO! (She
sinks to the ground and weeps.) How? Why? Why didn't
I know about it?

>   (ROGER tries to comfort her, but she
>   resists.)

ROGER: Now, Honey, take it easy, okay… please. I – I've
got some very good reasons – Honey, please understand.

ADELFA: (She sees the letters on the bed. She pores over
them.) Letters…telegrams… what are you, a monster?

ROGER: I only wanted to make sure you weren't lying to
me! I didn't want to lose you. I'm sorry.

ADELFA: You had me, you son of a bitch!

>   (ADELFA starts hitting him. ROGER
>   doesn't fight back.)

ADELFA: Come on! Hit me. Hit me back. I'm going to kill you. Angel is dead!

ROGER: Adelfa, I said I'm sorry.

ADELFA: I'm sick and tired of sorry. It's only a word.

> (ADELFA flings a closet open, takes out a suitcase and starts dumping her clothes into the case.)

ROGER: Where are you going?

ADELFA: Angel is dead. I want to go home, kneel at his grave and ask for his forgiveness.

ROGER: (Grabbing the suitcase.) I am your home. (He turns to hit her.)

ADELFA: Go ahead. But you better do a good job. This time tomorrow if I can still walk, I'm gone.

ROGER: (A beat.) I'll change. I am changing. I am getting better!

> (ROGER picks out a large red envelope from his attache case and gives it to ADELFA.)

ROGER: It's for you. You see that? I didn't open it, Honey. It came two days ago. Just before the telegram. I was going to give them both to you today. You've got to believe me -

(She grabs the envelope from his hand and throws it away.)

ADELFA: It's too late!

ROGER: No, it isn't. I'll go back to the Institute – find that therapist. I'll take the four-week treatment. Adelfa, give me one more chance!

ADELFA: I have nothing left to give you.

ROGER: I know you're very angry right now. I don't blame you. I understand.

ADELFA: I've heard this shit before!

ROGER: I've made your mother happy. I've done some good. You can't take that away from me.

ADELFA: And I've made you happy. We're even.

ROGER: All right. If you want to split, then split. Just don't do it out of anger. Give yourself time to cool off. The most important decisions in life take time, Adelfa. If I fail this time, I'll – I'll let you go. I'll even give you the money to go back home...

ADELFA: I don't believe you.

ROGER: What if the me you love – what if there's a chance of a lifetime without the demons. There's hope here. And where there's hope, there's stars. That's what you said.

(A long silence.)

ADELFA: I need time. And peace and quiet. Room to think it over. You understand?

ROGER: Yes.

ADELFA: I need to hear myself think.

ROGER: Take all the time you want. I promise to leave you alone. I'll check into a hotel. The place is yours.

(He turns to go.)

ROGER: You have no idea how much power you have over me. If you leave me, I'll die.

(ROGER exits. Lights change.

Smokey Mountain, 1985.

ANGHEL is working the trash. This is the Smokey before ANGHEL became its "king." He's carrying a large and heavy bag of trash, metal hook in hand poking, stabbing at hardened mounds of debris, face and head covered with cloth, the grime, the soot, the sewage clinging to his skin, his bare arms and legs, his soul. ADELFA is seen Downstage, in the present, in Brooklyn. She speaks her lines from where she is.)

ANGHEL: (Reading an empty tin can's label.) A-L-P-O! Alpo… for dogs … . Beef - bacon - ! (He mulls over this, gets it.) Pambihira.

ADELFA: (Something in the distance, offstage, has caught her eye.) Kuya! Kuya, look! Charing! The whole family… where are they going, Kuya?

ANGHEL: (Aloud. Waving.) Uy, Charing! Suerteng-suerte mo! Aba. Ang yabang. She's not even waving back. (Another whistle.) CHERRY PIE! Now she's waving back. Punieta. (To ADELFA) Someday I'll take you out of Smokey, too.

ADELFA: Cherry Pie? What's that?

ANGHEL: A cocktail waitress.

ADELFA: Why is she wearing white?

ANGHEL: It's the only color you can't wear in Smokey.

(ANGHEL, ADELFA watch in silence.)

ANGHEL: A whore. But look. The whole family... She doesn't care what people think. She'll do anything to get her family out of here. Even sacrifice herself. You know why? Because she's got a female heart. Pusong babae... (Putting his hand over her heart.) This. What you've got – right here – that's what makes you special. Pusong babae, Adelfa. A female heart beats only for the people it loves.

ADELFA: Is that why Itay left? Because he was a man?

ANGHEL: Hindi naman. A female heart is simply a tender heart. And a man can be just as tender as a woman.

ADELFA: I want to be like Mr. Paredes. Mr. Paredes knows so many things!

ANGHEL: Who put that idea in your head? No one from Smokey ever becomes a teacher!

ADELFA: I don't want to be a whore!

(ANGHEL laughs.)

ANGHEL: Whores make more money!

ADELFA: (Bursting into tears.) I don't want to be Cherry Pie!

ANGHEL: Aba. Ambitiosa.

ADELFA: Cherry Pie may not live her anymore but she's still living in Smokey!

(ROSARIO enters.)

ANGHEL: Ano?

ROSARIO: That meeting with Father Kintanar? Adelfa. Adelfa. She's a Sydney scholar.

ANGHEL: What's that?

ROSARIO: This Sydney gives money to the best pupils in Adelfa's school. Mr. Paredes recommended her. Kasi she's number 1 in her class. We've got to take her off the garbage.

ANGHEL: No, Inay. We can't! Six hands are better than four.

ROSARIO: Think! Think, Anghel. If she does well, she might even end up going to high school. High school!

ANGHEL: High school? Talaga ba? Ang suerteng-suerte mo, Adelfa.

ROSARIO: We'll work harder. We'll pick twice as much for as long as our bodies can take it. Adelfa, you're gonna be a salesgirl. At the mall. You've seen them. They're very clean, wear nice shiny shoes and pretty white dresses. They live with their Itay and Inay in rooming houses in Baclaran. You can do it. You're young and pretty and smart… you're the ticket.

> (Lights change.
>
> We are with ADELFA in the present, in Brooklyn, picking up letters strewn on the bed, examining each one, and sorting them in date order. As she nears the end of this sorting, she finds the red envelope ROGER had just given her, unopened. She picks it up and rips it open. She gives it a quick scan at first, reading a few phrases aloud.)

ANGHEL: "Last night I finally saw you clearly… walking in a pool of sunlight… caught a glimpse of your face… that same bold look in your eyes… I know now that what I'm going to do is the right thing.

Adelfa, we've wrecked our lives to save ourselves. It has to stop. I know Inay and Itay Ronnie will mourn for me deeply, as you will. But when that mourning is over, I want you to be glad. I've stopped taking the medication.

ADELFA: …"I've stopped taking the medication"?

ANGHEL: Use my life, my last gift to you…

ADELFA: …"I've stopped taking the medication" …

ANGHEL: You have two choices. You can stay with Roger and work it out. Or you can walk away and not look back. Goodbye, my dearest, Adelfa. Mahal na mahal kita. Your loving brother, Kuya Angel "

ADELFA: (Weeping.) Pusong babae… it was you all along. You're the one with the female heart!

(Lights change.

ADELFA is taking out other letters from the bedside table, gathering them together with the letters she had picked up from the bed, now a neat pack in her hand. She stands over the wastebasket.)

ADELFA: Basora.

(She drops all the letters into the wastebasket. They make a sound as they fall into the wastebasket. Then she turns around, giving the room one last look.)

ADELFA: Goodbye, Roger.

BLACKOUT

END OF PLAY

WOMAN FROM THE OTHER SIDE OF THE WORLD

By

Linda Faigao-Hall

WOMAN FROM THE OTHER SIDE OF THE WORLD

Premiered in 1996 with Ma-yi Theater Ensemble, Inc. in New York City.

Cast of Characters:

(All the characters are Filipinos or Filipino-Americans.)

Emilya Encomienda, mid-30's

Jason, her son, 9 years old

Isabel Albarracin, her best friend, early 30's

Ines Dacalos, late 50's, Jason's Filipina nanny

Gorge Ocon, Emilya's boyfriend, mid-30's to late 30's

PRINCESS URDUJA, late teens; a role performed entirely in dance by the character of Isabel

Time: Early 1990's

Place: New York City

Scene One

(Wednesday evening, around 6:00 in October.

A two-bedroom apartment in the Upper Westside of Manhattan.

Two main acting spaces: one, Down Stage, has a large white couch with two floor pillows, a telephone, a small table with a drawer that can be locked or unlocked, an intercom, a remote control, a joystick. Downstage Right and Left are windows defined simply by lighting. A wall stands behind the couch, Center, with a central opening covered by panels that can be raised or lowered. When they are raised, a bedroom is seen in the back. Lowered, the panels act as a scrim, as in shadow play. When the text asks for a scrim, only the sound cues are on and the visual cues are silhouettes of actors in a variety of activities described in the text. The rest of the time, it is simply a wall. Up Left and Right are used as exits and entrances.

When the scene opens, a telephone is ringing.

EMILYA ENCOMIENDA flies into the room, diving for the phone. She is light-skinned, a Filipino mestiza, her features more Latin than Malay. She is wired, like a coiled spring.)

EMILYA: Hello? ... Pam?... I just got in....What's that? A cellular. I will, someday... Tomorrrow? The Deputy Director? Okay. Okay. I'll be there.

> (She hangs up. She runs to her attache case and takes out all her files, laying them out on the table. JASON bursts into the room, a band-aid over his left eye.)

EMILYA: Jason! What happened to your eye? Where's Maria?

JASON: Maria's not coming no more.

EMILYA: Any more. What do you mean she's not coming anymore?

> (The intercom rings. EMILYA picks it up.)

EMILYA: Hello?... Maria? ...What?... Slow down. I don't understand... Why don't you come up and we can talk...

> (The phone rings. JASON picks it up.)

JASON: Hello...Tito George? Hold on. (To EMILYA.) Mom --- Tito George! He's waiting!

EMILYA: (Still on the phone.) I hope you mean Columbia University... Oh, no. Wait there. I'm going down! Jason, go play your Playstation!

JASON: (At the window.) You're not gonna make it. (Waving.) Goodbye, Maria!

EMILYA: (Running to the window.) Where's she going in a taxi?

JASON: Mom, where's Colombia?

EMILYA: Did she say she's coming back, Jason? Like tomorrow?

JASON: Not. (Waving.) Goodbye. Goodbye.

EMILYA: Six o'clock in the evening in the middle of the week and she's going back to Colombia. Who's going to pick you up from school tomorrow?

JASON: You.

EMILYA: I can't. The Deputy Director's coming!

JASON: How about Tito George. (Remembers. Goes to the phone.) Hello? Tito George?
(Hangs up.) Mom, he hang up.

EMILYA: He's working. (Pause.) Oh, Jason. Not another fight.

JASON: Mrs. Noonan called you at the office. Where were you, Mom?

EMILYA: I was out in the field. I'm sorry. How did it happen this time?

JASON: Vinnie started it. But I got him in the tummy, the mouth ---

EMILYA: Just tell me why it happened.

JASON: He called me a liar. I said I was Italian. He didn't believe me.

EMILYA: You said what?

JASON: You always say I can be anything I want to be. I wanna be Italian. So I'm Italian, right?

EMILYA: Why didn't you just say you're an American?

JASON: Mr. Shelby says every American has a… a… it's in my book bag.

EMILYA: (Opening his book bag.) And that's all. You hit a boy because he calls you names.

JASON: What's for dinner?

EMILYA: Don't change the subject. You don't hit someone just because somebody calls you names. You can be angry. And say angry words. But hitting is not acceptable behavior. Tell me you won't hit. Promise me.

JASON: Okay, okay.

EMILYA: Remember our agreement?

JASON: Mom, he called me a liar!

EMILYA: No Playstation for the week. That's it. That was the agreement, and we stick to it.

JASON: Oh, no, Mom. I learned some new codes today.

EMILYA: You should have thought of that before you hit Vinnie.

JASON: No fair.

EMILYA: This is serious, Jason.

(She opens a notebook.)

JASON: What's for dinner, Mom?

EMILYA: Pizza. We've got nothing in the fridge.

JASON: Why don't you get a microwave, Mom?

EMILYA: Someday.

JASON: (Picks up the phone. Dials.) Mom, can we get the large deluxe pan pizza with everything on it?

EMILYA: (Reading.)
"A heritage song... a costume..."

JASON: Tony?... This is Jason. We want the extra large deluxe with everything on it. Goodbye. Yeah... she's right here!

(He hangs up.)

EMILYA: So this is why you want to be Italian?

JASON: What's a heritage, anyway?

EMILYA: (Tentatively.) Something from your past you carry over to the present...

JASON: Like what?

EMILYA: Remember all the stories I used to tell you about home?

JASON: No.

EMILYA: The big white house on top of a hill surrounded with fruit trees?

JASON: What kind of fruit trees, Mom?

EMILYA: Tambis, and chicos, star apples, and mangoes... In the summer, the grounds would be strewn with them, all different colors, like a painting... All summer long, our house would smell of fruit...

JASON: Did I climb those trees? Did I? Did I?

EMILYA: The breadfruit tree was the biggest one in the orchard... Your father said his great grandfather had planted it... So right after you were born, Papa got the gardener to build a treehouse. It killed the tree eventually, Jason, but your father didn't mind. He loved you very much. That I could say for him.

JASON: A tree house! Cool! What else did he do, Mom?

EMILYA: (Pause.) Not now, Jason.

>(She picks up the telephone. JASON sits Center, facing the audience; he picks up the remote control, presses a button. Video music goes up. He begins to play with the joystick. He turns the music way up.)

EMILYA: (Dialling.) Pinch-sitters? Sandra... hi. I need someone for tomorrow....

JASON: (At the Playstation.) Come to Papa. No. No. No. Not this way. That way. No. No!

EMILYA: Send me Fiona. (To JASON) Turn that thing off!

JASON: You're history, Koopa. You're history… Yes… Yes! Yes! I beated it! I beated it! Mom, can I come as Super Mario?

EMILYA: (To JASON.) Now! (On the phone.) My son thinks Super Mario is his heritage.

>(JASON turns it off.)

EMILYA: (On the phone.) No. I think I'll arrange to stay home on Monday... Fine... Goodbye now...

>(She hangs up. JASON comes forward.)

JASON: James said he's gonna wear a...a... African thing... da --

EMILYA: Dashiki?

JASON: What am I gonna wear, Mommy?

EMILYA: (Wryly.) A g-string?

JASON: What's a g-string?

EMILYA: Never mind.

JASON: How about a song. You got a song, Mommy?

EMILYA: I don't got a song, Jason. I have a song.

JASON: Okay. Sing it.

EMILYA: Now?

JASON: I need a song for the Festival, Mom. Please, please, please!

EMILYA: All right, all right. Sit. (Pause.) Okay. I'll sing the whole song and then we'll go over it line by line. (Pause, collecting herself. Then singing.) "Planting rice is never fun. Bent from morn till the set of sun. Cannot stand and cannot sit. Cannot rest for a little bit ---'

JASON: No way. I'm not singing no song about planting rice.

EMILYA: Any song. I'm not singing any song about planting rice.

JASON: Me neither. And food. We have to bring food, too, Mom. What am I gonna bring? Patrick. He says he's Irish? He's bringing a boiled potato…

EMILYA: We can cook some adobo.

JASON: But it's just chicken. It's got to say something about heritage.

EMILYA: Well, it does.

JASON: What does it say?

EMILYA: (Pause.) I don't know what right now, but it does.

(The phone rings.)

EMILYA: Hello… George! … Oh…yes. I'm sorry. It's been a tough night… Call waiting? I should get call waiting. I ought to write all this down… Right now I'm trying to figure out if adobo can talk. Never mind… The Big Apple Circus?

(The doorbell rings.)

JASON: Pizza! (He exits. Offstage.) Twenty-one ninety, Mom!

EMILYA: George? Can I call you back? I'm sorry…'bye.

(She hangs up and exits. Offtstage voices heard.)

JASON: Twenty-one ninety. It's a large deluxe, Mom.

EMILYA: Jason, we always get the medium with pepperoni. I only have 15!

(They enter, empty-handed.)

JASON: Mom, it's so embarrassing. He took it back!

(The telephone rings.)

EMILYA: Damn this phone! (Picking up the phone. Furious.) HELLO! HELLO!

JASON: Don't worry. I'll have a peanut butter and jelly sandwich.

(JASON exits. Scrim on: silhouette of JASON fixing sandwiches.)

EMILYA: WHO? (A long pause.) Ramonito? Who's shouting? I'm not shouting... You're calling at a bad time... Call me at 3 in the morning. What?... who?... A yaya? For Jason? What are you talking about?

JASON: Mom, we're out of peanut butter!

EMILYA: Oh, shit! ...I said, shit, Ramonito, shit!

JASON: It's okay, Mom. We got hot dogs!

EMILYA: Jesus Christ, Ramonito, of course she's not here. And if she comes, I'll tell her to turn right back. I don't want a yaya. I don't need one. I have a babysitter... I had one... I don't have room.... I can't afford it... no, I don't need your help.

(A fire alarm goes off, strident and loud.)

JASON: Mommy! Mommy!

EMILYA: (Over the din, on the phone.) IT'S JUST THE FIRE ALARM! ... THE FIRE ALARM!

JASON: Mommy, HELP!

EMILYA: (On the phone.) I got to go.

> (She hangs up and runs out of the room. Scrim shows her and JASON jumping up and down, waving towels. A banging from the ceiling is heard; the door bell rings. EMILYA comes running out picks up the phone, finds out that isn't it, then discovers it's the doorbell. She opens it.

> A woman in black stands in the doorway. EMILYA gasps in fright, letting out a yell. Then the alarm stops ringing, the banging on the ceiling ceases. Suddenly, there is complete silence. The woman steps into the light, holding out her hand. She is in her late 50's. Something about her, even now, will always remain unruffled; she holds this self-containment without fuss.)

INES: My name is Ines Dacalos. Dr. Ramonito sent me. I'm Jason's yaya.

BLACKOUT

Scene Two

(A week later. EMILYA's apartment. There is a
small carpet on the floor. EMILYA is on the
couch, reading a book, listening to Gershwin's
Rhapsody in Blue.

The intercom rings. EMILYA gets up and speaks
into it.)

EMILYA: Yes, Mike...Who? Are you sure it's 3F she wants?
...Send her up.

(She turns down the music, fixes the pillows. The
doorbell rings. She exits.

ISABEL ALBARRACIN sweeps into the room. She
is in her early 30's; she's wearing a long batik
dress, an attractive headdress cut from the same
fabric, a straw bag; sandals. The outfit accentuates
her Malay features; she is dark to EMILYA's light.
)

EMILYA: What happened?

ISABEL: What do you mean what happened? Don't I look
multicultural?

EMILYA: American. You dress like that in Manila, they'd laugh
you out of the archipelago. What name did you give Mike? He
could hardly spit them out.

ISABEL: This week I'm Kayumangging Tagumpay. (Looking around.) It looks different. (Moving over to the alcove, taking a peek.) Ah - ha! The yaya is here.

EMILYA: She appeared last week at my doorstep, exactly the way Ramonito said she would.

ISABEL: (Turns off the music.) where is she? Where's Jason?

EMILYA: At the Museum of Natural History. Apparently it's Asian-American Week.

ISABEL: And I wasn't invited?

EMILYA: I don't know why he sent me a yaya. There was nothing wrong with my life the way it was.

ISABEL: You mean the one with the string of babysitters, the confusing love life, the stressed out working mother? Does she speak English?

EMILYA: She grew up at an orphanage. She was raised by the American nuns there. Then worked for the American consul in Cebu. She's never married. Last night she offered to stay with us until Jason goes to college.

ISABEL: Sounds better than a husband. Speaking of husbands -- how's Tito George?

EMILYA: Tito George is not anywhere near being a husband.

ISABEL: No? Two years and he's not proposed yet? Seems like your kind of guy. Knows when not to push it. We know what happens when a man gets close enough. Splat, you drop him like a hot patata.

EMILYA: Not true at all.

ISABEL: No? Let's see... Robert Dizon... Oswaldo Terra... Hector Hodel. John McCloskey. All patatas.

EMILYA: I had my reasons.

ISABEL: Don't you always? Oswaldo was too old. Hector too young. And John. Poor John. Went back home to Idaho. Idaho. You see what I mean? Patatas. But George. Don't let him get away, Emilya. Jason needs a father.

EMILYA: Jason needs a yaya and he's got one.

ISABEL: I have to admit. It's very brave of you sleeping wih a Pinoy. I wouldn't do it.

EMILYA: Why not?

ISABEL: I always imagine him jumping out of bed, rushing home to tell his buddies, one of whom will be a wife of a nephew of a neighbor who happens to be here for the summer, and with my luck, he'll be my mother's hairdresser.

EMILYA: George is American.

ISABEL: And I'm Polish.

EMILYA: Born and raised in Long Island. His mother died giving birth to him. His father remarried two years later. A pure Anglo.

ISABEL: Poor guy. He must be confused.

(The door opens. JASON flies into the room.)

JASON: Mommy! Mommy! A Filipino killed Ferdinand Magellan! (Sees ISABEL.) Tita Isa! (Kissing her.) Did you know a Filipino killed Magellan? He used arnis, Mommy. Arnis!

(He makes attempts at some arnis movements. INES appears in the doorway.)

EMILYA: Ines. This is ---

ISABEL: (Giving her hand.) Isabel Albarracin.

INES: Ines Dacalos. Ma-ayong buntag kanimo, Inday.[1]

(INES peers down at ISABEL's hand, holds it for a moment, as if she has divined something from it. ISABEL watches her quizzically, withdraws her hand and looks at it as well.)

INES: Kaga-an sa imong kalag, Inday. Gracias sa Dios.[2]

---

[1] Good morning, Inday.

[2] Your soul is light.

(ISABEL moves away, amused, curious.)

JASON: (Giving EMILYA a program.) Mom, we saw a program --

EMILYA: (Reading it.) "A Filipino dance-drama featuring --"

JASON: Mommy, the King of Spain sent Magellan to go around the world to look for -
(Looks to INES for help.)

INES: Sinamon, sili, luy-a...

JASON: But he found the Filipinos instead! A native king ---

INES: Rajah Kulambu.

JASON: That's right. This guy King Kulambu liked him a lot... gave him lots of gold and silver. Magellan was so happy he made everybody a Catholic! Then he went to Cebu to find more gold. But this guy Lapu-lapu, he didn't wanna give him nothing -- no way, Jose! So Magellan got angry and attacked his castle... but Lapulapu knew arnis... so he did this -- and this -- and this (Makes arnis attacks in the air) And Magellan fell down dead...

EMILYA: They said this?

ISABEL: Cool!

JASON: Then there was a princess --

INES: Princesa Urduja.

JASON: Yep. Just like Princess Zelda. And she knew arnis, too! Mommy, may I go to arnis instead of karate? May I, Mommy? May I? Please, please, please?

EMILYA: We'll talk about it later.

>(INES gives a slight bow, turns to JASON , and takes his hand.)

JASON: (To ISABEL.) Tita Isa, Nay Ines brought lots of pictures from the Philippines. But Mommy won't let me see them.

EMILYA: I'd rather we do it together. I haven't had time.

INES: I can show them to him, Mrs. Emilya.

EMILYA: How would you know all of them?

INES: That's true. (Taking JASON 's hand.) Come, Jason.

>(They exit.)

EMILYA: It's the first time I've heard her speak Cebuano.

ISABEL: That's very old Cebuano she's using.

EMILYA: What was that business with the hands?

ISABEL: She said my soul is light. Kaga-an sa imong kalag. That's what she said. How'd she know I'm a copy writer?

(Pause.) Nobody speaks like that anymore. You know what I think? She thinks I'm indigenous. And I don't blame her. Look at me!

EMILYA: Do you go to this new job dressed like that?

ISABEL: Of course not.

EMILYA: How do you like it?

ISABEL: I miss my old one. I liked teaching. (Taking on a teaching manner, as if in front of the class.) The verb "to be." Think of a universe without the verb "to be," Shaquana. People would sing and cry and run and walk and love and hate but they couldn't just be. The most profound thought in the English language: I am. You are. It is.

EMILYA: Sounds like I should be taking these classes.

ISABEL: The new job's going very well. I've been living in Manhattan for five years and it's the first time I'm working with white people. And you know what? Even their offices smell white. Did you know that? That white has a smell? Call me.

EMILYA: Are you staying for dinner?

ISABEL: No. I wanted to meet the yaya. (Pause.) Is that really how I look?

EMILYA: Multicultural is in, remember?

ISABEL: That's not multicultural, Emilya. That's Third World.

(ISABEL exits. JASON enters going over a batch of pictures.)

EMILYA: Jason!

JASON: Mom, Nay Ines said it was okay. I wanna see Lapulapu. Nay Ines says he was our relative.

EMILYA: He wasn't exactly --

JASON: (He looks to INES.) Look! She looks like Princess --

INES: Urduja.

JASON: Yeah. She looks just like Princess Urduja. Who is she?

INES: That's your Lola. Your grandmama.

EMILYA: (Taking it away from him.) Jason, please get dressed. Tito George will be here soon. We're going to the movies, remember?

JASON: Who's this?

INES: Oh. It's Alba. The witch. Alba the witch?

JASON: A witch? You mean a real witch? Cool! (To INES.) She doesn't look like a witch. She looks like you, Nay Ines.

EMILYA: She wasn't a witch, Jason. There's no such thing.

(She takes the rest of the pictures from him.)

JASON: Remember the game you got me for my birthday, Mommy? Desert Storm? This one looks just like the guy in Desert Storm!

EMILYA: (Flings the pictures to the floor.) I said get dressed! (To INES.) Why didn't you listen to me?

(INES and JASON watch her in shocked silence.)

JASON: (Angrily and in tears.) That's not acceptable behavior!

EMILYA: (A beat. Then she throws her arms around him.) I'm sorry. Jason, forgive me. Give me a kiss? Please, please, please?

(JASON hesitantly gives her a kiss.)

EMILYA: Now go and get dressed.

(JASON runs out of the room. INES starts picking up the pictures.)

EMILYA: Attend to Jason.

(INES walks away. Unnoticed, she turns to watch EMILYA who is picking up the pictures. EMILYA avoids looking at them at first, but something in them compels her to. She looks at one... then another... She looks at this last one longer; she sways a little, as if a gust of pain is passing over her body. Playwright's note to the actor: This is a picture of Alba.)

EMILYA: (Bursting into tears.) I'm sorry... I'm so sorry... oh, god... (With great effort, she chokes back her tears. She picks up another picture.) What do you think of that, Don Leon. Your son thinks you're a video game. A video game!

> (She tears it in two and throws them to the floor. A surge of violent rage rocks her body. She starts tearing up some of the pictures into pieces.)

INES: (Running to her.) Mrs. Emilya, no!

> (EMILYA, still caught in the violent trance, raises her arms as if to strike. INES involuntarily jumps back. EMILYA snaps out of it. With great effort, she tries to regain her composure.)

EMILYA: What did they tell you about me, Ines? What do you know?

INES: The tenants remember your acts of kindness.

EMILYA: And my family?

INES: They wonder why you never write or go home for a visit.

EMILYA: And Ramonito?

INES: That you needed help with Jason.

EMILYA: Good.

> (EMILYA sees the scattered pieces of torn photographs on the floor. She quickly scoops them up and throws them all into a drawer. She then takes out her keys from her bag and locks it.)

EMILYA: From now on, you can take weekends off. I should have taken him to the museum myself.

INES: You came home late last night. I didn't want to wake you up this morning.

EMILYA: It's not a problem. Good night, Ines. Don't ever disobey me again.

INES: Yes, Mrs. Emilya.

> (INES exits. EMILYA sits down on the couch, picks up the remote control and turns the music on. She leans back, soaking in the music.
>
> A few beats. INES comes back, head cocked, body taut.)

EMILYA: What's the matter?

INES: That music!

EMILYA: Gershwin?

INES: That's its name?

EMILYA: (Turning the music down.) You know Rhapsody in Blue?

INES: (She hums along for a few beats.) By heart.

EMILYA: How?

INES: Before I was brought to the Asilo, I lived with my uncle in Talisay, a fisherman. Our small hut stood next to a big house owned by a very rich family whose son went to school in America. He came home one summer. I was washing clothes out in the batalan when I heard this music from his bedroom window. It was like magic, Mrs. Emilya, right then and there, with all the dirty clothes. I didn't know who wrote it. Where it came from. What it meant... He played it all summer long, and everyday, washing clothes or not, I'd be out there in the batalan, wondering how easily the music made me forget who I was. When he left, I thought I'd never hear the music again. (Humming along with it.) I will be happy here, Mrs. Emilya. It will be as I have hoped. I've seen this place in my dreams.

EMILYA: I didn't mean to be harsh, Ines. I'm sorry. (Showing her the records.) You're free to listen to them any time you want. Good night, Ines.

> (EMILYA exits. INES goes over the stack of records. Her eyes widen with amazement.)

INES: So many Gershwins!

(She sits on the couch, listening. Something on the floor catches her eye. She picks up pieces of a torn photograph EMILYA has overlooked. She smooths them together and blows on them. She pulls the drawer open; it's locked. A few beats. Then she pulls at it again; it opens easily. She drops the photograph inside.)

INES: Pieces of yourself coming back...as if they just happened yesterday... I understand now.

FADEOUT

Scene Three

(JASON 'S bedroom. Later that night.

A dream sequence:

The sound of gongs, majestic, sonorous, spills onto an empty stage. PRINCESS URDUJA appears, resplendent in a native costume, dancing.

Then almost as softly as a whisper, other sounds intrude, then rise in volume, until their dissonance fills the air. At first, they sound like the synthetic, synthesized sounds of video games. But soon they turn strident and cacophonous as harsh bolts of neon and strobe lights flash, striking PRINCESS URDUJA with their sharp, jagged glitter. The princess puts up a brave fight but the noise and the light overpower her music, until it seems a spell is cast; PRINCESS URDUJA falls to the ground. JASON enters, running towards the princess. He tries to revive her but she doesn't respond. He screams.)

We see JASON thrashing wildly in bed.)

JASON: No! NO!

(INES enters. EMILYA is close behind.)

INES: Jason, hijo. Wake up. Jason!

EMILYA:
What happened?

JASON: Mommy! The princess! The princess... she's dead...

EMILYA: Shh...it's okay. It's okay... it was just a dream, Jason...

JASON: The monsters -- they did it, Mommy! They killed her!

(He falls back to sleep.)

FADEOUT

Scene Four

(Late Saturday evening the following week.

INES is seen sitting on a chair, chanting softly to herself. The door to the living room opens and

GEORGE, EMILYA and JASON come in. INES
greets them. GEORGE has JASON on his
shoulder. He lays him on the bed in the bedroom.)

EMILYA: He threw up. We had to leave.

GEORGE: (Laying him on his bed as INES helps JASON out of
his clothes.)
 Nothing but apples, rice or tea.

EMILYA: What did he have this morning?

INES: A hot dog and a Coke in the park.

GEORGE: Junk food, Ines.

INES: Junk? Hot dogs? (Undressing JASON .) All food is God's
grace, Mr. George.

GEORGE: I wish that were true.

INES: I'll take care of him now.

JASON: I missed the lions, Tito George.

GEORGE: There's the Barnum and Bailey. I'll take you and your
mommy next week.

JASON: Can Nay Ines come, too?

GEORGE: Of course.
EMILYA: (Kissing JASON .) 'Night, my love.

(She exits from the bedroom and walks into the kitchen. She prepares coffee. INES begins to massage JASON . Then she begins to chant. GEORGE stays rooted to the spot. There is a short pause. Down Left, EMILYA hears the chant and gasps, as if the sound of it is a solid thing, hitting her body like a blow. She walks to the living room to sit down.)

GEORGE: A Filipino lullabye, Ines?

INES: Sometimes. (To JASON .) How does that feel, Jason?

JASON: Good.

(She continues to massage his stomach.)

GEORGE: That's interesting. How you do it.

(INES takes GEORGE'S hand and peers down at them. Then she holds one of his wrists with her thumb and forefinger and jiggles his arm in the air. JASON and GEORGE laugh.)

INES: (She keeps jiggling his arm in the air, holding it by the wrist.) Let go. Let go. Let go. You see that?

GEORGE: I see one very limp wrist.

(INES drops his arm suddenly. It drops to his side with a thwack. JASON is beside himself with laughter.)

INES: Twice a day.

GEORGE: (Gives JASON a kiss.) I can see you're feeling better all ready.

JASON: Nay Ines, Tell Tito George about the people with the big white wings...

INES: The engkantos? Well, they want you to sleep now, because they're very tired and they want to go home...

JASON: Are they like angels? Like in catechism class?

INES: Yes. But unlike angels, they can cry and laugh...

JASON: Can they kill the bad guys?

INES: No, but if you get a cut, they can heal it with one touch of their wings...
JASON: What else can they do?

INES: When they fly through the air, music falls to the earth. The young man who hears it will marry a woman who will love him forever...

JASON: And if I hear it?

INES: (Laughs.) A boy can hear it only with his eyes closed.

GEORGE: (Tucking him in.) Good night, Jason.

JASON: Good night, Tito George.

> (GEORGE exits from the bedroom. Scrim off. GEORGE holds his hand by the wrist and lets it fall to the side. He does it once or twice until he's gotten it right. He sits down beside EMILYA.)

GEORGE: How come you never told me about the engkantos?

EMILYA: I'm surprised it doesn't scare the hell out of Jason.

GEORGE: I wish I grew up in the Philippines. The other day Jason asked me if I had ever heard of arnis. I never have. But Ines has. I'm glad she's here. She can answer all his questions.

EMILYA: And I can't?

GEORGE: Well, not really. You're not really Filipino. I mean, the way Ines is Filipino. You're very assimilated, Emilya. You're an American. You act American.

EMILYA: You mean I chew gum, love football and wear cut-offs?

GEORGE: No. I mean you never talk about it. What you left behind.

EMILYA: The past isn't important to me.

GEORGE: My Dad thinks the same way. He never talks about it, either.

EMILYA: I'm sure he has his reasons.

GEORGE: I know one of them. I think my Mom was a little ashamed she married a Filipino. So he made some very significant decisions early on in his life. He loved her very much. He'd do anything for her. Even forget who he was.

EMILYA: Is that what you think I'm doing?

GEORGE: I don't know about you. I know about my Dad. Mom never liked for us to visit with the Filipino relatives. It was only when I got older that I found out that his name was really Isidro Ocon, (pronouncing it the way a Filipino pronounces it) not Sidney Ocon. And that he grew up in Davao, came to New York in the 50's with a medical degree no one respected. My Mom's family gave her a hard time, but they forgave her when he was made Chief of Pediatrics. So now I always make it a point to tell people my Dad is Filipino. But I don't know anything about it.

EMILYA: Is that why you have a Filipino girlfriend?

GEORGE: Why are you twisting what I'm saying?

EMILYA: You're an American. Be proud of it.

GEORGE: I'm more than just that.

EMILYA: There are people in the world today who'd go through hell to be just that.

GEORGE: I'm an Asian-American. No. A Southeast-Asian Pacific Islander American. Okay... A Filipino-American... No -- I'm -- I don't know what I am!

EMILYA: Don't use my country to make you feel better about yourself. You can't borrow a culture, George. You're either raised in it or it isn't yours.

GEORGE: Emilya, that's not true.

EMILYA: It's not? You know what it was like listening to visiting Filipino-Americans? Their profound insights into the nature of the Filipino condition... the constructive criticism... the creative solutions, but only until the end of the summer, when they all had to go back to L. A. or New York or wherever they led their safe, comfortable lives. I used to envy them. Even their tortured confessions of their identity crises. Because at the end of the day, they were all simply Americans, weighing their options, and you know what, they always chose to come back here. They never fooled me. Thank god, I'm here now... I love this country more than I ever loved my own. I'd never go back there again.

GEORGE: Then help me to understand why you can say that.

EMILYA: What's the point? It's right now that matters. (Kissing him.) Right now. Do you understand, George?

GEORGE: All right. Good. So let's talk about it. Let's talk about right now. There are things I need to say. Things I've been thinking about for a long time now.

EMILYA: Like what?

GEORGE: Like you and me. And Jason. I know you said you wanted a lot of time.

EMILYA: Didn't we agree I'd be the one to bring this up?

GEORGE: But I need some guidelines here. What do you mean more time? A year? Five years? Ten?

EMILYA: I don't know.

(She takes his hand and kisses it.)

GEORGE: (He is not having any of it. Persistently.) After two years. I think I deserve better.

EMILYA: ((Pulling him to her, caressing him.) You do. You do, George. Don't you know?
The best things in life take time. What we do to each other... in the dark... Don't I please you? You please me.

GEORGE: But never in the light, Emilya? I never see you in the light. For once I want to make love to you with the lights on.

EMILYA: I never make love with the lights on.

GEORGE: I know.

EMILYA: It's a Filipino thing.

GEORGE: So you say.

EMILYA: We had such a nice day.

GEORGE: I want more than a nice day.

EMILYA: I asked you to bear with me a little while longer.

GEORGE: It's been a little while longer.

EMILYA: I have a long day tomorrow. I'm taking Jason to Sesame Place I want to avoid the rush.

GEORGE: Fine. So when can we talk?

EMILYA: Soon.

GEORGE: That's what you said the last time.

EMILYA: Then I'm saying it again, George. Soon. Stop. I can't stand this!

GEORGE: You can't stand this? You can't stand this! What do you think it's like for me? I know how to wait. But I'm not waiting forever, Emilya.

EMILYA: And what do you mean by that?

GEORGE: Maybe I'm the one who needs time.

> (A few beats. GEORGE: waits, but EMILYA
> doesn't say anything. He turns around and exits.

INES comes out of JASON 's room. She cocks her
head, listening.)

EMILYA: How's Jason?

INES: Asleep. No more hot dogs for him. Just as Mr. Ocon said.
(Pause.) What does Mr. Jorge do?

EMILYA: He's got his own business. He's an electrical engineer.

INES: Ah. That explains it. I see a lot of wires.

EMILYA: (Laughing inspite of herself.) Really?

INES: You're troubled.

> (INES takes out a small bottle from her side
> pocket, opens it, pours oil onto her palms and rubs
> her hands briskly with it.)

EMILYA: No!

INES: But this will soothe you.

EMILYA: I said no!

> (EMILYA turns to go, almost fleeing. INES begins
> to chant. It spills into the space, quietly; it's no
> longer a lullabye; it has a bird-like quality to it,
> unobtrusive but persistent. It cuts the air like a
> thin sharp knife; EMILYA stops in her tracks. She

is drawn to the sound against her will. It confuses her; she moves as if in a trance.)

INES: Lie down, Emilya... lie down.. Relax...there. Close your eyes. Lie on your stomach... there... good...

(EMILYA turns over. INES kneels on the floor, at the couch, bends over and lays her hand on EMILYA's back. She pushes down.

A sudden jolt rocks INES' body, as if she has touched something hot. Her hands hang motionless in the air, her body braced, as if in shock. She tries again, and again, she's thrown backward, pushed by a force that leaves her shaking.

A few beats. Then she begins to hum an ordinary love song from home; words, commonplace and familiar, tumble out of her mouth. The spell is broken. EMILYA sits up, as if awakened from a deep sleep.)

EMILYA: It's too sad.

INES: All love songs are sad. You think because I'm old and homely, I don't know anything about love.

EMILYA: I don't think you're old and homely, Ines.

INES: My cousin Nena used to take me away from the Asilo every summer. I remember when I turned 15. Nena was pregnant with her first child. Her husband Danilo was a jeepney driver. He was so grateful that I could help with the chores. Nena was craving for bocayo every night, and he wasn't always there to grate the coconut. You know, if you don't satisfy the cravings, the baby comes out deformed.

EMILYA: That's not true, Ines.

INES: A week after I arrived, Danilo started acting strangely. He'd follow me around with his eyes, and sometimes, he'd stare at me and burst into tears. It didn't take long before Nena and I realized he had a craving himself.

EMILYA: What was he craving for?

INES: A virgin.

EMILYA: A what?

INES: A virgin.

EMILYA: No.

INES: Yes.

EMILYA: Who?

INES: Me.

EMILYA: You! Yeah, right. (Laughing.) One craves for food, Ines. Food. Shredded coconut. Mango ice cream.

INES: You can crave for anything. The moon. A flower. When Nena had her second child, she craved for roses. Big, red American roses. But they couldn't afford them. So the baby was born dead.

EMILYA: Oh, Ines!

INES: He craved for me. A virgin. We didn't know what to do.

EMILYA: I bet you didn't!

INES: So we went to the elders in the sitio and they all agreed that something had to be done.

EMILYA: Like what?

INES: (Getting to her feet.) They held a dance, and everyone was invited. Then they told Danilo to dance with me. Just me. All night. It so happened it was my birthday. So the night I turned 15, I danced with the handsomest man I ever met. I still remember the touch of his hand, the faint smell of hasmin in his breath, as if he'd been eating flowers... (Singing the same song. Swaying to the music a little.) The next day, the craving had passed. It was the most beautiful baby the sitio had ever seen. They named the baby after me. Nena said that way, they'll remember me forever.

EMILYA: But what about you? Wasn't it painful for you?

INES: Is that what happened? It was too painful?

EMILYA: What?

INES: Mrs. Emilya, it's your turn to tell your story.

EMILYA: (Flustered.) But -- but I was talking about you, Ines. What story are you talking about? I don't have any stories.

(EMILYA rises to her feet and leaves.)

INES: That's not true... (Pause.) Poor Jason!

(She stands Center, deep in thought as lights

FADEOUT

Scene Five

(The next day. Afternoon, around 3. GEORGE and INES are in the living room.)

INES: There's so much pain inside her, it hurts my bones to touch her!

GEORGE: What? Is she sick? Ines, if she is, I'll take her to a doctor! Dad will see her!

INES: No. No. It's not the kind of pain your doctors can heal.

GEORGE: This is America. We have a doctor for every kind of pain. My father's a doctor.

INES: It's a pain that finds its home inside. In the dark. It sits there and takes up space until it takes over that person's soul.
GEORGE: I don't understand.

INES: She's hiding something. And it's killing her. That's why she can't marry you.

GEORGE: Oh. That. Ines, it's nothing unusual. It's called fear of commitment. But I don't think it ever killed anyone. If it did, everybody my age in New York would be dead.

INES: Don't take this lightly.

GEORGE: I'm not. We have a cure for it. It's called therapy. You go to someone who will help you talk about it.

INES: But what if you don't want to?

GEORGE: You take Prozac. I don't know… Ines, I walked out telling her I need time and here I am, back the next day.

INES: This is no time for being proud. I called you because she needs your help.

GEORGE: I know about the others who've loved her before I did. She let them all go, Ines. I don't want to be one of them, but I'm lost here.

INES: First, learn how to use your hands.

GEORGE: I'm sorry?

> (INES flaps GEORGE's arms in the air, as before. She keeps at it until his wrists hang in the air completely without resistance.)

INES: Now rub your hands together until they feel hot. Hard. Good. Good. Now follow what I do.

> (She begins to massage her own forehead, moving her thumbs from the center of the forehead, away from each other, down to the temples and then pushing her open palms against the temples. He follows her every move.)

INES: Now do it to me.

> (GEORGE massages INES' forehead.)

INES: Relax. Gently… gently… too light. Too heavy… no...

GEORGE: (Frustrated.) I'm useless at this!

INES: Practice. You need to practice.

GEORGE: I've always hated being in the dark. Literally. Up until the age of eight, I used to carry a flashlight everywhere I went. Never went to bed with the lights off. My friends had baseball cards. I had a flashlight. I was the only kid in the block who hated Halloween. In fact the idea of becoming a painter appealed to me more than once. Painters worked in the light. Created all this cool stuff out of light. Problem was I couldn't draw. Nevertheless, I make a living lighting things up. Banishing shadows with a flip of the switch. Then a woman like Emilya comes along -- I haven't a clue.

INES: Maybe these will help you… Her brother Ramonito asked me to bring them with me.

(She walks over to the table and pulls the top
drawer. It's locked. She pauses, pulls it once
again. It opens easily. She takes out the pictures.)

GEORGE: (Picking one up.) Who's this?

INES: (Peering over his shoulder.) Alba. A witch.

GEORGE: No way.

INES: I don't really know why they'd have a picture of her. It's a
mystery. She died in a fire.

GEORGE: I'm sorry.

INES: Why? Did you know her?

GEORGE: No.

INES: (Giving him another picture.) Her mother. She died
when she gave birth to Emilya.

GEORGE: Really. She's never told me this. (Studying the
picture.) Lovely...the same proud face... the sad eyes...

INES: (Showing him another photograph)…and that's Dr.
Ramonito… her brother …manages the hacienda himself. Those
hacenderos. They're a bad lot, most of them. But not him. The
tenants love him. He doesn't even have a private army! Imagine
that. No private army!

GEORGE: (He picks up a photograph.)And who's the Anglo?

INES: Her husband... Don Leon. When he married Emilya, he became the biggest sugar landowner in the province. He died of a stroke a few months after Jason was born. May God have mercy on his soul...

GEORGE: I never thought…

INES: (She picks up another.) The house she lived in.

GEORGE: House? It's a mansion! What a far cry from a two-bedroom co-op.

INES: She took nothing from him after he died, not even what was hers as his wife.

GEORGE: We've got so much more in common than I thought. There's hope --

INES: If and when you earn her trust. Then she may tell you about her pain.

GEORGE: I have a f-- damned headache!

> (INES plucks small leaves from an ivy, squashes them in her hand, spits at them.)

GEORGE: What are you doing?

INES: (She spits at them some more.) I thought at first it was the coleus but the ivy is better.

GEORGE: (Moving his head away.) Ines! Just give me some Tylenol.

INES: I can't open it! (Pressing the leaves on to his temples. They stick.) Your headache will be gone in a few minutes.

GEORGE: And if we fail, Ines?

INES: Then take the Tylenol.

GEORGE: No! I mean if we can't reach her... if we fail!

INES: Then we'll ask Isabel.

GEORGE: Isabel. What can she do?

INES: That's for me to worry about.
GEORGE: I should just run for my life. Now!

INES: And Jason?

> (The door opens. EMILYA stands in the doorway. INES, with swift and agile grace, scoops the pictures up and throws them back into the drawer except for the ones GEORGE is holding in his hand which she overlooks. She pushes the drawer shut.)

EMILYA: I was on a site visit. I finished sooner than I thought.

INES: I'm just getting ready to pick up Jason.

EMILYA: Okay, Ines.

(INES exits.)

GEORGE: Hello, Emilya.

EMILYA: Hello, George. (Pause.) Headache?

GEORGE: Oh.

(He takes off the leaves from his temples.)

EMILYA: I have some Tylenol.

GEORGE: My headache's gone...! (Pause.) I was in the neighborhood. No, actually I was seeing an architect on Pine St. I thought I'd drop by. New contract. The builder's from Hongkong. Wants state-of-the-art electronics.

EMILYA: Pine Street? Isn't that on Wall Street? I'm confused.

GEORGE: Yes, I suppose you would be. Actually that makes two of us.

(EMILYA sees the pictures in his hand.)

EMILYA: What are those?

GEORGE: (Showing her one of them.) You have her eyes.

EMILYA: I never knew her.

GEORGE: (Holding up another.) Don Leon.

> (EMILYA grabs it from him. She looks at it, quizzically. She tries pulling it apart. It doesn't tear, remains intact and whole.)

EMILYA: I tore this up!

> (She walks over to the table and tries to open the drawer but it's locked.)

GEORGE: (Looking at the drawer quizzically.) I could have sworn... (Tries opening the drawer, but it remains shut.) I didn't know your father was Spanish.

EMILYA: What else did she say? What lies has she told you about me?

GEORGE: What?

EMILYA: She's up to something. She's spying on me. That's why Ramonito sent her.

GEORGE: Emilya, why would she be spying on you?

> (EMILYA walks away.)

GEORGE: (Pulling her back.) Emilya, talk to me!

EMILYA: What about? That times were hard? Profits were down -- the price of sugar plummeting, Americans cutting their quotas. We had to do with less. Except Don Leon. He was buying up all the land. He wanted ours, all of it. Papa wanted to hold on. But it was impossible.

> (GEORGE leads her to the couch and begins to massage her forehead. Then somewhere from the depths of the house, a soft chant is heard, inaudible, a mere whisper, gentle but pervasive. EMILYA yields to GEORGE's touch.)

EMILYA: So when Don Leon offered to buy the land, my father said he'd sell it to him only if he married me. Papa said it was the only way to keep the family from losing the hacienda. It didn't matter that I didn't love him. That he was old enough to be my father. Of course, I refused. Then one by one, they came - rich cousins and poor onesbegging, pleading, scolding, Marry Don Leon, you will learn to love him. Listen to your Papa. God will bless you for your sacrifice. We must never let go. This land. This precious heritage. I stood firm. Until Ramonito. My favorite brother. Sweet, kind Ramonito. The doctor in Bacolod. With his free clinics, his social causes, his political activists. Great wealth is a source of great power, he said. The power to do good. Marry Don Leon and the good I do can continue. Give up our birthright and you give up the privilege of helping the poor. He brought the tenants with him... all one hundred-thirty-two of them... Five generations of theirs to five of ours, tied to the same land... They said, Marry Don Leon and you will save our lives... the poor need the rich... abandon your clan and you abandon us... (Pause.) So I married him. How could I say no? My life was warp and woof to a fabric woven long before my time...

GEORGE: Emilya... (He pulls her close to him. He kisses her.) I'm so sorry. I didn't know.

EMILYA: Come to me. Don't go to Ines. Promise me you won't talk to her about any of this again.

GEORGE: I promise.

FADEOUT

Scene Six

(Three weeks later. Scrim. INES is in the kitchen. Sound cues only. There's a loud bang. EMILYA runs out of her room into the kitchen.)

INES: Madre de dios! Uy, hala! Tan-awa ang saging![3]

EMILYA: You're microwaving a banana?

INES: It should work. Look. 30 minutes.

EMILYA: Thirty minutes! Seconds, Ines. Seconds. What a mess!

(The intercom rings. EMILYA enters and speaks to it.)

EMILYA: Yes? ... Who? Elizabeth Blake? I don't know any Elizabeth Blake. Okay. Send her up.

---

[3]Look at the banana!

(She goes back into the kitchen. Scrim. Sound cues.)

INES: I'm sorry. It won't happen again. See? It's clean. Good as new.

EMILYA: It is new.

(INES opens a box.)

INES: (Counting.)
One...two...three...

EMILYA: What are you doing?

INES: If I cook 23 pieces of macaroni, Jason eats it all up. So there's no left-over...five...six...

(She runs out of them. She takes out another box, a new one, from the brown paper bag and struggles to open it. She puts it aside.)

EMILYA: Sometimes, I don't know whether to laugh or cry. I'm running late, Ines. Jason's play date is over in fifteen minutes.

(The door opens. ISABEL comes in, dressed impeccably in a suit.)

ISABEL: Tada!

(She turns around, showing off her clothes.)

EMILYA: Isa!

ISABEL: (Shaking her hand.) Elizabeth Blake. How do you do?

EMILYA: And I'm Mary Tyler Moore.

ISABEL: Armani.

EMILYA: How can you afford it?

ISABEL: Hand-me-down.

EMILYA: From whom? Imelda Marcos?

ISABEL: So what do you think? Elizabeth Blake. It's my name for the week. I'm going mainstream.

EMILYA: What?

ISABEL: Blake is from my favorite poet. And this is only the beginning. I've enrolled at NYU for diction classes.

EMILYA: What for?

ISABEL: I wanna speak with an American accent.

EMILYA: You've got a charming accent.

ISABEL: Don't you believe that crap, Emilya. You know the only accent Americans find charming is French. (Approximating a French accent.)Could you please tell me how to get to the Museum of Modern Art? (Lapsing into her own accent.) They'd walk you there. But ask in a thick Filipino accent, they'd think you're going there to sweep the garden.

EMILYA: Isa, you don't look like an Elizabeth Blake.

ISABEL: When I was Isabel Albarracin, Rupert, my boss, didn't read any of my copy. He's English, you know. The week I was Elizabeth Blake, he thought mine was the best. I wrote exactly the same thing. Explain that to me.

EMILYA: I don't know about this one. I think I liked you better when you were Kayumangging Tagumpay.

ISABEL: There's this account. American Express. But there's this blonde, blue-eyed Bennington grad who wants it as well. She was doing a crossword puzzle at lunch time. She looks at me with her big, innocent blue eyes and says, I was going to ask you about a word but you're from the Philippines. You don't do crossword puzzles. I say, Give me your best shot. She says, a three-letter word for `iota.' I say, `Tad.' She says, a six-letter word for `din.' I say `racket.'

EMILYA: How did you know all this?

ISABEL: I'd done it that morning. So Rupert, eating a pastrami sandwich, chimes in, You know you're much too clever for an immigrant. I've never met a Filipino with your mastery of the American idiom. Are you sure you weren't born in L.A. or somewhere like that? I'm probably the only Filipino he's ever met. So I say, What's with the pastrami, Rupert? The way you're wolfing it down, you sure you're not from Bensonhurst?

(They burst out laughing.)

ISABEL: American Express will give me a direct route to production.

EMILYA: You just got this job. You're already thinking of a promotion?

ISABEL: I plan early. Is Nay Ines here? I want to know what she thinks.

EMILYA: So now she's got you, too. Don't get too comfortable. She's still on probation.

ISABEL: You sound like a prison warden. Emilya, how can you possibly not want her?

EMILYA: I think she may not be good for Jason.

ISABEL: Jason loves her!

EMILYA: He has nightmares. I think her stories overexcite him.

ISABEL: Are you sure it's not those games he plays with? Have you seen Mortal Kombat?

EMILYA: She interferes. She meddles.

ISABEL: How? (A pause.) Well?

EMILYA: I just know she does. (Putting on her coat) Stay for dinner. If George gets here before I do, tell him we'll be back soon.

ISABEL: Again? That's three times this week, isn't it, Emilya? Is there something I should know? Should I mention the unmentionable?

EMILYA: We're talking.

ISABEL: You're talking! About what? Buying a Honda Civic? Moving to New Jersey? A 30-year mortgage?

EMILYA: Isabel, I'm not an open book.

ISABEL: No, you're not. You're very cool, Emilya.

EMILYA: Good. Jason likes cool.

ISABEL: Jason's nine. (Peering closely at her.) You know it's nice being obvious once in awhile.

EMILYA: That's you, Isabel.

ISABEL: I'm always obvious. Being obvious is my idea of living dangerously.

> (EMILYA exits. INES enters. She's wearing denims. She turns around, showing them off to ISABEL.)

INES: K-Mart!

ISABEL: Not bad. Not bad at all! (Offering her hand) Elizabeth Blake. How do you do?

(INES takes it and squeezes it very tightly.)

ISABEL: (Screaming in pain.) ARAY!

INES: Elizabeth Blake.

ISABEL: You did that on purpose!

INES: Sometimes I don't know my own strength.

ISABEL: Okay. Do it again. Come on, Nay Ines.

(INES squeezes her hand again.)

ISABEL: OUCH!

(They both laugh.)

INES: Miss Isa, please teach me how to operate the microwave. Mrs. Emilya thinks I'm ignorant and can't handle anything more complicated than a broom!

ISABEL: She didn't say that.

INES: She thinks it. She also thinks she's unhappy with me but it's not really me she's unhappy with.

(She goes into the kitchen as ISABEL follows. The
following scene is behind the scrim. Sound cues.)

ISABEL: I have the same model. Look. See. This is the timer...
seconds... minutes... and this is for popcorn.

INES: (Giving her a plantain.)
Do they have a button for bananas?

ISABEL: Oh. What's this?

INES: Morcon. Here. Take a bite. (Comes out with a cup of
chocolate and a saucer with the plantain, ISABEL behind her) I
went to 9th Avenue yesterday. Look!

> (INES gives her something wrapped in green
> leaves.)

ISABEL: Fresh chocolate! I didn't know they sell them like this!

> (ISABEL takes out a lump of pure dark brown
> chocolate and smells it.)

ISABEL: I can't imagine life without you and I don't even live
here. (Sits on the couch, taking a sip.) Oh. (Takes another sip)
How this brings it all back... Meriendas at 3:00... roused from
the noonday siesta… out in the veranda where it's cool...
bougainvilleas burning in the sun... scarlet blossoms on green
grass... mangoes... succulent, fragrant... like yellow flowers on a
white plate... and chocolate... steaming... thick ... so rich it made
you dizzy...

INES: Magbabalak. That's what you are. A poet.

ISABEL: How strange that you would say that, Nay Ines.

INES: Why?

ISABEL: Because I am a poet. I was. I mean one day I was, and the next, I wasn't. Just like that. All the words came up hard as stones... I remember waking up in the night, my heart pounding, as if I had been dreaming of something... I couldn't remember what it was... all I knew was that something was over...

INES: What did you do?

ISABEL: Left for the country, stayed in the mountains for a year... nothing... I gave up. Quit my job, let it go... the teaching, the poetry quarterly, the volume of poems I'd been working on... I bribed a couple of bureaucrats to get me a businessman's visa and that's how I ended up in New York writing about Imodium A-D.

INES: Imodium A-D? Imodium A-D! I use it. It works. It really does.

ISABEL: Imodium A-D! It works! It really does! ...Nah.

INES: You will be very successful. But not here. Somewhere else.

ISABEL: You can see the future, Nay Ines?

INES: Sometimes.

ISABEL: What do you see for me?

INES: Everything you desire.

ISABEL:
(Breathlessly.) Really?

INES: But you've got a curse on you and you have to get rid of it first.

ISABEL: A what?

INES: When your mother was pregnant with you, she made enemies with someone with great power. This person laid a curse on your mother, but because she was pregnant with you, the curse went to you instead.

ISABEL: You're joking. You said my soul was light!

INES: A light soul can have a shadow over it.

ISABEL: This is Manhattan. The air's so polluted. Maybe you're getting all the auras mixed up? Nay Ines, you're giving me the creeps.

INES: I can get rid of it for you but only if you do something for me in return.

ISABEL: I should really go back to the habit of eating in my own place. Good night.

(ISABEL runs out. INES goes into the kitchen
behind the scrim and comes back out again as
ISABEL does the same.)

ISABEL: Okay. Okay. Let's say it's true. Let's believe for a
moment that I do have a curse on me. What do I have to do?
Not that I'm going to do it. But let's just say, I'm game. How do I
get rid of it? Don't for a minute think I'm going to do it, because
I'm not.

INES: (Giving ISABEL an egg) You must move it to this egg.

ISABEL: (Giving her back the egg as if it were hot) You mean
that egg.

INES: Then go to the park early in the morning before sunrise
and get a handful of soil.
ISABEL: Park? What park? You mean Central Park? You want
me to go to Central Park at five o'clock in the morning to pick
up some soil? Are you crazy?

INES: Then a pinch of coffee.

ISABEL: Sanka okay?

INES: And a piece of bread.

ISABEL: Whole wheat?

INES: Every morning and night for seven days, rub the egg all
over your body. (Rubbing the egg over her body.) Say an

oracion. Then before you go to bed, put it in a brown paper bag with the coffee, the bread and the soil and place it under your bed for seven days. (Moving the egg over ISABEL's body.) Kaluy-i intawn, Guino-o, ang mga sala sa akong guinikanan... ang bugtong sala sa akong inahan... ang sala sa akong ka-ugalingon...Kaluy-i Santa Maria... On the eighth day, throw everything out. Except for the egg. Bring the egg to me.

ISABEL: And I'm bringing me to my apartment. Now.

INES: Then you have to do something for me.

ISABEL: Give you my soul? (Pause.) I'm kidding.

INES: Ask Mrs. Emilya to do the same thing. She will listen to you.

ISABEL: Really. Like hey, Emilya, how about rubbing yourself with this egg? (Pause.) Is she cursed, too, Nay Ines?

INES: She may as well be. You're the only one who can save her now. I can't do it. And Mr. George thinks the job's done. It isn't.

ISABEL: What job, Nay Ines?

INES: She thinks she's strong. She's not. She's just hard. You're easy. You're all air and space inside.

ISABEL: That's a museum, Nay Ines. (Pause.) She may be neurotic, but at least she's not crazy. I'm crazy.

INES: But if it works?

ISABEL: If it works, you and I are going to Bellevue!

(She exits laughing.)

INES: New Yorkers! Not very bright.

BLACKOUT

Scene Seven

(Sunday after dinner. INES is at the kitchen. JASON is drawing on the table. ISABEL and EMILYA are having dessert in the living room.)

ISABEL: Pinakbet... pancit. Then torta with hot chocolate for dessert. (Sinking deeper into the cushion) Last night, she gave me the best massage I ever had. I slept like a baby.

JASON: (Rising from his seat, holding up his drawing. Coming over to EMILYA.)
 Look, Mom. Juan Tamad under the banana tree. You see his mouth wide open? He's waiting for the banana to drop into his mouth.

EMILYA: (To ISABEL.)Lazy Juan. (Addressing INES at the kitchen.)
 Not exactly a role model for the 90's.

ISABEL: Emilya, folklore is not about making it, okay. Let me see.

(JASON shows her the drawing.)

ISABEL: Oh, look, there's more. Who's that?

JASON: The tikbalang, half-horse, half-man.

EMILYA: A tikbalang? Let me see that. That's great!And this is --- don't tell me. It's a duwende, right? (To ISABEL.) A duwende.

ISABEL: Well, why not. The Greeks have their minotaurs We have ours. The Irish have leprechauns, we have duwendes. I'm not sure about the engkantos though. I think the Spaniards brought them over. They're blond, you know.

EMILYA: And who's sitting on the roof?

JASON: The manananggal. At night time, she splits in two and the upper part flies all over Fifth Avenue and finds a pregnant woman so she can suck the baby's blood.

EMILYA: Dios mio.

JASON: But it's okay, Mom. Because Juan Tamad pours ash all over the other half that's left behind. That's how he kills it. And that's how Lazy Juan becomes Brave Juan.

ISABEL: I haven't heard that story.

JASON: I made it up. You can't be lazy all the time. Sometimes you have to kill the bad guys. And this is an agta. The giant that lives in trees.

EMILYA: There's no such thing!

ISABEL: There is, too. What an imagination! You deserve a piece of chocolate. (Rising, looking for her bag.) Where's my handbag?

EMILYA: (Stirring from the chair.) Oh. (Finding it on the chair she's sitting on.)
Is this it?

JASON: (Leaps for the bag and opens it. He takes out a paper bag.) Is this it, Tita Isa?

ISABEL: (She grabs the bag.) Jason, no!

> (JASON pulls the paper bag back and inadvertently tears it apart. An egg falls to the floor. ISABEL lets out a yell. INES comes rushing out.)

INES: Madre de dios! (To everyone.) GET OUT! (To ISABEL.) What have you done?

ISABEL: You said to wrap it in paper. I forgot all about it.

EMILYA: You have a raw egg in your bag?

INES: Go into your rooms! Quickly!

ISABEL: (Peering down at it, then drawing back in horror.) Blood! And hair! Oh, my god! (Looking at everyone.) I was just joking, Nay Ines. Emilya, blood and hair! Do you see it?

INES: It's the curse. A spell Isabel has broken. Miss Isa, it worked! It worked!

> (JASON runs towards the egg and INES wrestles him to the floor.)

EMILYA: Let go of Jason! Let go!

> (She pulls JASON away. INES falls to her knees and begins to chant. EMILYA pulls INES up.)

EMILYA: Stop this nonsense! Stop it! (To JASON .)Go to your room. Right now. (To ISABEL.)
Isa, stay with him.

JASON: The egg! The egg! Mom, it's magic!

ISABEL: It's not her fault, Emilya. I encouraged it.

EMILYA: (To ISABEL.) Leave this matter to me. (To INES.)
They have to stop. The stories. Everything. Engkantos who live in the sky. Tikbalangs. Spells and potions. I will not allow it!

INES: I'm sorry, Mrs. Emilya.

EMILYA: Don't you understand? There's no magic here. This is America.

JASON: That's not true!

(ISABEL drags him away. JASON resists and
stays within earshot.)

INES: Jason is hungry for stories. And these are the only ones I know.

EMILYA: Your stories frighten him.

INES: No. Not mine. It's those stories he watches on television. And the video games!

EMILYA: He's got plenty of books in his room.

INES: Those books have nothing to say about his country.

EMILYA: This is his country.

INES: He doesn't know anything about the Philippines.

EMILYA: So what?

INES: He doesn't know who he is!

EMILYA: I will be the judge of that.

INES: How can you judge?

EMILYA: I'm his mother!

INES: But I'm here with you. There's a reason for it. Something very powerful has brought me here.

EMILYA: And what's that, Ines?

INES: Fate.

EMILYA: Fate didn't send you. Ramonito did. And I let him. It's got nothing to do with fate.

INES: You're so blind!

EMILYA: Blind! How dare you speak to me like this. Don't you know I have the power to send you back?

> (JASON bursts into the room.)

JASON: No! No!

> (JASON lunges at EMILYA small fists flying in the air.)

EMILYA: (Slapping him hard. He falls back, more taken aback than hurt.) Nobody hits me! Nobody hits me!

JASON: I hate you! I hate you!

> (ISABEL drags him away. She throws EMILYA an astonished look. They exit. INES stands, dumbfounded.)

EMILYA: (Controlling her fury.)
Leave my house. Leave it. I will tell Ramonito I'm sending you back.

(She leaves and runs after JASON . Scrim on. INES
exits. ISABEL enters as INES comes back in with
gloved hands and some rags. She bends down to
wipe the floor clean of the broken egg. They
exchange glances. Nothing is said. INES exits.
EMILYA enters.)

ISABEL: How's Jason?

EMILYA: He'll feel better tomorrow. (Pause.) She has to go.

ISABEL: Not over this. It's my fault. I encouraged her.   Don't be
rash, Emilya, please.

EMILYA: Did you see how he tried to hit me? I've never seen
him do that before. I've never hit him before.

ISABEL: Where's she gonna go?

EMILYA: Back home where she belongs. And you. A curse! Are
you out of your mind?

ISABEL: How do you explain that egg? I saw it. With my own
eyes! We all did.

EMILYA: It's a fertilized egg.

ISABEL: A hundred million eggs in New York City and I had to
pick that one.

EMILYA: It's not impossible. How long have you been carrying that egg around in your bag? One more week and you'd have hatched it.

ISABEL: Every night I went through the chanting, the rituals, feeling stupid and at the same time compelled... I couldn't not do it... Think of it, Emilya. Once upon a time, one's words and thoughts were so powerful, they could take on a life of their own... take root in someone's else's body, live in time and space...

EMILYA: She got to you.

ISABEL: I've forgotten how there's so much to wonder about. That life is extraordinary. That's what Ines does for me. You can't hold that against her.

EMILYA: I like ordinary reality. I thank God for it everyday.

ISABEL: But you have to admit there are things that are inexplicable.

EMILYA: Like what? Next thing you know you'll be telling me the microwave is magic.

ISABEL: It is magic, Emilya.

EMILYA: Oh, for god's sake!

ISABEL: Look at it through her eyes. We call it electromagnetic radiation. But what exactly is electromagnetic radiation? How do you explain photons of light making food molecules vibrate? How do we explain photons? Molecules? Atoms! Do you realize that when you come down to it, it's all energy. And what is energy? A force. A force you can't see. Touch. It's just there. And it does things.

EMILYA: Now you sound like Star Trek.

ISABEL: Ines calls it magic. We call it energy and because we have a name for it, we're no longer awed by it. People like Ines. Like us. Filipinos. We can shift gears. That's a strength, Emilya.

EMILYA: People like us.

ISABEL: There are many kinds of reality.

EMILYA: That's right. There's this reality, and the rest is creative writing. I understand that both are important. But let's not fudge the boundaries.

ISABEL: Why not?

EMILYA: Because it'll drive you crazy.

ISABEL: You're the one who's seen too many movies.

(Scrim on. INES is seen in shadow.)

EMILYA: I know someone driven mad because the boundaries were fudged. Her name was Alba. She lived alone. She always wore black. Black shoes. Black handbag. Black umbrella. Rain or shine. And she walked. She was always walking. Because jeepney drivers knew of her, and they never picked her up because they were afraid of bad luck. And so the more everyone rejected her, the more she withdrew. Everyone began to believe she was really a witch. All the yayas used to scare us by calling on her. Eat your carrots. Take a bath. Say your prayers. Or Alba will get you. I was 18 when I met her face to face. She came to the house, selling rosaries. I knew why she was selling them. Witches were supposed to melt if they touched holy things. But it didn't do her any good. She didn't melt, you see. But it didn't change anybody's mind. One night years later, after I'd left town, her house caught fire. No one helped to put it out. She died in it. That's what happens when you shift gears. You can kill people doing it.

(JASON enters.)

JASON: Mommy, I finished my book. (Pause.) I don't like 'Goosebumps' anymore.

EMILYA: Give Tita Isa a kiss, Jason. It's way past her bedtime, too.

ISABEL: (Kissing JASON .) One of these days, I 'll read you one of my favorites, " The Lion, the Witch and the Wardrobe. " It's C.S. Lewis, Emilya, very mainstream.

(EMILYA and JASON exit.

ISABEL turns to go. INES, catches her at the door. ISABEL gasps in fright, but seeing it's only INES, regains her composure.)

ISABEL: I'm sorry, Nay Ines. I tried --

(INES puts something in her hand.)

INES: An anting-anting. A gift. You did your best.

ISABEL: An amulet? (Examining it.) In the shape of a hand!

INES: Keep it next to your skin.

ISABEL: Nay Ines, enough! Don't you think we've caused enough trouble?

INES: (Fiercely.) The stories will stop but my work must continue.

ISABEL: What is this supposed to do?

INES: It will open what is closed.

ISABEL: Sounds like trouble I don't need, Nay Ines.

> (She puts it back in INES's hand. She exits. INES stays put, as if waiting.
>
> The door opens again. ISABEL comes back in. She takes the amulet from INES.)

ISABEL: Oh, what the hell.

> (She exits. INES is left alone. She sees the drawings JASON has left on the floor. She picks them up. She looks at all of them. Something in a

sheet catches her attention. She cocks her head, deep in thought.)

INES: Maisog... Maisog! Of course!

FADEOUT

Scene Eight

(A dream sequence. Silence. Stage is pitch black.

Then gradually, lights go up; we see PRINCESS URDUJA prone on the ground, the same harsh music keeping her down. Whispers. Low rumblings. Moans. Screeches. The stage is filled with shadows. We see JASON holding an arnis stick; he has come to rescue the PRINCESS. But the shadows fall on him, a swirling, black shape -- the agta. It swoops down on JASON . He struggles; he puts up a fight, but it engulfs him, pinning him to the ground. The music screams.)

JASON: No! NO! NO!

(Lights go up in JASON 'S bedroom.)

EMILYA: Jason! Jason!

JASON: (Crying hysterically.) The agta. The agta! (Pointing at the corner of the room.)
See? Look! Look!

(EMILYA turns on the overhead light. INES follows close behind.)

EMILYA: It's just your teddy bear. Look. (She takes it to him.) See it's good old Timmy. There are no agtas. They're just make-believe.

JASON: But I saw it! I saw the agta! He was trying to kill me! I just wanted to save the Princess!

EMILYA: No, Jason. It's just a dream.

JASON: I tried to save the Princess... but the agta... he tried to kill me.

EMILYA: (To INES.)You see?

JASON: It killed Papa. So it's gonna kill me, too.

EMILYA: What?

JASON: Nay Ines said that when Papa built the playhouse in the breadfruit tree, the agta who lived there got very angry, so he put a curse on him and that's how he died.

EMILYA: (Addressing INES as well.) Jason, that's not true. The agta didn't kill your Papa. Ines was just telling you a story. It's all made up. A pretend story. And I promise you, Jason, she will never tell you stories like that again.

(INES withdraws.)

JASON: So why did he die? Why?

EMILYA: He was sick. He had a bad heart and one day, he had a stroke. You must believe me. (Pause.) Go back to sleep. I'll stay with you until you fall asleep, all right?

JASON: Okay, mommy...

EMILYA: (Hugging him tightly.)
I love you very, very much. I will never let anything come between us again.

JASON: Tell me a story, Mommy...

EMILYA: You're all I've got, Jason...

JASON: How about Tito George? And Nay Ines. And Tio Ramonito... Lola and Lolo... those people in the pictures? Mommy? Mommy. You're crying...

EMILYA: Go to sleep, hijo, go to sleep...

FADEOUT

Scene Nine

(The following week. EMILYA is on a cellular phone.)

EMILYA: Your mother was sick... and you're back?

(The bell rings.)

EMILYA: Will you hold on, Maria? (She picks up the intercom.) Yes? (Pause.) Okay.

> (She presses the button, opens the door and goes back to the phone.)

EMILYA: Maria? It wasn't right, the way you left .   I have someone working for me now... but she'll be gone in a few weeks' time... I have to go. We'll talk again, okay? I'll call you. 'Bye, Maria.

> (She hangs up as ISABEL enters, carrying a carton. She is wearing denims, a sweatshirt. She is simply herself.)

EMILYA: So did you get the account?

ISABEL: No.

EMILYA: I'm sorry. Did our Bennington lady get it?

ISABEL: Yes... But I got Rupert.

EMILYA: Rupert. The Rupert?

ISABEL: He's in love with me. And I love him, too!

EMILYA: When did this happen?

ISABEL: It's so confusing. I'm in love with a man named Rupert. How did this happen?

EMILYA: What's wrong with Rupert? I like it.

ISABEL: He wants me to meet his parents.

EMILYA: Really.

ISABEL: I don't like the English. And he'll never want to live in the Philippines. The English never do. The Irish. Germans. Italians. They love it there. But the English. I don't know why but they don't.

EMILYA: So who's going to the Philippines?

ISABEL: I am!

> (ISABEL drops the carton on the couch. She flings it open. In it are loose sheets of paper. EMILYA picks one up and begins to read.)

EMILYA: I, Lapulapu? Bow my head and lay down –

ISABEL: my sword.
  For those whose hilt like that of their god
  This blade I offer when they land on shore
  Blow on the conch the call to battle
  What runs in their veins is it not blood?
  Let's bathe the earth they touch in crimson ---

EMILYA: (Picking up another sheet.)

where will you take me now -

ISABEL: my dusky sparrow
i give you my hand so you might lead me
into what regions of the heart descend
you and i where no loves are forbidden

what rhythms and turns shall wind
what paths we seek, what edges
shall we push back, whose hearts shall we break
into the night into the night ---

EMILYA: (Picking up another.)
Who brought this succubus to my sleep?
The dark clouds, the thunder & the lightning –

ISABEL: A halfway house between the real
& imaginary. Whose dream is this? Who
is behind the turns & the windings?
Who lives behind this veil of night
in a white attic room next to the centenary tree.

EMILYA: (And another.)
one with so many faces
like a crystal
with so many cut sides

what you see

depends on the angle
from where you look

ISABEL: I took the week off. I sat down and the whole thing came out -- like vomit,Emilya. Vomit...and piss and shit. Poem after poem after poem. It's been there all along. It never left me. I can't stay here. I need to be home. I'm myself again!

EMILYA: What?

ISABEL: A poet needs to write in her own country.

EMILYA: What are you talking about? You can be a poet here, too.

ISABEL: An Asian-American poet. But in the Philippines, I would simply be a poet.

EMILYA: But Rupert --- ?

ISABEL: It's no use. He'd die there. It's too hot. And if I stay, I'll end up writing poetry and stashing it away in the drawer. I'll be like the rest of us. Someone with a fucking hobby.

EMILYA: You've been saying all along that the time has finally come for people like us. Everyone who never had a voice is finding one.

ISABEL: Nobody's listening, Emilya.

EMILYA: I'm listening!

ISABEL: So now I'm writing again. Big deal. They'll pick a few poets my color and it will be good for their conscience until the next slogan. Multiculturalism. Bullshit. Someday it will be old hat and nothing will have changed. We'll still be on the outside looking in. We will always be.

EMILYA: Oh, no. Not the victim speech. It doesn't become you.

ISABEL: I'm a goddamn clerk. I write one line of copy about diarrhea and the rest of the day, I'm pushing paper. Before that, I was teaching GED. Yes, I'm a victim. A victim of diminished expectations.

EMILYA: What do you want, Isabel?

ISABEL: A place at the table.

EMILYA: You're assuming there's only one table to sit at. You're the poet. Extend the metaphor. Build your own table. Find friends who'll do it with you. Then sit down and eat. The thing this country gives you is room to do it. The rest is your problem. You're not entitled.

ISABEL: You think I'm talking about entitlements?

EMILYA: Where in this planet would you rather be? Can you imagine being a woman anywhere else in the world today? A homosexual? A black man? A Jew. You can't even be a Buddhist in Tibet anymore, but oh, yes, they're all in Boulder, Colorado. Never mind political dissidents. Remember Ismael Escudero in the 70's? Marcos threw him in prison and shoved electrodes up his ass. He came to America and they gave him a grant. The truth is it's very good here. We all know it. We use it. Then we lie about it.

ISABEL: You believe the hype. You talk like that because you live on the Upper Westside. I can show you neighborhoods just across the park where your ideas are merely chic. And as for the rest of the country, you think New York is America? There's 7 million of us, but there's 255 million more out there who think New York is a city from hell. You're a Filipino. In Kentucky you'd still be a gook. And don't you forget it.

EMILYA: Well then stay and change it!

ISABEL: I need to choose what I can accomplish in a lifetime because that's all I have.

EMILYA: That's a cop-out. Going home would be easier.

ISABEL: You're right. Staying here would be too dangerous. Because at the end of the day, what do you become? Who are you? What are you?

EMILYA: A person. First and last. Not a gender. Not a race. Not the color of my skin. I'm your English lesson, Isabel. I am. You are. It is.

ISABEL: Precisely. It's too academic. I left because I thought I lost something that was important to me. What did you lose, Emilya?

(INES enters.)

INES: Good evening, Mrs. Emilya. Miss Isabel.

ISABEL: Good evening, Nay Ines. Where's Jason?

155

EMILYA: (To ISABEL.) Jason has a sleep-over with a friend. (To INES.) Did they tell you when we are supposed to pick him up tomorrow?

INES: I'm sorry. I forgot to ask.

EMILYA: It's okay, I'll give them a call.

(EMILYA exits.)

ISABEL: It worked, Nay Ines. (Giving her the amulet back.)

INES: So are you really in love with this Rupert?

ISABEL: Why, are you gonna give me another amulet?

INES: I've asked a friend to come and help me out with Emilya. He has great power and maybe he can do something for you as well. But you have to be absolutely certain that you love this Rupert because if you fall out of love with him, you're stuck. That's the way it works.

ISABEL: Sounds terminal.

INES: (She shows her a CD player.)And he loves music, too! Mrs. Emilya gave this to me for a going away present. My own CD player. And all my Gershwin's. (She turns it on.) Mrs. Emilya and I are getting along better. She's right. It's best that I leave. Mr. Ramonito's taking care of everything. The plane tickets –

ISABEL: So why can't we go home together, Nay Ines?   STOP
HERE

INES: (Hushes ISABEL to be quiet.) Come. Lie down. Close
your eyes. His name is Maisog. I must warn you. He's not very
polite. The first day he arrived, he simply found his way into
the kitchen and helped himself to the cocoa.

ISABEL: Maisog. From the Philippines? Where is he? When did
he get here? Does Emilya know?

INES: Not yet.

ISABEL: But he's already been here for some of your cocoa?

INES: She won't be displeased. Especially if she knows he's
come to help her. I don't know about you, though. He chooses
the people who can see him.

(A long pause.)

ISABEL: (Sitting up, turning off the music.) Do you mind if we
listen to Gershwin some other time? What did you say, Nay
Ines?

INES: I didn't think they could travel so far. But they do.

ISABEL: He's a relative of yours?

INES: Oh, no, no. He's a duwende.

ISABEL: A duwende. You mean a real one?

INES: (Laughing.) Of course. What do you think?

ISABEL: A duwende, right here in this house? (Pause.) What does he look like?

INES: Well, you know.

ISABEL: No.

INES: Small and short. Long dark hair. Powerful arms.

ISABEL: Where's he now, Nay Ines?

INES: Oh, he comes and goes.

ISABEL: Comes and goes! Oh, we can't have that. Did you tell him you don't just come and go in America?

INES: He's a powerful friend to have. And he gives good advice.

ISABEL: He talks to you?

INES: He told me that Jason is God's blessing and someday the pain in Emilya's heart will go away.

ISABEL: I talk to myself, too, you know. You'd think I had a thousand duwendes in my room. I have talk shows in there. Panel discussions. Conversations with Bill Moyers. But it's all in my head.

INES: Maisog is not in my head. He's as real as this chair is real. As you are real. Sit. You will meet him. (Leaning forward, head cocked, listening.) He's here! It's time!

> (INES exits. ISABEL is left alone. She sits on the
> couch. A few beats. She leans forward as well,
> peering into corners, over her shoulder. She gets
> up and walks towards the kitchen and stops,
> changes her mind and goes back to the couch.
> INES enters carrying a bowl with a mound of rice
> in it. On top of it are pieces of herbs. ISABEL
> watches in silence. INES goes to the window and
> places the bowl on the floor. Then INES exits.
>
> EMILYA enters.)

EMILYA: Isabel ---

ISABEL: (Jumping to her feet.) Jesus, you scared me.

EMILYA: I'm looking forward to getting my life back... I'll never know what she was up to... Something about her --- so obstinate. So determined. And nobody sees it but me...

ISABEL: You mean you've seen something? Someone, maybe? Someone short? Emilya, have you been seeing anything strange lately?

EMILYA: Like what?

ISABEL: Nothing.

EMILYA: Would you like some cocoa?

(EMILYA walks towards the kitchen.)

ISABEL: (Pulling her back.) NO! Not there. Not the kitchen. Emilya, don't ever go into the kitchen from now on!

EMILYA: What? What's wrong with you tonight? (Spots the bowl of rice on the floor.)
What --

ISABEL: It's for the duwende.

EMILYA: What?

ISABEL: Nay Ines says there's a duwende in this house. It's travelled all the way from the Philippines. Goes by the name of Maisog. Talks to her. Emilya, he talks to her all the time. Now I know I said I'm multicultural and I'm all for shifting gears, but I draw the line on hearing voices. Oh, god, Emilya, what are we -- - you going to do?

> (INES appears in the doorway, wearing a patadyong; she carries a bowl of flowers. She stands framed in dim light, cocooned in quiet power.)

INES: He's here... (Turning towards the window.) Emilya... can you hear him?

EMILYA: (Her back turned.) No. Please, Ines...no!

(A long pause. Then faint music spills into the space --- and stardust and moonlight, sigh of wind and wing.

EMILYA sways, as if something light has settled very gently over her body. She turns around, entranced; she drifts towards the window; she looks out.

She sees it.)

EMILYA: Don't you remember the stories, Isabel?... Our yayas told us about them ... we were raised on these stories... spirits flying through the air, nourished in the roots of trees... in the bottom of rivers... and in all the spaces where the sun could not reach... (To the spirit.)
Don't come into the light... they have names for you in the light... you'll die in the white light and its iron heat... here in the white light where they have a name for everything...

(EMILYA falls to the floor. ISABEL runs to her. INES blocks her way. INES begins to chant as ISABEL as if in a trance, exits. INES turns off the lights. Stage is dark except for the circle of light coming in through the window that falls on INES and EMILYA.

INES lays the bowl of flowers on the floor. INES bends down and lays her hands on EMILYA's back. There's a jolt. She looks up towards the window. A shadow passes over her. Then she lays her hands on her again, and this time, it happens. She can take it.

EMILYA moans in pain, her cries muffled. But as the exorcism proceeds, her body begins to twist and contort; she wails in anguish, its sound rending the air in two.

Then silence takes over. And very gently, INES takes off EMILYA'S clothes. INES takes a handful of flowers from the bowl and rubs them against EMILYA's body until it is completely covered by them. Something of this scene must remain primal, primitive. For this is how it must have been once: woman healing another in the soothing safety of darkness, mending bones, shedding tears.

Then INES covers EMILYA with a shawl, carrying her gently into the bedroom. Here, votive candles have been placed on the windows and on the tables; INES lights them all until the whole room begins to look like a shrine. INES produces the box of pictures and gives them to EMILYA. EMILYA picks them up one by one, tacking each one to the wall. Each picture brings fresh pain, INES' chanting gathers force, candlelight burning with ferocious intensity.

Then it's over. EMILYA sits on the chair, exhausted. INES leaves.

The silence is thick, like smoke. Votive candlelight flickers, throwing shadows on the walls.

Then one of the shadows moves, takes shape. It is GEORGE.)

GEORGE: (Gently, like a whisper.) Emilya? Emilya...

(He finds her sitting in the darkness.)

GEORGE: What is it? What happened? Isabel called me --

EMILYA: Ines and I...

GEORGE: What's going on here?

EMILYA: The time has come.

GEORGE: For what?
EMILYA: She came to heal me, George, but I wasn't ready... the first time Leon hit me... a week after we were married... the first blow... like lightning... he struck, palm spread apart from nowhere... I remember the blinding flash of pain in my head... the ringing in my ears... taste of blood in the mouth... Was it something I did? Something I said? Why? Or was it me? Something about me? He hit me often and everything set him off... a month's quota not met... a silk tie he couldn't find... a rainy Tuesday? I couldn't tell anyone. The shame of it... the secret shame of it... until Alba. Alba the witch. Black crow with the sad, soulful eyes. She came to comfort me... heal me... oil of biatelis, sap of narra... smoothed over broken bones... poured over cut flesh, hands strong as steel, but soft as silk... And then

one day something moved inside me.. A child... I was going to have a child! Leon was overjoyed. He didn't hit me once... not once for a whole year... Then exactly the day Jason was three months old… he came to my room, black with rage over something... I bore a year's worth of fury that night...

> (She takes down her shawl and in the harsh, yellow light reveals a body marked by old scars.)

EMILYA: The next morning, I told the servants to take the day off. I served him his hot sweet tea. He died with the poison I put in it. Alba's poison. There he lay… an old man coughing up blood and vomit, drowning in his own piss and shit... I held him down with my bare hands. It took so long for him to die! When it was all over, I washed and cleaned him up. So when the servants came back that night, he looked as fresh and immaculate as Sunday morning. No one knew how he died. He'd built a playhouse in the breadfruit tree in the backyard and the old people assumed he died because he had angered the agta. The doctors thought it was his heart.

> (She gets up. She sits on the bed. She waits. But GEORGE doesn't make a move.)

FADEOUT

Scene Ten

> (Three weeks later. Late afternoon. ISABEL is at the window. EMILYA: dressed in beige and cream, enters with a pot of bright pink flowers. It is spring.)

EMILYA: Jason's arnis class is over by seven... Take an hour and a half for the cab...we should get there early enough. So are you all packed?

ISABEL: I've been packed for weeks.

EMILYA: You better be the best goddamned poet the Philippines ever produced or I'm going down there myself and drag you back.

ISABEL: Don't bother. Rupert says he's dragging me back if I'm not out with a volume by Christmas.

> (She moves over to the window; EMILYA joins her.)

EMILYA: She's out there somewhere. Why did she leave like that? Left with only the clothes on her back and the CD player I gave her.

ISABEL: Her work was finished.

EMILYA: But where did she go? What's going to happen to her?

ISABEL: She promised to keep in touch, remember? You read her note.

EMILYA: But she didn't need to leave at all. I'm no longer the person I once was. Why didn't she give me a chance to make it up to her?

ISABEL: You don't need to. She knows. If it makes you feel any better, I gave her my address book. I don't know about yours, Emilya, but all my friends need every help they can get.

EMILYA: Your friends! Is she ready for them, Isabel? Is she ready for New York?

ISABEL: The question is -- is New York ready for Ines! You know who's under `A'? Abbott. Rupert Abbott. With Ines behind me, I think that poor man is going to end up living in the Philippines. (Pause.) It's you I worry about. I'm sorry, Emilya. I thought for a while there both you and George would pull through.

(EMILYA remains silent.)

ISABEL: It's his loss. And you'll have some peace around here for a change.

(The intercom rings. ISABEL picks it up.)

ISBAEL: Hello...fine. (Hanging up. To EMILYA.) I'll go ahead.

EMILYA: Is that the cab? It's too early.

ISABEL: Wait here. I'll ring when I'm ready.

(She exits. A few beats. The door opens. JASON comes rushing in, holding a trophy.)

JASON: Mom! Mom! I won the tournament! Look!

EMILYA: A tournament? In arnis? Why didn't you tell me? Oh, Jason! You mean I missed it?

JASON: But Tito George didn't!

(GEORGE enters.)

JASON: He's been watching me play, Ma. Every week, he comes to see me. He said not to tell you. It was our secret. (Holding his trophy in the air.) Mommy, Mommy, let's put it up on the shelf!

(He runs out. A long silence.)

EMILYA: The day I killed my husband was the day I decided to come to America... the safest country in the world... I got away with it, George... I intend to keep it that way...

(GEORGE makes no move towards her. Both stand apart, framed by window light.

(Lights go down.

DR, the PRINCESS is seen once again, prone on the ground. JASON whirls into view, an arnis stick in his hand. In this dream, he is invincible, easily banishing the shadows away. ThePRINCESS rises, is set free. She leaps into the air, resplendent as the first time we saw her. And in this dream, JASON: runs straight into her arms. The music, Gershwin fused with the age-old sound of gongs explodes.)

BLACKOUT

END OF PLAY

GOD, SEX AND BLUE WATER

by

Linda Faigao-Hall

GOD, SEX AND BLUE WATER

Premiered in 2009 with Living Image Arts Theater Company
In New York City.

Cast of Characters

Clarita Kintanar, Asian or Filipino, 23 years old

Brian Andersen, Caucasian-American, early to mid-30's,

Laling Kintanar, Clarita's mother, early 50's

Max "Dadong" Saavedra, Laling's brother, mid-50's

Time: Early March until a week after Easter Sunday, Spring
2001.

Place: Hoboken and Manhattan,

(Action unfolds in the following spaces:

a room in DADONG's apartment in Hoboken with a shrine, an icon of the Blessed Virgin, surrounded by votive candles, a window that opens to a view of the street;

BRIAN ANDERSEN bedroom, also with a picture window that opens to a spectacular view of Wall Street;

a neutral space for other scenes described in the text: a church, a hospice, a loft etc.)

Scene One

(Philippines. Monday, Holy Week. 1999

At rise, LALING is seen on a hospital bed.

Female voices chanting softly in Cebuano[1]:

Matam-is nga Hesus,
tungud sa pagtubus Mo sa Kalibutan
 nagpasakit Ka sa Krus;
Nangamuyo kami Kanimo,
nga tungud sa Imong mapa-it uyamut nga mga kasakit,
luwason Mo and kalag ni Eulalia
sa mga kasakitan nga giantus niya
 ug papahulayon Mo
sa Imong himaya, nga walay katapusan.[1]

      The chanting continues and fades out. CLARITA
      enters, and stands at LALING's bedside.
      CLARITA, is in her 20's; at first glance, there is

something ethereal about her beauty, but up close, tempered by an acute awareness of her surroundings, she has a grounded self-assurance. She 's dressed very simply although nothing of her look would suggest a lack of style. What she really lacks is a sense of irony. She means exactly what she says.)

CLARITA: (Bending down to kiss LALING's hand.) Mama?

LALING: Kinsa na?

CLARITA: Si, Clarita, Ma. Ni-a ming tanan. Giampo-an ka namo, Ma.

LALING: Ha-in ka, anak?

(CLARITA walks over to the window and pulls the shades up a little. Soft light streams into the room.)

LALING: Kalu-oy sa Dios.

CLARITA: (Hushing her.) Pahuway, Ma.

LALING: Ma-o na kani? (Making the sign of the cross. Praying.) Matam-is nga Hesus,
tungud sa pagtubus Mo sa Kalibutan... (She begins to cry.) Nahadlok ko, Inday...Nahadlok ko...ayaw ko ug baya-i. (Is this it? Sweet Jesus, because you have saved the world from sin-- I'm so scared, Inday. I'm scared. Don't leave me!)

CLARITA: Kahibalo ko, Nay. Ni-a Siya karon. Gihigugma ka niya. Dili gyud ka biya-an.

(CLARITA holds her in her arms.)

Matam-is nga Hesus,
tungud sa pagtubus Mo sa Kalibutan
 nagpasakit Ka sa Krus;
Nangamuyo kami Kanimo,
nga tungud sa Imong mapa-it uyamut nga mga kasakit,
luwason Mo and kalag ni Eulalia
sa mga kasakitan nga giantus niya
 ug papahulayon Mo
sa Imong himaya, nga walay katapusan.[1]
        (The sobs subside.

(A few beats. Then CLARITA takes out a gold pyx from her suit pocket, opens and takes out a wafer.)

CLARITA: Ginoo, dili ako angay nga mokalawat Kanimo, apan ipamulong lamang ug mamaayo ako. Ang lawas ni Cristo.

LALING: Amen.

(CLARITA brings the host to LALING'S lips and she takes it and eats it. And as she does, a river of light floods the room. Caught in a sharp instant of time, CLARITA becomes something not quite of this world, an apparition surrounded by a corona of light.

Then CLARITA lays her hands on LALING'S head. A few beats. Then she utters a cry of pain as she slips into a trancelike state, head raised, eyes closed. LALING begins to shake, her body seized by spasms. She cries out, then suddenly falls silent.

CLARITA falls backward onto the chair, her head thrown back, eyes closed. Pools of blood appear in the palms of her hands. The light around her shimmers with a savage glow, a contrast to the meditative pose, the closed eyes, the soft, languid look in her face.)

BLACKOUT

Scene Two

(Hoboken, New Jersey. Two years later. Spring, 2001.

The living room in DADONG's house that same evening. DADONG is singing "Achey Breaky Heart" karaoke style in front of a state-of-the art stereo system. LALING is pacing the floor, rosary in hand. There is an elaborate altar of a statue of the Virgin Mary. The phone is rining. LALING picks it up.)

LALING: Hello... Father Knickerbocker!... Yes, Father. I will.

(LALING hangs up. DADONG doesn't hear her over his singing. LALING turns off the music. DADONG stops. exasperated. LALING dials another number. She listens for awhile. Then she hangs up.)

LALING: No one's answering. Dadong, Clarita really needs a cell phone.

DADONG: Why? She's not a yuppie. Who was it?

LALING: Father Knick.

DADONG: What does he want now?

LALING: He needs her tomorrow at St. Luke's. At eight.
(Resumes pacing and praying the rosary. To Dadong) Dios mio,
what time is it?

DADONG: (Stops his dancing.) You're cramping my style.

LALING: She's not here yet!

DADONG: She's across the street.

LALING: I don't even know these people. They're not from the
parish. (Looks at her watch.) It's twelve o'clock! She's never
been out this late!

DADONG: Laling, you're not in Cebu anymore.

LALING: She's never been to an American party before!

DADONG: It's about time! St. Luke's . It's unhealthy being with
all those parish people. She should be going out more. Will you
put that away, please. No one's going to mug her crossing the
street. Lighten up.

LALING: I'm light. (Prays.)

(He pokes her gently. LALING puts her hand with
the rosary inside her pocket. She sulks, but
continues to move her lips in silent prayer.
LALING's ability to move from silent prayer to
casual conversation and back to prayer again is
one of her god-given talents.)

DADONG: No sulking.

LALING: Clarita and I could've stayed in Cebu. Even move to
Manila. But no. We had to come to the States! See the world! See
Hoboken! (Prays.)

DADONG: For good reason. The farm gone. The whole island
in the bottom of the sea. Manolo in it. You're my sister. With
nothing left to your name! And Clarita. That girl needs a life! A
future!

LALING: You were quite happy minding your own business all
by yourself here in the States. All of a sudden you're so
interested in her future. (Prays.)

DADONG: Listen, I never forgot a single birthday. Every
Christmas, I sent you a container of gifts!

LALING: Don't get me wrong. We'll always be in your debt.
You helped Manolo buy the farm after all. (Prays.)

DADONG: It's just my luck it's in the bottom of the sea.

LALING: But you said you'd sell the grocery store and come
home! Retire in Cebu. Set up a real estate business. What

happened to all those plans? (Prays as she looks at her watch again.)

DADONG: I can't find a buyer.

LALING: But Mr. Lee calls you every day.

DADONG: That cheapskate. $200,000! That grocery store is at least twice that. I have a business I started from the ground up, and if I sell, I'll do so on my own terms. (Pause) You talk as if I never went home.

LALING: Ten years ago.

DADONG: But there was just me and Nena. Who was going to watch the business for us if we went home?

LALING: You could have closed the store for a month. You're the boss. It's only money.

DADONG: It's only money, she says. Ay, dios mio. We close the store for a month, how would we pay for our trip.

LALING: Why didn't you bring her home when you found out she was sick? We might have cured her cancer. You never know.

DADONG: Who might have cured her cancer?

LALING: The Philippines. The air. There's no pollution there.

DADONG: She was a Filipino-American, Laling. She was born in Brooklyn.

LALING: It doesn't matter. Lots of people go to the Philippines and if they're sick, they recover.

DADONG: No, they don't. That's the end of karaoke practice. I don't want to sing anymore.

LALING: So why didn't you come home after she died. There was nothing to stop you.

DADONG: What would have been the point? You know what they're like - shaking their heads, feeling sorry for me. Wife dead... no kids... so what if he's got his own business? What's business without a family? Wa gyuy swerte intawn. Kalu-oy ni Dadong, 'Sus, kalu-oy. No way am I going to put up with that.

LALING: We never even met Nena. She was just pictures in letters you sent home. She was pictures and you were a gift box. What time is it?

DADONG: I think I know what's going on here. It's Clarita's first evening out and that's why you're making all this noise.

> (DADONG starts putting away the sound system. LALING pulls out her hand and resumes fingering the rosary. She watches him, praying in silence, her lips moving.)

LALING: Aren't you giving that up for Lent?

DADONG: What?

LALING: Your karaoke. Aren't you giving that up for Lent?

DADONG: Giving up karaoke for Lent? Me? The Hoboken Karaoke Champion of 2001?

LALING: So you got the gold medal already. What more do you want?

DADONG: This year, Hoboken. Next year, New Jersey! (Pause.) If I win, I'll offer it up to God. You like that?

LALING: But you still have to give up something.

DADONG: Bacon. I'll give up bacon. (Looking at his watch.) This conversation's making me nervous. I'm going to bed.

LALING: Uy, Dadong, I've to start making plans!

DADONG: What plans?

LALING: There's more I have to do for Lent.

DADONG: The Virgin in our living room. Evening prayers until Easter Sunday. No bacon. What else do you want to do?

LALING: Dadong, build me a cross.

DADONG: What?

LALING: You were the best carpenter we had. You were good with coffins. The mayor himself, was buried in one of yours.

DADONG: That was years ago. Before I immigrated.

LALING: The baranggay is holding a pasyon right here in Hoboken.

DADONG: A WHAT?

LALING: Imagine that. It will be the first pasyon to be held in Hoboken. Maybe in the whole country.

DADONG: A pasyon. In Hoboken. Whose crazy idea was that?

LALING: What's crazy about it?

DADONG: You didn't.

LALING: I didn't what.

DADONG: Laling, how could you?

LALING: We can do it in the churchyard. Kasi, we need penitentes, flagellantes -

DADONG: Flagellants. You're gonna have flagellants. Oh, Jesus.

LALING: Neil said he'll do it.

DADONG: Neil Cayabyab wants to be a flagellant. That man won't even see a dentist! And a crucifixion? Are you crucifying anyone? (Laughing.) Hey, I hear back home, they're using Black and Decker pneumatic drills. The nails go in and out. No problem. Very high-tech.

LALING: Who ever heard of a pasyon without a crucifixion?

DADONG: I was kidding...?

LALING: And you're building the cross.

DADONG: You're joking, right? Please tell me you're joking.

LALING: Am I laughing?

DADONG: Who's doing the hanging? (Pause.) Oh, no. Laling! Oh, my god....

LALING: I don't do the feet. Just the hands.

DADONG: Just the hands? Just the hands?!

LALING: Black and Decker pneumatic drill... what a good idea!

DADONG: You're not nailing yourself to a cross, you hear me? Don't you dare –

LALING: You can't stop me.

DADONG: Laling. Listen to me. (Holding her face.) Focus. You're in America. It's different here.

LALING: What's so different about it?

DADONG: You can't pray in a classroom without some lawyer going to court.

LALING: But this is my devotion. Since Clarita was born. Never missed. Not once. And you're telling me I can't do it anymore because I'm in Hoboken?

DADONG: You're damn right, it's because you're in Hoboken. You can't hang from a goddamn -- you can't hang from a cross. Everybody in Manhattan will be coming with their camcorders. We'll be the laughing stock of the whole country.

LALING: Let them laugh. This is not about them.

DADONG: No way am I sticking around for this. I'm gonna make sure I'm out of town!

LALING: What do you mean? Where are you going?

DADONG: North Dakota! I'll go to North Dakota. Filipinos don't know where it is.

LALING: The Magbanuas live in North Dakota. I'm inviting them.

DADONG: We have relatives in North Dakota? Why?!

LALING: Dadong, only you can build this cross.

DADONG: I'm telling you, I'm not building anything.

LALING: Fine. I'll go to Washington Street. There's furniture people there. If they can build a bookcase, they can build a cross.

DADONG: You mean Isaiah Wood Works? But they're Jewish!

LALING: So what? They don't know how to build a cross?

DADONG: Laling, we're not going there.

LALING: We're not imposing it on anyone. It's in the constitution. Isn't that why those people came on the Mayflower. For freedom of worship. Neil says if we don't get a permit, he'll go to the ACLU. What's that?

DADONG: ACLU? You're gonna ask the ACLU to support your right to get nailed to a cross on Washington St.?

(He turns to go.)

LALING: Dadong, our prayers!

DADONG: And that's another thing. I'm gonna video these prayers. So every evening, we'll just turn on the VCR and we can all go to bed early.

LALING: You're ashamed of us!

DADONG: No, Laling. I'm not.

LALING: I can't break a vow!

DADONG: What vow?

LALING: Don't you remember I was married five years before Clarita was born?

DADONG: I remember you wrote and told me the doctors said there was something wrong with Manolo. Well obviously they didn't know what they were talking about.

LALING
They were all useless. I even went to the albulario. Blackberries boiled in pig's blood. Sap of narra. Oil of biatelis. Eaten at the stroke of midnight. A whole month of midnights – nothing. Then on a January day, I took a boat and went to dance at the Feast of the Sto. Nino. I danced, Dadong, for nine days and nine nights, chanting, Pit Senor! Pit Senor! And vowed. If you give me a child, I will take up the Cross every Lent for the rest of my life. Nine months later, Clarita was born.

DADONG:
You should just have given money. That's what people do. They give money. Why take up the cross, Laling. Dios mio... I thought you only do that to atone for big sins. Graft and corruption. Bribery!

LALING: I was desperate. I wanted to do something hard – that demanded pain and suffering I could offer up. She's more than my child. She's God's gift. She's special, Dadong. When the volcano erupted, she saw it in her dreams.

DADONG: She saw it in her dreams?

LALING: After Manolo died, I thought my heart would break…
I was sick for a long time… I thought I was going to die. She
saved my life, Dadong.

(A long silence)

DADONG: I'm sorry, Laling. Let me handle this. I'll talk to
Father Nick. You can't just go barging in there proclaiming,
Father, I want to get crucified. He's from Wisconsin, he won't
understand.

(The door bell rings.)

FADEOUT

Scene Three

(Same time as Scene Two, in Hoboken, across the
street.
A room in a house.

Offstage, we hear the sound of a loud and raucous
party; dance music is blaring.

CLARITA is seen eating from a small plate from
which she's piled mounds of food in plates set on
the table.

BRIAN ANDERSEN is seen Down Right, coming
into the room, closing the door behind him,
talking on his cell phone. The music goes down a
little.

CLARITA sees him and stops eating. She watches

him, studying him.)

BRIAN: Amnesty International got involved... the charges? Crew intimidation... persecution... abuse. And two crew members got very sick... No. Let's keep out of it... You heard me. None of our business. (He sees CLARITA.) Lindsay? Call me back in 15.

(CLARITA turns away.)

BRIAN: No. Five. Make that five.

(He puts the cell phone back in his pocket. He walks over to her.)

BRIAN: Hello. Have we met? Didn't see you out there.

CLARITA: Too loud.

BRIAN: Too crowded.

CLARITA: I'm hungry.

BRIAN: Jane and her pot luck.

CLARITA: Pot luck? (Pointing at a few dishes.) This is lucky. This... this... Not this.

BRIAN: (Laughing.) Guacamole. You don't like guacamole.

CLARITA: Gua..ca..molee... sounds exactly how it tastes.

BRIAN: (Very amused.) You don't like avocado?

CLARITA: I love avocados. What did they do to it?

BRIAN: What do you do to it?

CLARITA: Mash them, put milk and sugar, chill them. If silk were fruit, it would taste like avocado.

BRIAN: Really. I can taste. What did you bring?

CLARITA: Bring?

BRIAN: You didn't bring anything. (Laughing.) That makes two of us.

CLARITA:
I'm supposed to bring something. I'm sorry I didn't know

BRIAN: Never heard of pot luck.

CLARITA: Back home, when you're invited to a party, you don't bring your own food.

BRIAN: I wouldn't either. And where's home?

(The sound of a jazz selection wafts into the room.)

BRIAN: That's more like it –

(CLARITA shushes him.)

CLARITA: What is that?

BRIAN: Brubeck.

CLARITA: Brubeck...

(A few beats.)

CLARITA: It's wonderful.

BRIAN: Jane and I go a long way back. I've never met you.

CLARITA: I'm a new friend. I teach choir at St. Luke's. She's in it.

BRIAN: Jane's not very religious.

CLARITA: She loves Bach.

BRIAN: hat would you say about a man who likes this kind of music.

CLARITA: It's new to me.

BRIAN: No one in this planet is new to jazz.
CLARITA: I'm from the Philippines.

BRIAN: I was in Hongkong last year on business. The best jazz band in town was from Manila.

CLARITA: I'm not from Manila.

BRIAN: So where are you from?

CLARITA: A small island in the South Pacific off the coast of the Visayas. It was destroyed in a volcanic eruption last year. It no longer exists. You never heard of it, and it never heard of jazz.

BRIAN: I didn't get your name.

CLARITA: Clarita Kintanar.

BRIAN: Clarita. Exquisite. And I'm Paul Gauguin.

CLARITA: You're named after the French painter who lived in the South Pacific?

BRIAN: It eventually killed him but I can't think of a better way to go, can you?

CLARITA: I beg your pardon?

BRIAN: I'm sorry. I was being facetious. Brian Andersen. Are you seeing anyone?

CLARITA: For what?

BRIAN: I mean boyfriends. Do you have a boyfriend. Forget that. Are you married?

CLARITA: No.

BRIAN: Would you like to have dinner with me?

CLARITA: Why?

BRIAN: In this country when a single man meets someone attractive, he asks for a date.

CLARITA: That's a lot of dates.

BRIAN: Life is short. Are you free tomorrow evening?

CLARITA: We don't know each other.

BRIAN: I'm from Iowa. I moved to New York 10 years ago. I'm 32, never been married. That means no ex-wives, alimonies, kids in private schools, in-laws.
CLARITA: That's good?

BRIAN: Yes, you could say that. It means I'm free.

CLARITA: To do what?

BRIAN: To take you out?

CLARITA: You didn't say anything about a religion. Do you have one?

BRIAN: No. But I'm a Leo. Does that help?

CLARITA: You don't practice any faith?

BRIAN: No. My parents used to be Lutheran. Hardly went to church though. I'm not a fan of organized religion.

CLARITA: Organized religion is only a means to an end. It can be useful. Do you believe in God?

BRIAN: Is this a test?

CLARITA: Do you believe in the soul?

BRIAN: Do you want me to?

CLARITA: What happens when you die?

BRIAN: You die, that's it. To tell you the truth, I've never really seriously thought about it. In fact, this is the longest conversation I've had about the subject since college. But I'm open to suggestions. I'm perfectly willing to discuss this again over dinner.

CLARITA: Is this a date?

BRIAN: You bet.

CLARITA: I've never been on a date.

BRIAN: I believe it.

CLARITA: My Saturdays are very busy.

BRIAN: Oh? How?

CLARITA: I'm a Eucharistic Minister for my parish. I give Holy Communion to the sick. I start around 8:00, don't finish until noon. Help out Sister Kathleen at the Sisters of Mercy until four

-

BRIAN: And what is it you do there?

CLARITA: I give comfort. Then I teach choir at St. Luke's until 8:30.

BRIAN: Busy day.

CLARITA: What do you do on Saturdays?

BRIAN: I'm probably hung over. I sleep late.

CLARITA: What do you do when you wake up?

BRIAN: See friends.

CLARITA: You have many?

BRIAN: No.

CLARITA: What do you do after you've seen them?

BRIAN: Are we finally talking about hobbies? Good! I build things! In fact, you're sitting on one of my chairs. I gave it to Jane for her birthday.

          (CLARITA gets up and examines the chair she's sitting on.)

BRIAN: White birch. Ribs out of unsplit saplings. No nails, screws, rivets... root lashings hold it together.

CLARITA: Where I grew up, we built our own things. So I know what it's like working with wood. The feel of it... its strength. Its texture.

BRIAN: The warmth and the beauty. No such thing as dead wood. One can make any piece of wood come alive. Once upon a time, that's all what I wanted to do.

CLARITA: Then you grew up and decided to make money instead.

BRIAN: It's a long story. I'll tell you over a bottle of Cristal.

CLARITA: What's that?

BRIAN: I keep doing this wrong.

CLARITA: Besides money what else do you believe in?

BRIAN: I don't believe in money. I just make it. Like organized religion. It's only a means to an end.

CLARITA: What end?

BRIAN: A two-bedroom condo over Battery Park. A summer house on the Cape. ... Comfort.

CLARITA: Besides comfort, anything else?

BRIAN: I believe in working hard. Doing my best.

CLARITA: But if you don't believe in God or the soul, why would you want to do your best?

BRIAN: For myself. For the people I love.

CLARITA: You love many people?

BRIAN: Just my Dad. I've had my share of relationships. I've loved many women and many women have loved me.

CLARITA: Then you're very blessed.

BRIAN: You mean I think I have a life but when you strip it down there's really nothing there. (Pause.) How did we get here?

CLARITA: Wood is better.

BRIAN: I'm sorry?

CLARITA: Dead wood. The more you strip it down, the more attractive it becomes.

(The cell phone rings.)

BRIAN: Excuse me. (Answering it.) Lindsay? Dammit, Lindsay, go home and get a life, okay? ...Yes. Drinking water was contaminated with diesel. Two crew members got sick. Didn't I say to leave it alone, Lindsay? Call the P & I guys... 'bye, Lindsay.

(He turns it off and puts it back in his pocket.)

BRIAN: I'm a broker. Ocean marine. You have a ship, you call me if you want it insured. I'll find you the underwriter with the best rates. It's very uninteresting.

> (Just then the music changes. The thin wail of a sax solo wafts into the room.)

BRIAN: (Holding out his arms.) May I have this dance?

CLARITA: I'm not sure. I don't know -

BRIAN: Just follow my lead.

> (She steps into the circle of his arms. She is unsure about what to do, and he shows her.)

BRIAN: That scent you're wearing... lovely.

> (They dance.)

BRIAN: May I take you home afterwards?

CLARITA: I live across the street.

BRIAN: We can take the longer route if you want.

CLARITA: Why?

BRIAN: Clarita, I'd really like to see you again. You remind me of Iowa.

CLARITA: I'm sorry?

BRIAN: Do you like movies? There's a Meryl Streep Festival at the Film Forum. You like Meryl Streep?

CLARITA: No.

BRIAN: All right. There's this bistro on Park Avenue.

CLARITA: Bistro?

BRIAN: How about coffee? You like coffee? Everybody likes coffee.

> (CLARITA slips her hand from his and places it on his heart. Then turning away, she clasps her hands together.)

CLARITA: I need to sit down.

> (CLARITA goes back to the table. Her arm sweeps a glass off the table and it crashes to the floor.)

BRIAN: Are you - Oh, my god, you're bleeding!

> (He stares at her hands, then grabs a handful of paper napkins on the table. She presses them between her open palms. She closes her eyes, biting her lips, head bent over in pain.)

CLARITA: Just give me a moment...

BRIAN: It looks nasty. How did that happen? (Turning to go.) Wait here. Jane keeps her – let me get you something -

CLARITA: Don't make a fuss.

BRIAN: Then let me take you home.

> (He pulls her up, her hands clasped against each other, a pained expression in her face, her eyes tight shut. He puts his arm around her and they exit.
>
> The telephone rings. The sound of the party overpowers it.)

BLACKOUT

Scene Four

> (DADONG'S house. CLARITA and BRIAN enter. CLARITA comes forward to kiss both LALING's and DADONG's hands. A blood soaked tissue falls to the floor. LALING picks it up quickly and shoves it into her own pocket.)

CLARITA: Tio, Ma, Brian Andersen.

BRIAN: (Shaking DADONG's hand.) Good evening.

DADONG: (To BRIAN.) Max Saavedra. Clarita's uncle. You can call me Dadong.

LALING: Eulalia Kintanar. Mrs. Kintanar. Clarita's mother.

DADONG: (To CLARITA.) What happened to your hand?

CLARITA: An accident.

DADONG: Again?

BRIAN: She cut her hand with a glass. I didn't really see it. It happened too fast.

LALING: Excuse us.

CLARITA: (To BRIAN.) Thank you.

BRIAN: I'm glad I was there. I hope it heals nicely.

> (CLARITA and LALING exit. Lights go Up Left. CLARITA lies down on the bed.

> LALING enters a few seconds later, with a first aid kit. LALING begins to dress CLARITA's hands.)

CLARITA: I was dancing with him. That's when it happened.

LALING: Why?

CLARITA: He's an unbeliever.

LALING: Clarita, Father Nick called. You're needed at eight tomorrow at the hospice.

CLARITA: Yes, Ma.

LALING: You look tired, anak.

> (LALING sits on the chair, and CLARITA rests her head on LALING's lap. LALING begins

untangling CLARITA'S hair, picks up a brush and
begins brushing her hair, singing a soft, gentle
hymn.)

CLARITA: Do you miss home, Mama?

LALING: More than my heart can bear. And you?

CLARITA: It feels like a dream now. All of it.

LALING: But it was real. More real than this place.

CLARITA: I miss the sea… the colors – grey, green and blue –
especially the blue – when it was blue, it was the bluest sea
you'd ever seen -

LALING: I remember the sky. Everywhere you looked, every
time of day, you knew it was there. In Hoboken, I'm hardly
aware of it.

(They fall silent, each in her own thoughts.)

CLARITA: Do you think it's time to tell Tio Dadong, Ma?

LALING: Didn't the sisters warn you about the world, Clarita?
When you left the convent, and before we left, they asked you
to renew your vow of silence. I don't think it's wise.

CLARITA: But he's family, Mama.

LALING: He's become an American. He's got a long way to go
before he's worthy to hear the truth.

CLARITA: Poor Tio…

LALING: Don't feel too sorry for him. Besides he's enjoying himself. We amuse him.

CLARITA: You can't see what I see. He's soul is still Filipino. The rest is just Macy's. Please see to Mr. Andersen, Ma.

LALING: Yes, Inday.

DADONG: May I offer you a drink, Mr. Andersen.

BRIAN: Thank you, but I'm afraid it's getting late.

(His cell phone rings.)

BRIAN: I'm sorry. (On the phone.) Lindsay, didn't I tell you to go home? … Is that right… All right. I'll talk to Cambanis tomorrow. I'm turning this off. 'Bye.

(He puts the phone away. To DADONG.)

BRIAN: No rest for the wicked.

DADONG: What do you do?

(BRIAN gives him a card.)

DADONG: (Reading the card.) "Ocean marine insurance…"

BRIAN: Blue water. Tankers as opposed to tugboats. That would be brown water.

DADONG" "Twenty Wall Street…"

BRIAN: It's old. This time next month, we'll be moving to new quarters. Just down the block.

DADONG: Thanks for bringing Clarita home.

BRIAN: She's very lovely. I've never met anyone like her before. I asked her out and she wanted to know if I believed in God.

DADONG: She did? I'm so sorry. I'll speak to her about it.

BRIAN: I found it refreshing.

DADONG: And that's what she is. Fresh off the boat, Brian. Grew up in a convent. Very sheltered. The ways of the world still baffle her.

BRIAN: Now I understand.

> (He spots the shrine. He looks at the Virgin closely.)

BRIAN: Made from one piece… I don't recognize the wood.

DADONG: Narra. Philippine hardwood. An antique.

BRIAN: Beautiful piece of work… such fine detail… oh…the Madonna's nose –

DADONG: We come from an island that drove out all the Spanish friars in 1838. We kept the faith. And the icons. But we cut off all their noses to make them look Filipino.

BRIAN: Fascinating.

(LALING appears UL, unobserved.)

DADONG: Are you interested in antiques?

BRIAN: I work with wood. A hobby of mine.

DADONG: What kind of things do you make?

BRIAN: Mostly furniture.

LALING: Can you make a cross?

(BRIAN and DADONG turn around.)

BRIAN: I'm sorry?

LALING: A cross. Can you make one?

(DADONG makes gestures for her to keep quiet.)

LALING: It should be easy. For the church. For Lent. Ten -- fifteen feet high.

BRIAN: Big.

DADONG: I'm sure Mr. Andersen is very busy.

BRIAN: Well, I don't really mind. I think it would be --

DADONG: My sister. She's – she's an FOB, you know. Thank you very much, Mr. Andersen. It was nice meeting you.

BRIAN: Well, I better be going then. Thank you.

(He exits.)

DADONG: Are you crazy?

LALING: FOB? What's that?

DADONG: He's a master of the universe!

LALING: What are you talking about?

DADONG: The first man to bring Clarita home and you ask him to build a cross.

LALING: He said he works with wood! And don't you encourage him. She's not interested.

DADONG: Chill, Laling. She's not going to marry the first man who brings her home.

(Lights dim. CLARITA is in prayer in front of the altar.)

CLARITA: His eyes... I never thought that eyes could be blue the way the sea is blue or the sky is blue... I've never known anybody... anybody close... And all the time, inside, I've always been the same. Where it's quiet and nothing happens... I accept it... all for you... I do it all for you...

FADEOUT

Scene Five

(DADONG'S house. Next day, Saturday.

Down Left, DADONG is seen singing to "Achey Breaky Heart" in the stereo while sanding pieces of hardwood, each about a foot wide and ten feet long. There are tools on a work table. Now and then, he pauses from his work to improvise a dance move. CLARITA enters. DADONG looks up.)

CLARITA: So have you spoken with Father Nick?

DADONG: I've an appointment to see him later this week.

CLARITA: Mama's very grateful. She didn't think you'd see it her way.

DADONG: She's got her reasons. Old school, you know.

CLARITA: They give her comfort. That's reason enough. She's given up everything to come here.

DADONG: She told me about your dream.

CLARITA: Ash, smoke, lava. A wall of water as high as the convent tower. The sea in my mouth. I woke up screaming.

DADONG: What did you do?

CLARITA: I told Mother Superior. She called a cousin in Manila who worked for a newspaper. The cousin told his boss and the boss called someone at the Weather Bureau. The Bureau reported some unusual activity. So someone there called Hawaii. Hawaii said there was more than unusual activity. The whole island was evacuated a week before the eruption. Twenty-five nuns from the convent and all 83 people from the island.

DADONG: That's creepy.

CLARITA: Mother Superior believed me. And Mama.

DADONG: And Manolo? What really happened there, Clarita. I'm afraid to get the details from her.

CLARITA: We got separated during the evacuation. We found out later from a neighbor that he had gone back to the island to look for us. He didn't make it out. It was that which broke our heart.

DADONG: All the same, it's a good thing you weren't in Hoboken. I'd have told you to go back to sleep. You can't go around believing in your nightmares. You'd be a nervous wreck. Does this happen often, Clarita.

CLARITA: It was the one and only time.

DADONG: A coincidence!

CLARITA: Mama says it was a miracle.

DADONG: And you? What do you think?

CLARITA: It doesn't matter what one calls it.

DADONG: A coincidence, then. This is America. There are no miracles here.

CLARITA: Two days later, the island was gone. And Mama and I – we couldn't see it through our tears. Papa. The convent. Our lives. As if we were never there... We wept for days.

DADONG: A blessing in disguise. You can't live like that, cut off from the world. It's not natural.

CLARITA: Don't exaggerate. It was only a two-mile walk on the foot bridge.

DADONG: That's what I mean. A foot bridge.

> (CLARITA passes her hand over the wood's surface.)

DADONG: Smooth as a baby's ass. No narra. So I got oak.

> (He picks up a jar of oil.)

DADONG: Hasmin... you know what's so strange? I've been smelling it a lot lately... at first I didn't know where it was coming from...

CLARITA: Do they have hasmin in America, Tio.

DADONG: Maybe Manhattan. You know you can find anything in Manhattan.

CLARITA: My favorite flower. Mama's, too. She told me that when she got married, she carried a bouquet of them. What kind of flowers did Tia Nena have, Tio, when you got married?

DADONG: An orchid. A cattleya. From Hawaii. Every year, on our anniversary, I go to Manhattan and buy one and lay it on her grave. Hand me that piece of cloth, will you?

> (CLARITA picks up a piece of cloth and gives it to DADONG who dips it in the jar of oil. He rubs the board with the cloth. He takes a few deep breaths)

DADONG: How are you doing, Clarita? Are you enjoying yourself here in America?

CLARITA: Oh, yes, Tio! It's so - different. It's as if I'm in another planet.

DADONG: No. You're the one – I mean, go out more, Clarita. What you did? Going to that party? Letting that Mr. Andersen bring you home. That's good.

CLARITA: There's so much I don't know. Brubeck, Crystal –

DADONG: What? Who?

CLARITA: It's a drink?

DADONG: Never heard of it. Do you know the secret to living happily in America? Avoid extreme behavior. Remember your Manong Peping? He came here in the 70's with his family. One day he and his wife went to see "Hello, Dolly." He saw all the hookers in Times Square. The blonde ones. Wouldn't you know it. He disappeared for six months. No one knew where he was until some resourceful nephew tracked him down to an SRO hotel on Eighth Avenue. Fifteen thousand dollars, he blew it all. When they brought him home, he had 200 dollars left in his wallet. His wife took the kids and split. A few years ago, over a glass of beer, I finally got bold enough to ask him about those six months. You know what he said? 'Dadong ... it was the best six months of my life...' Now all he's got is cable.

CLARITA: It's something in the air. The minute the plane hit the ground. It was noon when we arrived. In the middle of summer - hot, noisy, crowded... everything breathed. Even the ground I walked on seemed to jump up at me.

DADONG: Where was this?

CLARITA: Newark.

DADONG: (Laughing.) Newark! Clarita – you and your mother. You're all I have. God spared both of you for a reason.

CLARITA: I wonder what it is.

DADONG: You'll know soon enough. As long as you keep an open mind - what life brings. Ordinary stuff. Like falling in love. Getting married. Children.

CLARITA: I have choir practice, Tio. I have to go.

(CLARITA exits.)

DADONG: Dios mio. Can't even talk about it.

(DADONG goes back to sanding the board, singing "Achey Breaky Heart" again. A few beats. LALING: enters.)

LALING: Is this true Mr. Lee raised his offer to $300,000. And that you still rejected it? Dadong, that's a lot of money!

DADONG: That's because you keep multiplying it by 50 pesos. You can't set up a gated housing development in Cebu for less than a million dollars.

LALING: Dios mio, what are you thinking?

DADONG: An island.

LALING: What?

DADONG: The one off the coast of Argao. Where I used to play when I was a boy. Isla Kambing. That's mine.

(DADONG opens a drawer and takes out a batch of blue prints and lays them out on the table next to the cross he's building.)

DADONG: This is why I came to America. And this is what it will take to get me home.

LALING: Isla Kambing? There's nothing there but goats! What are you going to do, make caldereta?

DADONG: I've got it all planned. Down to the last tile in the jacuzzi An American-style gated community. 4.8 hectares. Cebu City's first residential tower! (Going over the blue prints.)... the Lifestyle and Entertainment Complex... the restaurant. Here... Prada, Coach, Salvatore Ferragamo... McDonald's. Swimming pool. Spa.... and right here, a waterfall.. I'm calling it Isla de Esmeraldas.

LALING: God won't like that. It's like you're building heaven on earth. So what's the point.

DADONG: And He told you this personally. You got a hotline? Give me the number. I wanna talk to Him.

DADONG: God himself will want to retire there. I've done all the research. Ageing baby boomers from Australia, the US, Germany. Filipino-American retirees.

LALING: Forget the island with the goats, Dadong. With your luck, it's got a volcano in it. There's plenty of things you can do with three hundred thousand. Didn't you tell me you've got some savings? A few more years and you'll be retired and you'll be getting money from Uncle Sam. With all that money you can run for president. You're so greedy. What's wrong with you?

DADONG: What's wrong with me? You were gonna ask Brian Andersen to build it.

LALING: He just called. I told him Clarita was at choir practice.

DADONG: He called her back? He must be interested. Clarita likes him, too.

LALING: Forget it. Clarita's answered for.

DADONG: She was a novice. She almost married Jesus. But she didn't. That volcano erupted just in time.

LALING: There are things you still don't know about Clarita.

DADONG: Like what?

LALING: (Beat) She's in the business of saving souls.

DADONG: And you don't think Brian is a perfect career move.

LALING: Why are you singing that song? Don't you remember how we sang an oracion while the carpentero built it?

DADONG: I need to practice!

> (DADONG resumes singing along as LALING begins chanting. The two songs don't go together.)

LALING: Buot ni Pilato buhian si Jesus,
            ug busa misulti siya pagusab ngadto sa mga tawo
            pan misinggit sila pagtubag kaniya Ilansang siya
            sa Krus! Ilansang --

DADONG: Okay! Okay!

(He turns down the music, rifles through his CD collection. He takes one from the pile and gives it to her.)

DADONG: They're monks.

LALING: Let's just keep quiet.

DADONG: Okay. (Relieved.) Quiet is good.

(They resume working. Then LALING lies down on a piece of board, spreads her arms, lowers her elbows as DADONG measures the span.)

LALING: Straight out. Like this.

(DADONG marks one of the pieces. LALING raises her knees a little, both her feet resting on the ledge.)

LALING: Make sure it's a foot and a half wide. Don't you remember?

DADONG: I don't want to.

LALING: My whole weight must rest on it, so I don't end up hanging from my hands or I'll choke to death!

DADONG: I thought that was the point.

(LALING gives him a look.)

DADONG: Just kidding! I guess you had to be there.

LALING: (Correcting the angle.) No. No. 45 degrees from the ground. What's the matter with you?

DADONG: What's the matter with me?

LALING: You never take anything seriously.

DADONG: You sure hit the nail on the head. You know what my problem is with Jesus? He's always hanging from a cross or looking for lost sheep or knocking on doors. He needs to lighten up. Have you ever wondered why there's a laughing Buddha? Squatting on the floor, beer belly hanging out, looking like he's had a few. You can even touch his belly for good luck. Who can't relate?

LALING: Jesus turned water into wine. He had his moments.

DADONG: And that's not one of them. All I get out of that story is he's bossing His mother around. "Woman, what is that to me?" No Filipino mother would put up with that.

LALING: (Smiling at the thought.) I'm sure he laughed when Peter tried to walk on water and began to sink. You know what Jesus probably said? "Oh, you of little feet." (Laughing uproariously.) You get it? Feet? Oh you of little feet?
DADONG: Wow, Laling. I didn't know you had it in you.

(LALING picks up two coils of rope. She ties them around each end of the arms of the cross.)

DADONG: Now you're thinking. You're just gonna put your hands through these. No nails.

LALING: I'm just practicing. My arms get so tired now that I'm older.

DADONG: Never mind. I hope to God you're right about this, Laling. I can see it now. The New York Post - Nailed!

(LALING gives him a light slap. Then she, too, begins sanding the wooden boards. DADONG opens the bottle of hasmin and sprinkles it on the wood. LALING begins to hum, softly. DADONG recognizes the tune, an old forgotten hymn from his past. He hums along with her until a kind of hushed silence settles over them, broken only by the rhythmic whisper of sand paper on wood mingling with the smell of jasmine.)

FADEOUT

Scene Six

(At St. Luke's Church. Later that same day around 5:00 in the afternoon.

A chanting is heard:

Kyrie, eleison

Kyrie, eleison

Kyrie, eleison

Christe, eleison

Christe, eleison

Christe, eleison

BRIAN is seen at Left. A few beats. CLARITA
comes forward.)

BRIAN: I was in the neighborhood. (Pause.) That's a lie. I called
you on the phone. Your mother said you had choir practice. I
figured it would be near where you lived. I'm very good with
details. I'm a broker.

CLARITA: Have you come to see the church?

BRIAN: Yes! (Pause.) No. But I've never been inside before.

CLARITA: Built in 1823...

(A pool of stained glass light falls to their Left.)

CLARITA: They say Easter Sunday in 1934, all the colors turned
golden... The southern wing... a fire in '48 completely destroyed
everything in it. Except for this...

(Spotlight on a statue of the Virgin Mary.)

CLARITA: They found her, untouched by the fire, surrounded
by ash and smoke. Back home, devotion to Mary is as strong as
worship of her Son. It wasn't easy. Many American women

object to her humility. They think her passive. But look at her feet. She's crushing the serpent's head.

> (A choir of voices:
>
> Gloria in excelsis Deo
>
> Et in pax hominibus bonae voluntatis
>
> Laudamus Te.
>
> Benedicimus te.
>
> Glorificamus te...

BRIAN: There's Jane!

> (He waves. Then he turns around and picks up something from a pew.)

BRIAN: There's a flower shop in the building where I live. I found these... they remind me of you. They're jasmine.

CLARITA: Hasmin! Hasmin - you do have them!

BRIAN: Clarita, let me into your life. You believe I have a soul. Save it.

CLARITA: I can't save something you don't believe in.

BRIAN: Then prove to me God exists.

CLARITA: Tomorrow. Noon. I'll meet you here.

(BRIAN leaves. Lights go down. Spotlights on
CLARITA and the icon of the Blessed Virgin.)

CLARITA: So this is why you've sent him to me... so that when
I show him what I am, he will believe? And then what? I never
see him again? Or are you testing me? Why? Don't I always do
Your will? I obey you... I'm prudent... I've always been
prudent. In thought, word and deed... that incident back
home... that big scandal... The college senior who broke up
with her boyfriend... went up the school tower... jumped to her
death...love letters on the window sill... my friends passing
them around... talking about the things they did and said to
each other... all the details... Sister Erlindis pleading with us to
burn them... burn them! Occasions of sin, she called them...
Estelita Perez giving me a page... I'm holding it in my hand, it's
hot in my hand, burning my hand, and then, a gust of wind
blows it wide open... I give it a quick glance... my eyes fall on a
word... just one word.. 'mouth'... it said 'mouth'... I let go, the
wind sweeps it up into the sky, days afterwards, I keep seeing
blue-black letters on a white sheet of paper and the word
'mouth'...

BLACKOUT

Scene Seven

(Three weeks later. Two spotlights. CLARITA is
seen praying in front of the icon of the Virgin
Mary.)

CLARITA: The first time was coffee. Then long walks in Central
Park. A Broadway musical the name of which I've forgotten. A
visit to the Cloisters that moved me to tears. And movies. All

jumbled together... fighting for space in my head... crowding out others -- pictures of home, my convent, my life, and in my heart, so without incident and faith so easy, like breathing. The time has come. Tomorrow, I'll show him who I am. You'll be there, watching over me... one more lost soul brought home to You... I have found him which once was lost. joy shall be in heaven...

BLACKOUT

Scene Eight

(The next day, Tuesday evening, Holy week. BRIAN's apartment. BRIAN is at the study table peering at a computer screen. CLARITA, seated on a couch, is looking at pictures in a photo album. The music is on.

Up Center is a partial view of Wall Street through a large window. The speaker phone is on.)

BRIAN: Two people died, Mr. Cambanis!

CAMBANIS (VOICE OVER): My lawyer – he say they already sick when they on board. One diabetic. Brian, I pay premiums every month. Never late.

BRIAN: This is not about premiums. It's about people.

CAMBANIS: This is P & I business, Brian. You handle only hull and machinery, no?

BRIAN: The P & I people can't get through to you. They know your Dad and me go a long way back. He was my first client. Clean up the act, please, sir. These labor violations tarnish the old man's image.

CAMBANIS: Mr. Andersen, what is this you're telling me?

BRIAN: Send me a fax. Please say this will never happen again. I want it in writing. Now.

CAMBANIS: You want me to send you fax?

BRIAN: Yes. But not for me. For your Dad. Tell Amnesty International you will sit down with them.

CAMBANIS: Fifty years in this business, no one ever asked me for showfax. Did my father ever give you showfax?

BRIAN: There never was a need.

CAMBANIS: I am saddened and surprised. Okay, okay. I send showfax now.

BRIAN: We're in the throes of moving to the new office. Send it to my home fax number, will you, Mr. Cambanis? Thank you very much.

> (BRIAN hangs up, walks over to a sound system and turns on the music and then sits next to CLARITA.)

BRIAN: I'm so sorry.

CLARITA: I understand.

(The music comes on.)

BRIAN: Oscar Peterson's Bach's Blues.

CLARITA: Bach?

BRIAN: Inspired by him. What do you think?

CLARITA: Fascinating. Bach and jazz!

BRIAN: Made for each other... (Pointing at a photograph) My home.

CLARITA: As big as my convent!

BRIAN: Built turn of the century... 1825... the first Andersen - from Norway bought the first 10 acres that would become Chestnut Hill Farm six generations later...The view from my bedroom window... four hundred and fifty acres of the richest most blessed spot on earth... When I was a boy, I thought we owned the world and was responsible for feeding it... Mom...leukemia... she died the day of the foreclosure... Dad. On happier days... He died two years ago, a shell of the man I once knew as a child.

CLARITA: I'm sorry.

BRIAN: So am I. He'd seen the land crash and burn in his watch. While his father and his father's father before him saw it through natural disasters, a civil war, two world wars, the Depression. It couldn't survive Dad's poor judgment. He'd borrowed too much, bought too much. Then hit a brick wall called the '80's. I was there. That foreclosure taught me the most important lesson I've ever learned. I discovered where the world was going, and I made sure I was in it.

CLARITA: And how has it turned out?

BRIAN: Extremely well. As you can see. (Laughs.) I like making money…the highs and lows…the risks. Even the losses. The rush. And of course, the comfort it brings, the freedom. Money is the closest thing to divine energy, Clarita. You can have all the faith in the world, but when it's time to move the mountain, you need money. Dad always used to ask me, Yeah, but are you happy? And I would always say, You know what, Dad? I am. Pissed him off every time.

CLARITA: I'd have asked if it's made up for all the loss.

BRIAN: No. Nothing will ever make up for it. (Shows her a tea table.) But I have this. The only thing I took from Chestnut Hill. Stripped it myself.

CLARITA: (Studying the table closely, peering down at a spot, tracing it with her fingers. Reading.) "Rhys and Margaret. 1910." How beautiful.

BRIAN: My greatgrandfather carved that himself when my Dad was born. Story was lightning had struck the tree on his wedding day. See the burn? Straight to its core. He'd always point it out to me, show me what lightning can leave in its wake. Much like what he thought happened to us. But all I see is how something beautiful can be made from ruin. No mortised joints, not even tenons. Just corner blocks and scarfed splices. It's a wonder it holds up. Like magic. That was the difference between my father and me.

CLARITA: You have a hobby. Every person I meet in America has one. My uncle is passionate about karaoke.

BRIAN: (Pouring her a glass of wine.) To America. To life, liberty and the pursuit of hobbies. And why not? Every time you find something you're passionate about, you discover something new about yourself. Pursue it and you end up mastering yourself. And isn't that what it's all about?

> (BRIAN takes her hand and leads her to a large curtained window, Up Center. He pulls the curtains apart. A view of Wall Street is seen, magnificent in the night.)

BRIAN: If God made the world exactly the way it's written in the Bible, He must have got up early Monday morning to look at His handiwork and say, Wow, it is good. And then split. And we haven't heard a word since then. So it's been mainly up to us. And look at it, Clarita. It's just as good, don't you think so? (He flings the windows open.) A work of art. A piece of sculpture fashioned out of iron, steel, glass. Stuff men's dreams are made of, and money built it. A year ago, the firm wanted to send me to London. Run their ocean marine. I turned it down... This is my world and I live in the heart of it. Smell that air, Clarita. Everything ends and begins here. Every living soul in

222

this planet has a stake in its survival. The Dow Jones dips and a waitress serving burgers in Singapore is let go. This is as simple as it gets. I told you I have no faith. But I do.

CLARITA: In what?

BRIAN: Free market economics.

CLARITA: There are other values to live by.

BRIAN: There's only one other I know.

CLARITA: And what's that?

BRIAN: Natural selection.

CLARITA: What would you say about someone who gives up his life for others? Isn't that how heroes are made. Don't you think it's a paradox? That the strongest who survive aren't necessarily the ones we admire. There must be something more to us than breath.

BRIAN: But it doesn't matter. Because that's not the right question to ask. It isn't - does God exist? Or does the soul exist? But - does it matter? And the answer is no. The problem with God is that nothing really happens to you if you don't believe in Him. You can choose not to believe. But stop making money, and there's hell to pay. People lose their jobs, marriages fall apart, children suffer. Civilizations die.
Jane, our mutual friend, runs a dance company in the Lower Eastside. My firm subsidizes her performance space. She can't take a flying leap without corporate grants. Yet artists like her

keep bashing people like me. The truth is every person's first act of social responsibility is to make money. Without it, he's useless

CLARITA: It doesn't teach you how to die.

BRIAN: What?

CLARITA: Money. It doesn't teach you how to die. I respect its power to seduce, but in the end you're exactly right. It doesn't matter.

BRIAN: So you mean nothing I've got impresses you. (Pause) I was right about you.

CLARITA: My Tio Dadong tells me to be open.

BRIAN: Perhaps I know something that might captivate your heart.

CLARITA: What would that be?

BRIAN: A passionate relationship with a man.

CLARITA: I know nothing about men.

BRIAN: (Trying for a lighter tone.) How do they make out in the Philippines? I mean, date. Get to know each other - woo each other. I don't believe this. I'm using words like 'woo.'

CLARITA: They go to the movies. My aunt had a boyfriend who used to take her to the movies. They took me along as a chaperone.

BRIAN: I thought you grew up in the convent.

CLARITA: I was a novice. I was permitted to spend a few days in town every year during Lent. The chairs. They were wicker. Every time my aunt and her boyfriend moved, you heard it. Sophie's Choice was showing.

BRIAN: But you said you didn't like Meryl Streep.

CLARITA: I don't. Every time I watch her, I hear wicker. (Pause.) We didn't really talk about movie stars. Ana Maria Goretti. We talked about her.

BRIAN: Who?

CLARITA: Patron saint of virgins. She suffered 49 stab wounds from a man who tried to rape her. The nuns used her story to teach us the virtue of chastity. We had a picture of her on the wall. Right next to the Pope and Corazon Aquino, a dark-haired virgin with deep, soulful eyes, clutching a knife thrust to the heart, pleading with the man who had just stabbed her 49 times. There was blood all over her lilywhite hands. We loved that story. She was the most popular saint in school.

BRIAN: (Laughing) She sounds Italian.

CLARITA: Yes! How did you know?

BRIAN: (Pulling her to him, kissing her very gently) That's how a real man does it.

> (Then with a suddenness that takes their breath away, blood gushes from CLARITA's hands. She pulls back, raises her arms, palms facing upward. She closes her eyes. A stillness settles in the room, as if something heavy has dropped, an invisible blanket muffling all sound. BRIAN sits, immobilized. A few beats. Then he jumps to his feet.)

CLARITA: Don't be frightened.

BRIAN: What - ? (A long pause.)

CLARITA: I bear the marks of Christ.

BRIAN: What?

CLARITA: I bear the marks of Christ.

BRIAN: The marks – ?

CLARITA: My parents sent me to a hospital in Manila –

BRIAN: Please. Stop. Give me a moment.

> (A long silence.)

CLARITA: I lived there for two years… Doctors studied and examined me… I was poked at, monitored, tested… In the end they couldn't find anything wrong with me. They couldn't stop it, or explain it. So my parents sent me to a convent. I was happy there. It was peaceful... my refuge from the world... from those who insisted I perform miracles on the sick and the dying... But even after I left, His marks continue to come every year at Lent.

BRIAN: Every year at Lent...?

CLARITA: The blood can heal the sick. Or if they die, they die peacefully... I have no control over who lives or dies... I can summon it at will, but sometimes it surprises me. When we met at Jane's house, I didn't expect it.

BRIAN: You summoned it at will. Just now. Why, Clarita?

CLARITA: You wanted to know if God exists. He does! Bear witness. These are His signs. He is here!

> (CLARITA holds up her hands. BRIAN staggers back.)

CLARITA: Brian?

> (BRIAN moves away, doesn't answer. CLARITA looks down at her hands. A few beats.)

BRIAN: Does it hurt?

CLARITA: Yes.

BRIAN: (Taking deep breaths.) It's here again... that scent, that's you, isn't it?

CLARITA: Yes. Bring me a towel, please.

> (BRIAN exits. We hear the sound of his being sick, then a toilet, flushing. A few beats. He enters with a towel in his hand.)

CLARITA: Take me home, please.

BRIAN: Clarita -

CLARITA: Take me home!

BLACKOUT

Scene Nine

> (An hour later. DADONG's apartment. The door opens and CLARITA and BRIAN enter. CLARITA: has bandages on both her hands. She lies down on the couch.)

CLARITA: Don't let me keep you.

BRIAN: Is there anything you need?

CLARITA: Ginger ale? Down the hall to your right.

> (BRIAN gets up and walks down the foyer. He has a fleeting glimpse of a huge cross with LALING hanging from it. He walks by and exits. A few beats. Then he comes back. He peers up at the

cross. LALING has her eyes closed. She has her
hands through loops at the end of the arms of the
cross, her feet set on a ledge. BRIAN stares up at
her. He tentatively touches the drape of her skirt.
The movement awakens her from her meditation.
Both LALING and BRIAN yell out. LALING pulls
her arms out. She gets off the ledge. They stare at
each other for a few beats. BRIAN staggers back to
the living room.)

BRIAN: Clarita?

CLARITA: Yes?

BRIAN: Your mother is hanging from a cross.

(CLARITA leaps to her feet and runs to the foyer.
She sees LALING in front of the cross.)

LALING: Maayong gabi-i , Inday.

(LALING sees CLARITA's hands. She stares at
them in silence. Then she makes the sign of the
cross. She kneels down to kiss her hands.
CLARITA pulls them away.)

CLARITA: Please go to your room. (A beat. LALING stares at
her.) Please, Mama.

(LALING exits.)

BRIAN: (Sitting down.) What a day I'm having.

> (Then he bursts into a paroxysm of nervous convulsive laughter.)

CLARITA: You don't know anything about us.

BRIAN: No, I don't.

CLARITA: My mother hangs from a cross.

BRIAN: Clarita, Jesus Christ hangs from a cross!

CLARITA: It's the pasyon, a Filipino Lenten practice. She's preparing herself for the actual crucifixion.

BRIAN: The actual – crucifixion?

CLARITA: The crucifixion. She's nailed to the cross.

BRIAN: Nailed. Nailed! Like real – nails? Oh god, there's more.

CLARITA: Back home, the plaza is filled with penitents for days.

BRIAN: She does it in public?

CLARITA: She stays up there from Good Friday until Easter morning.

BRIAN: And then what? She dies and goes to heaven and comes back again?

CLARITA: (Now at last, the irony.)Yes. She's actually a ghost. She does it every year. Obviously, she doesn't die from it.

BRIAN: Every year? How is that possible?

CLARITA: The wounds heal. There's a correct way of doing it so that – you don't want to know, Brian.

BRIAN: Was this the cross -- oh, no. You mean I almost built --

CLARITA: Yes, you did. But Tio Dadong didn't think you'd understand. When the Spanish came to the Philippines in the 1500's, they brought with them practices of a medieval Catholicism. The pasyon was one of them. Many years later, the Church banned it, considered it sacrilegious. But ours was an isolated island, so it escaped reform. It remained a practice up to the day it was buried in the eruption.

BRIAN: (His cell phone rings.) My Nokia! My Nokia 5120i, 79 grams light, top-of-the-line premium category dual band, just came out in December. (Answers it, turning around, out of earshot.) Hello…. Lindsay. Oh, Lindsay. How are you, Lindsay. Everything okay? …How are the girls? Good. They're at NYU! That's fantastic! …Me? I'm fine… No, I'm not sick… I'm just glad you called… ah, the aframax! God bless the aframax tankers…a strong freight market would do that… you're doing great, Lindsay… Lindsay, have you ever been on a date from hell… never mind… as a matter of fact, yes, I've spoken to Cambanis. He's a good man, Cambanis. He's sorry those crew members died… give it another day. That's right. Goodbye, now, Lindsay. (He puts his cell phone away.) This is mad. I'm

231

mad. You're mad. And so is your Mom. I'm so sorry, Clarita.
I'm so sorry. But this has all been a terrible mistake.

> (A few beats. Then he turns around and exits.
> LALING enters.)

LALING: Did you break your vow of silence? To this man?
Why, Clarita?

CLARITA: I thought it would make him a believer.

LALING: He's already got everything he needs. He doesn't
need a soul.

CLARITA: It's not for us to judge what a man needs.

LALING: But we're not talking about his faith. He's attracted to
you. Are you attracted to him?

CLARITA: I don't know! I'm so confused!

LALING: My poor child... I was expecting this to happen. I just
didn't think it would be so soon.

> (She sits on a chair and holds out her arms.
> CLARITA doesn't move.)

LALING: America is a dangerous place. You need to be strong
to live here. What's wrong, Inday? You think I don't
understand? Passion is a powerful thing. Your father loved me.
So I've been there myself. Why don't you answer?

CLARITA: Maybe – I don't want it.

LALING: What?

CLARITA: Maybe I want to be normal. Ordinary.

> (LALING shoots out of her chair, pulls CLARITA to the window and flings it wide open.)

LALING: Normal. Like everyone else! Can you smell them? Look. Bob... people tell me he was in Desert Storm. Have you looked into his eyes? He's still there... Sonia... all five kids in foster care. Her current boyfriend... this one beats her... and over there... the lady who has no name, like a heap of old clothes someone had discarded.

CLARITA: We had poor people, too.

LALING: Hungry for food. But full in spirit. What do you think keeps me going? The typhoon, that damned volcano, your father dead, and here, everything familiar ripped from my heart. Yet I go on.

CLARITA: So do I. That's why I left the convent, Mama. You'd been through so much while I hadn't been through enough. I was safe. And useless. I had a gift and it meant nothing. God has sent this man to me. Nothing happens without His will.

LALING: How do you presume to know how He thinks. Perhaps He's testing you.

CLARITA: Why? Can't I love someone and someone love me back?

LALING: You belong only to God.

CLARITA: Why didn't He ask me, Mama? He should've asked me. I decide! I choose! Otherwise, I'd only be an instrument of His will. That would mean He doesn't care what I think. Certainly who I am. What I want.

LALING: This is how it begins. One day, you know who you are. Where you're going. Where you've been. Then a man who believes in nothing lays his eyes on you and all of a sudden, you're asking questions. You're from two different worlds, Clarita. And there isn't a bridge to connect them.

CLARITA: Love will be my bridge.

LALING: What do you mean by that?

CLARITA: Brian has seen who I am. If he comes back, it means God has given him the grace to love me exactly the way I am.

LALING: And then what?

CLARITA: I will offer myself to him.

LALING: What do you mean? (Grabbing at CLARITA.) What do you mean? You wouldn't dare! I forbid it! God forbids it!

CLARITA: God allows it. He is Love himself!

LALING: (Fiercely.) Then for your sake I hope and pray he won't come back. How do you think you look in his eyes. How can you even think he'd want to make love with you. You bleed, Clarita. You're right. You're a freak!

> (CLARITA takes a step back, stunned by the ferociousness of LALING's words. She wavers, suddenly unsure of herself.)

LALING: What does a big man like him want to do with someone like you? Dress you up in fancy clothes and take you to his fancy parties? And when you're eating your fancy food, what will you say if you bleed? How will you explain your blood on the salad? How long after that he'd want to keep you home, until you turn into a doll he plays with after work?

CLARITA: Stop it, Mama! Stop. Please!

LALING: (Seizing CLARITA'S hands.) Do you know how much I envy you? These are mine. They're my wounds! I give Him my complete devotion. I take up His cross and follow Him. All these years, I suffer unbearable pain. I do it all for Him. Do you know to this day I ask Him this -- why you?

> (LALING suddenly releases her hold and the force of it catches CLARITA by surprise.)

LALING: Why do you think I sent you away... Every time I laid eyes on you, I saw God mocking me... I still do... but every day I fight it... every day I ask His forgiveness... and so must you. So must you.... My child, my angel.

(LALING walks up to the cross and picks up a whip from the base. She gives it to CLARITA.)

LALING: Do this for me.

BLACKOUT

Scene Ten

(Holy Wednesday.

Down Center, CLARITA, stripped to the waist, her back to the audience, whips herself. Ribbons of blood flow down her back.

Agnus Dei, qui tollis peccata mundi: miserere nobis.

Agnus Dei, qui tollis peccata mundi: miserere nobis.

Agnus Dei, qui tollis peccata mundi: dona nobis pacem.

BRIAN appears DL. He is unshaven. He looks tired and for the first time since we've seen him, something of his self-assured air has been diminished. He watches the scene with growing consternation. Then he comes forward and takes the whip from CLARITA's hand. He takes off his shirt and covers her with it. He helps her up and they exit.)

BLACKOUT

Scene Eleven

(The same evening. An hour later. BRIAN's
apartment.

He is seen dressing CLARITA's wounds. He and
CLARITA are in his study, windows wide open,
piles of books on the floor and on the worktable;
notes scattered about, on the couch, on the chairs.)

BRIAN: You can cry, Clarita. No need to put up a brave front
with me... There... it's done.

(BRIAN prepares the couch for her. Then he exits,
CLARITA lies down on the couch, on her stomach.
BRIAN comes back with a cup of tea. He gives it
to her. She takes a sip. A few beats.)

CLARITA: In Argao, they use sea water to wash the wounds.

BRIAN: Pile it on. See if I care.

CLARITA: Mama said you could never love someone like me.

BRIAN: Are you kidding? First time I saw you, I wanted you.

CLARITA: I saw it in your eyes. I was surprised it didn't make
me feel ashamed or guilty. I simply thought to myself -- so this
is desire -- what a wonderful thing – desire.

BRIAN: Desire… I don't believe I'm saying this, but you know what. I can wait.

CLARITA: God allows it.

BRIAN: He does? (Pause) Well, you know Him better than I do.

CLARITA: I've never seen a naked man before.

> (BRIAN takes her hands and guides them to undress him. She takes off his shirt.)

CLARITA: And you were made in God's image. And you please me.

> (He pulls her gently to him. He sits on the edge of the couch. He places her on his lap, and face to face, he lets her straddle him, her back to the audience, faint traces of blood on her whip-lashed skin.)

BRIAN: (Kissing her.) Your hair. Your eyes. Your skin. But the best thing about you is your mouth.

BLACKOUT

Scene Twelve

The next morning. Holy Thursday. CLARITA and BRIAN are in bed, asleep. CLARITA wakes up first. She contemplates BRIAN, asleep. Then she gets out of bed, gets dressed. It is noon. There is light everywhere. Then she walks over to the window.

BRIAN stirs, sits up, sees CLARITA. He watches her in silence. CLARITA moves away from the window, walks around the room, no longer shy, with an ease and looseness to her movements; she touches everything she can lay her hands on, the curtains, the pieces of furniture, the computer, the phone, a pile of books, open notes, seeing them all as if for the first time.

> Then something catches her eyes; there's a shift in her scrutiny. She reaches for a book.)

BRIAN: Good morning.

CLARITA: You've been busy. (Reading.) On Continual Psychogenic Purpura... Dr. Leo Handszer... (Reading the book's jacket.) "...one of the greatest clinical writers of the 20th century..."

BRIAN: He was referred to me by a psychiatrist friend. He gave me a list of books to look up. Stop with the books. Come here.

> (CLARITA walks over to the bed and tumbles into his arms. They kiss. CLARITA begins to laugh.)

CLARITA: I thought the world would look a little different.

BRIAN: (Laughing.) Clarita, I'm not that good. (A beat.) How do you feel?

CLARITA: Ordinary.

BRIAN: What?

CLARITA: That's a compliment. You were patient and generous.

BRIAN: And you were curious.

CLARITA: Everything about you is new to me.

(She sits down on his lap.)

BRIAN: And everything about you is driving me nuts. Clarita, I'm so lost.

CLARITA: Why did you come to my house last night?

BRIAN: I wanted to understand.

CLARITA:
And do you? It horrifies you, doesn't it. You think it's - barbaric. You can say it. I saw it with your eyes. That first time – our date from hell.

BRIAN: What was it like, the first time you – they appeared. When did it happen?

CLARITA: I was six years old. Good Friday. At 3:00. On the dot. My mother was up and I stayed with her. I wanted to keep her company. Then I saw them ... in my own hands. Like roses... I remember thinking... like red roses in full bloom.

BRIAN: How did you feel?

CLARITA: Ashamed. I didn't deserve it. I wasn't good like my mother. I felt unworthy.

BRIAN: You weren't even scared?

CLARITA: My island was full of rituals. The pasyon was just one of them.

(The phone rings.)

BRIAN: I'm not answering that.

CLARITA: It might be important.

(BRIAN presses a button and the speaker phone turns on.)

GARLAND (V.O.): Brian, get back here now. Brian? Goddammit, forty vessels, close to ten million dollars in premiums! And your boys lost it!

BRIAN: (Picking it up.) What are you talking about?

GARLAND: We lost Cambanis!

BRIAN: What?

GARLAND: You heard me.

BRIAN: (Turning on the PC again.)But the strike's been settled. He's sat down with Amnesty International and they've dropped their suit.

GARLAND: You're damn right. But we lost Cambanis. I hear one of your boys asked for a showfax. A fuckin' showfax. Who's the goddamn bastard?

BRIAN: What do you mean?

GARLAND: The son-of-a-bitch who asked for a showfax. The P & I guys are fit to be tied. Board's pissed. They're meeting this afternoon, and I need you here for damage control. I want Plan B in place.

BRIAN: Plan B?

GARLAND: The whole team. Out.

BRIAN: The whole team?

GARLAND: And we've got eight people in Chicago. Let's use this mess to downsize it. The Board will like that. Call Lindsay and get the financials on Plan B. And by the way, ask Cambanis who asked for the showfax.

BRIAN: I asked for it.

GARLAND: You? What the fuck for? The P & I guys were handling it!

BRIAN: Not very successfully.

GARLAND: It wasn't your call.

BRIAN: Two people died, Garland!

GARLAND: You're telling me we lost ten million dollars because you wanted to be a fucking Boy Scout?

BRIAN: It was a business decision. You alienate the crew, they sabotage the ship and you end up with a total loss. It's happened before. Northern Star. Aegean Queen --

GARLAND: That's it. I need you. Get down here. Tell me the story. Start to finish. I'm terminating your team.

BRIAN: I'm responsible. They had nothing to do with this! Terminate me.

GARLAND: You're in no goddamn condition to negotiate.

(He hangs up. A few beats.)

BRIAN: Two people. Dead. I thought it had gone far enough.

CLARITA: What's going on, Brian.

BRIAN: A ship's crew had been on strike over unfair labor practices. I asked the shipowner for assurances to settle it and put it in writing. It's called a showfax. It's risky. Shipowners don't like it. Think asking Bill Gates himself to write you a letter promising to be a good boy. It's risky.

CLARITA: But people were dying?

BRIAN: But I don't do people.

CLARITA: You don't do people.

BRIAN: I just do hull and machinery. Cargo. It wasn't my call.

CLARITA: Whose call was it?

BRIAN: P & I. Protection and Indemnity. But they were useless. They couldn't get through to Cambanis. He doesn't talk to anyone. Guards his privacy like a madman. He's like Fort Knox. I took a chance. His father and I – we were tight.

CLARITA: So you did the right thing.

BRIAN: Unfortunately, it's not always about the right thing.

CLARITA: It's always about the right thing, Brian.

BRIAN: (He peers at the screen.) I've never lost an account as big as this. You know what's funny? My first impulse was to do it to impress you. Then I meant it. It was the first time I saw crew as people.

CLARITA: But crew are people.

BRIAN: (Dialing.) Not where I live.

CLARITA: Crew are people. Even in business, Brian.

BRIAN: The whole team? Miriam. Lindsay. Lindsay has two girls in college – what the hell did I do? What was I thinking?

CLARITA: I don't understand…

BRIAN: It is what it is, Clarita. Don't try to understand it.

CLARITA: But it's wrong!

BRIAN: I understand you think that. But let's not rush to judgment.

CLARITA: Why not? I make very few of them, and when I do, I make them freely. There are very few true things in the world. That one acts with compassion for the poor, the sick, and the dying is one of them.

> (BRIAN is hastily getting dressed, grabbing his coat.)

BRIAN: Where I live it's not as simple as that. But fortunately for you, you don't have to live there. I do that. That's why we're so perfect together. Stay. Please? Wait for me. I'll be right back. Here. (He gives her a book.) Read it. Read them all. Remember what your Uncle Dadong said? Keep an open mind...

> (He gives her a kiss. Then flies out of the room. CLARITA picks up the book and reads.)

BLACKOUT

Scene Thirteen

> (DADONG's house in the living room. CLARITA enters, carrying the same book. LALING is seen hanging from the cross. LALING gets down.)

LALING: I can smell you.

CLARITA: There's no blame in it.

LALING: No one's to blame for the smell of sin on you?

CLARITA: Is it a sin to be human, Mama? .

LALING: What has he done to you?

CLARITA: I make my own choices.

LALING: You've lost your fear of God.

CLARITA: I was never afraid of Him.

LALING: Then I'm afraid for you.

CLARITA: Do you think I have your kind of faith, Mama? Simple? Like a child's? I worship with you because it makes you happy. But what I have is a power beyond all understanding. It doesn't belong to you nor me. It simply works through me. It's the same power behind all of nature. Roses, brain cells. Stardust. Unless. Unless it's something else altogether.

LALING: I don't understand what you're saying.

CLARITA: Dr. Leo Handszer... (Reading the book's jacket.) "...one of the greatest clinical writers of the 20th century..." (Reading a manuscript.)"Current literature on the subject tells us that there are three certified stigmatics known today... their case studies... She's a housewife living in North London, a devout Anglican... she's an African-American Baptist living in South Carolina. He's the third one.

LALING: Padre Pio.

CLARITA: Yes. You would know that.

LALING: But I've never heard of this Dr. Handszer.

CLARITA: (Opening another book. Reading) Portraits of classic stigmatics... wounds to the hands and feet as well as to the side. No inflammation... no infection... nothing to indicate physical trauma. But I only have them in my hands. This says its psychogenic purpura... this was induced by hypnosis. Extreme skeptics say they're clever hoaxes, and others are schizophrenics, or people with multiple personality disorder.

LALING: You mean you're crazy. We've been told that. Yet here you are. Tell me something new.

CLARITA: (Picking up another book.) "There are countless studies that point to mechanisms in the brain that can turn belief into an agent of biological change... it is actually possible that you can suspend the natural and organic processes that govern the human body..."

LALING: God works through the brain cells. You just said that.

CLARITA: All of the literature say that stigmatics bleed any time or bleed at no particular specific time. I only do it at Lent.

LALING: Because you're unique.

CLARITA: (Reading.) "The first event is usually marked by profound physical or mental stress..." Profound physical or mental stress, Mama. How old was I the first time I saw you on the cross?

LALING: It's begun...

CLARITA: How old was I the first time I saw you on the cross?

LALING: It's too long ago.

CLARITA: Three?

LALING: I don't remember.

CLARITA: Four?

LALING: I don't know!

CLARITA: Maybe earlier? (Raising her voice.) Tell me, Mama!

LALING: You can't talk to me this way. I'm your mother!

CLARITA: And I'm God's chosen.

LALING: You be careful - so proud and so cruel.

CLARITA: Yes, I am.

(LALING gives in.)

LALING: Your father... he was there... he was supposed to be there... he always watched over you. Made sure you didn't see it. The priest and the doctors... they thought you'd be too young to understand...

CLARITA: So you do remember.

LALING: How can I forget? You were four. We'd keep you in your room and he'd watch over you. But that Good Friday – there was a drought that year, the heat was unbearable... you were fussing... he was so foolish... he left you alone in the room... he wanted to get a glass of ice cold water next door... he was only gone for a few minutes... but when he came back... you'd wandered off... the plaza was filled with penitents... we had no idea how long you were lost, walking by yourself... a neighbor recognized you and brought you to where I was being laid on the cross... she was so stupid... ignorant...

CLARITA: What happened then?

LALING: I don't know... the neighbor got caught up in the moment... you know what it's like... everyone's in a trance... gripped by the Holy Spirit...wailing and weeping... she forgot all about you... someone found you hours later... on a bench next to the wall of hasmin... you had passed out... the heat... they brought you home.... You were unconscious for three days... The doctors could hardly hear your pulse... we thought you were going to die...

CLARITA: Blood on the hasmin...

LALING: Blood on the hasmin?

CLARITA: Hot - so hot - so much glare it hurts the eyes... scorching heat in the dead of noon... the sun, sharp as a whip on my back...

LALING: April – Good Friday – the hottest day of the year –

CLARITA: Mama... what are they doing to you...no! no! No! I'm screaming... but you can't hear me... no one hears me... the sharp thwack of the hammer... pounding... pounding... pounding... smell of blood... taste of dust in my mouth... smell of hasmin... I'm going to be sick ...

(CLARITA slumps on the bed.)

LALING: The following year, we let you watch. The priest thought it was time to explain it to you. That's when the wounds came.

(DADONG comes rushing in. He's excited, and trying hard to keep his excitement in check, but his delight, or perhaps relief overpowers him and it comes out in laughter mixed with dismay.)

DADONG: Father Nick... I just spoke with Father Nick... Laling, he kicked me out of the rectory! He forbids you to do it. He said it's a blasphemy. A mortal sin! You can't go through with it! (To CLARITA, overjoyed inspite of himself.) A mortal sin, thank God! (Checks himself, turns to LALING.) I'm so sorry, Laling. I'm so sorry.

(LALING and CLARITA look at him in silence.)

DADONG: What's wrong? What's going on?

LALING: Then we will do it here. Right here in the privacy of our own home.

(She pulls CLARITA up from the bed. CLARITA as if in a daze does not protest. LALING nudges DADONG towards her.)

LALING: Guard her with your life. Don't you dare let her out of your sight.

BLACKOUT

Scene Fourteen

(Later that evening. DADONG'S house. LALING is seen dressed in a long silk robe, kneeling in front of the shrine, arms outstretched. There is chanting in the background. The whole room is lit

with votive candles. A large wooden cross is
behind a scrim. A few beats. BRIAN enters, sees
LALING: and stands, waiting. LALING feels his
presence. She turns around and rises to her feet.)

LALING: What do you want?

BRIAN: Where is she, Mrs. Kintanar?

LALING: Where you can't find her.

BRIAN: She deserves to be happy.

LALING: She is happy doing God's will.

BRIAN: You mean yours.

LALING: How do I deserve your disrespect?

BRIAN: I'm simply being honest.

LALING: You don't think I wish I had a grandchild to hold in
my arms? But God gave me Clarita.

BRIAN: Where is she?

LALING: Haven't you done enough harm?

BRIAN: She needs me.

LALING: No, she doesn't! This has nothing to do with either of
us.

BRIAN: You can't give her what I've got.

LALING: And what is that, Mr. Andersen?

BRIAN: A life with me. A man. No more. No less. Don't get me wrong, Mrs. Kintanar. I know she thinks there's a God. I respect that.

LALING: She thinks there's a God?

BRIAN: I'm not asking her to give it up. I simply love her. I'm in love with your daughter.

LALING: You love her. But not her faith.

BRIAN: Faith? That's not faith, Mrs. Kintanar. What she's got isn't faith. It's certainty. She is sure He exists because she has proof. But people like me. I don't have anything.

LALING: Yet you see it with your own eyes.

BRIAN: I see blood. She sees God. This is proof for her. But not for me.

LALING: So there's no divine nature to her affliction? But she's nothing. God makes them happen. He works through her. Only He can heal the sick. The dying.

BRIAN: We keep people from dying everyday! We have our miracles, too. But we call them CAT scans. MRI's. Zoloft! We're mapping the human genome, for god's sake. Has it ever occurred to you there are good people in the world who don't have a need to believe in God? And that some even manage to believe in things bigger than themselves. You want causes, Mrs. Kintanar, we've got them. Gay rights, women's rights, PETA people and tree-huggers – a good number of us even want to save the planet! The planet!

LALING: Hobbies. They're hobbies, Mr. Andersen. Things you do to fill up your time because you have too much of it. Now go! Go! Leave her to God.

(LALING opens the door.)

BRIAN: Your God is small!

LALING: Small! And you're so big.

BRIAN: Don't you dare judge me. You don't know me!

LALING: But I do. You're a rich white man who thinks he can have it all.

BRIAN: You're dangerous, Mrs. Kintanar. You need help.

LALING: Then that makes two of us. Because nothing you have impresses her. Your good looks, your money, your houses, your business. You take her with you, and you will lose them all. She will grind you down until you feel like dirt under her feet. Do you think she loves you for yourself? She loves you because she looked into your eyes and saw nothing there. You're her job, Mr. Andersen. Her business. Big proud man.

(She walks across the room and lights go up.

The Lenten practice of the pasyon begins. The following scene is ritualized.

LALING is nailed to the cross. The cross is raised.)

Agnus Dei, qui tollis peccata mundi: miserere nobis.

Agnus Dei, qui tollis peccata mundi: miserere nobis.

Agnus Dei, qui tollis peccata mundi: dona nobis pacem.

BLACKOUT

Scene Fifteen

(Easter Sunday. Noon. A room at St. Luke's. DADONG is seen, agitated, pacing the floor, still dressed in his Sunday suit, his tie undone. CLARITA enters.)

CLARITA: What happened? Where's Mama?

DADONG: It must be her heart! I'm waiting for Dr. Samson.

CLARITA: But her heart is strong! I know it.

DADONG: I'm so stupid. I should have seen it coming. I'm a goddamn fool! Father Nick. Father Nick. How could he do what he did? A man of God! Easter Sunday mass at that! Your mother and I go up to take communion. I'm right behind her. He skips her. That's what he does. He skips her. She thinks he's made a mistake. So she stands there, trying to catch his eye.

Nothing. He ignores her. Your mother remains standing in front of the congregation, even after the communion is over, I'm in my pew, unable to move; there's 500 people in the church and not a sound. As if everyone's holding his breath. And then Father Nick walks up to the pulpit and he gives this sermon, accusing her of heresy. Blasphemy! Dear God forgive me. I run towards her, just in time. She falls into my arms.

CLARITA: I need to see her. Now.

DADONG: Why didn't I see it? My poor dear sister... so lost... she's so lost. And I'm so blind. I should never have asked both of you to come... I've been selfish.... I'll never forgive myself... where's Dr. Samson? What's taking so long?

    (DADONG exits.

    Up Center behind a scrim is a bed with LALING in it.

    CLARITA walks over to the bed. She lays her hand on LALING's head.)

CLARITA: In my distress I called upon the Lord and he heard my voice!
    I will love thee, O Lord and my strength
    The Lord is my rock and my fortress, and my deliverer;
    My shield, horn of my salvation and my high tower!
        (CLARITA walks over to the window and pulls
        the shades up a little. Soft light streams into the
        room.)

CLARITA: (Hushing her.) Three days without food and water. It's different here, Mama. You can't keep it up.

(There is no movement from the bed.)

CLARITA: But don't be scared. I'm here. Lord, I am not worthy that Thou shouldst come under my roof, say but the word and my soul shall be healed... Lord, I am not worthy that thou shouldst come under my roof, say but the word and my soul shall be healed...

(CLARITA lays her hands on LALING'S head. A few beats.

The moment ends. Nothing happens.

CLARITA opens her eyes. She looks down at her hands.

A sound escapes from her lips, a wail, pulled from the depths of her being; it rips the air apart.)

BLACKOUT

Scene Fifteen

(Easter Sunday. Noon. A room at St. Luke's. DADONG is seen, agitated, pacing the floor, still dressed in his Sunday suit, his tie undone. CLARITA enters.)

CLARITA: What happened? Where's Mama?

DADONG: It must be her heart! I'm waiting for Dr. Samson.

CLARITA: But her heart is strong! I know it.

DADONG: I'm so stupid. I should have seen it coming. I'm a goddamn fool! Father Nick. Father Nick. How could he do what he did? A man of God! Easter Sunday mass at that! Your mother and I go up to take communion. I'm right behind her. He skips her. That's what he does. He skips her. She thinks he's made a mistake. So she stands there, trying to catch his eye. Nothing. He ignores her. Your mother remains standing in front of the congregation, even after the communion is over, I'm in my pew, unable to move; there's 500 people in the church and not a sound. As if everyone's holding his breath. And then Father Nick walks up to the pulpit and he gives this sermon, accusing her of heresy. Blasphemy! Dear God forgive me. I run towards her, just in time. She falls into my arms.

CLARITA: I need to see her. Now.

DADONG: Why didn't I see it? My poor dear sister... so lost... she's so lost. And I'm so blind. I should never have asked both of you to come... I've been selfish.... I'll never forgive myself... where's Dr. Samson? What's taking so long?

(DADONG exits.

Up Center behind a scrim is a bed with LALING
in it.

CLARITA walks over to the bed. She lays her
hand on LALING's head.)

CLARITA: In my distress I called upon the Lord and he heard
my voice!
I will love thee, O Lord and my strength
The Lord is my rock and my fortress, and my deliverer;
My shield, horn of my salvation and my high tower!

(CLARITA walks over to the window and pulls
the shades up a little. Soft light streams into the
room.)

CLARITA: (Hushing her.) Three days without food and water.
It's different here, Mama. You can't keep it up.

(There is no movement from the bed.)

CLARITA: Lord, I am not worthy that Thou shouldst come
under my roof, say but the word and my soul shall be healed...
Lord, I am not worthy that thou shouldst come under my roof,
say but the word and my soul shall be healed...

(CLARITA lays her hands on LALING'S head. A
few beats.

The moment ends. Nothing happens.

CLARITA opens her eyes. She looks down at her hands.

A sound escapes from her lips, a wail, pulled from the depths of her being; it rips the air apart.)

BLACKOUT
Scene Sixteen

(The next day. The same room. CLARITA sits in the dark. Something is gone from her, though we can't say exactly what it is - maybe it's simply the absence of light in this small, hard room. BRIAN enters. He rushes to her and wraps her in his arms.)

BRIAN: I've been looking for you. I came as soon as I got your uncle's call... Oh, my love, I'm so sorry... I'm so sorry.

CLARITA: She only came to when Father Nick came for the last rites. I begged him to come. I was fierce with him. That was the only thing I could do for her.

BRIAN: You said the blood can heal the sick. You have no control over who lives or dies... but if they die, they die peacefully... You gave her that.

(CLARITA flings her arms, palms wide open, pale, small and clean. BRIAN sees them and stares at them. Then it hits him. He takes her in his arms.)

BRIAN: Oh, my love...

CLARITA: I've squandered a gift... I'm drowning, Brian.

BRIAN: Hang on to me.

CLARITA: A light has gone out... something very lonely and cold is taking its place... so this is what it's like...

BRIAN: I'm here. For you. I'll never ever leave you.

CLARITA: How do you know? When the wave hits, how do you know we'll be around for each other? Or if we are, how do you know we won't both drown? This is what it means... To live in the midst of a storm and hope someone will be there for you. To believe in something – anything and not know. Now I understand... I have a choice to make, and you put me here.

BRIAN: What choice are you talking about?

CLARITA: What if I need to live in the world, but not be of it. What if loving you means being of it? What if this means I can't love you and remain who I am because of who you are. And what if - what if you were sent to me, because I need to choose?

BRIAN: But you've already chosen. That's why they're gone. You're free, Clarita. Don't you understand?

CLARITA: What if I believe I will get them back if I give you up?

BRIAN: What? No, Clarita! That's not what this means!

CLARITA: Don't you see? Everything was to get me here, to this very moment now. So I can choose.

BRIAN: This is madness!

CLARITA: For love of you or for love of Him. All things of great value demand supreme sacrifice.

BRIAN: It's not going to happen. It was a sickness. Now it's gone. Because that's the way it works. Doubt happens. And then everything is changed forever.

CLARITA: But you're not certain.

BRIAN: I don't. I do know this. People do what they can. Visit the sick. Give to the poor. Bury the dead and mourn them. While the rest of us remain stuck being human. So you hope to find someone you can be human with. If you find each other, you're lucky. We are.

> (BRIAN rains her with his kisses. CLARITA submits.
>
> A few beats. Then CLARITA pulls back. A few beats. BRIAN watches her, rooted to the spot.
>
> Then she slowly with great effort, struggles free of his embrace.)

BRIAN: No, Clarita!

CLARITA: You will thank me for this someday.

BRIAN: Don't be rash. Don't do this. Give it time. I will wait.

CLARITA: Pray for understanding.

BRIAN: I don't know how to pray!

> (She comes forward and puts her hand over his heart.)

CLARITA: Somewhere inside you is a space. It's quiet there. Nothing happens. Not memory. Nor desire. Not even a fragment of a thought. Find it.

> (Something passes from her to him. But unlike the first time, he doesn't pull away. He closes his eyes, taking it. Then she pulls away.
>
> She exits. BRIAN is alone.

BLACKOUT

Scene Seventeen

> (Two months later. A loft space, bare except for a table and a chair, a few books, a computer. There are two signs on the floor, face down, a suitcase next to it. CLARITA is seen at the computer, typing on the keyboard. A few beats.
>
> DADONG enters. Gone is the look of casual informal air about him, though he still wears his seriousness lightly. He is also dressed for travel.)

CLARITA: Sister Kane asked me to install Quickbooks before we leave this morning.

DADONG: Cab will be here in fifteen minutes. You ready?

(He surveys the room.)

DADONG: It's so bare.

CLARITA: But not for long.

DADONG: It's hard to believe I had crates of tomatoes right where you're sitting. And here, the cash register. And there the ham and pastrami... From grocery to hospice... what a leap. (Picking up a "Hoboken Fresh Foods" sign. Behind it, we see another sign, "Eulalia Kintanar Memorial Hospice.") A Mother Teresa wannabe. I can see it now. A chain of hospices throughout the United States. Today, New Jersey. Tomorrow, the world! Jesus Christ, Clarita. When we get back, we're gonna need funding! Where's Brian when we need him?

CLARITA: He left for Chicago last week.

DADONG: I know he called to say goodbye. Are you sure about this?

CLARITA: No. But I do need to stay where I'm needed the most.

DADONG: But you never know what tomorrow will bring...

CLARITA: He's moved on, Tio. And so have I.

DADONG: Laling. She will approve, won't she…what we're planning to do… she will love it, right Clarita? Her ashes spread where the island used to be… she will look down on both of us, smiling and giving her blessing. She will see how my heart is pure… she'll forgive me, won't she… Damn, I forgot to call Neil Cayabyab to do my taxes… How about the application for the 501C3?

CLARITA: I mailed it yesterday.

DADONG: Where's my rolodex. I didn't pack it, did I? Where is it? (Rifling through the drawers.) Is it here? Where did I put it? (He begins to cry.) Where the fuck is my rolodex? I can't lose that rolodex. (He is weeping now.) I never told her how I loved her… how grateful I was… when I lost Nena, I realized she – you – were the only family I had left… All these years, I was never there for her… and yet when I needed her, she came, and you, and how it was this that made me want to sing… Forgive me, Inday. Forgive me. Dios mio! Wa gyud nako kasulti-i. Magpasalamat ako. Pagkamatay ni Nena, siya ang bugtong igso-on uyamut ang nahabilin… pagka walay kasingkasing ang akong pagbakho…

(He sinks to his knees, his face in his hands.)

DADONG: Pasayloa ko, Inday. Pasayloa ko. Kadako sa akong sa...

CLARITA: (Helping him up.)Unsay imong sa, Tio?

DADONG: Laling, pasayloa ako.

CLARITA: Nakahibaw siya, Tio. Naminaw siya karon.

DADONG: Way bili ang akong pagkaPilipino. Ang dakong gracia sa akong mismong atubangan. Ang bugtong ko nga igsoon Kadako sa akong sala. Pilipino lang gihapon ang akong kalag… My soul is still Filipino. Everything else is just Macy's…

>(CLARITA pulls him up. He rises to his feet, composes himself, picks up the suitcase and exits.)

CLARITA: I didn't choose Brian. Even though my hands came up white and empty. I still let him go. (Spreading her hands wide, white palms facing up.) Because I will get them back. Maybe not today, nor tomorrow… But I have faith. And faith is an act of the will and I've only just begun. I will find You. I will seek You out. I will not rest until You come back to me!

>(Then as in Act One, Scene 1 of the play, light comes flooding into the room with ferocious intensity.

>BLACKOUT

>END OF PLAY

Playwright's Notes

Baranggay - a local district

Carpentero - a carpenter

Flagellante - a flagellant, in the Catholic Church, one who whips
                        himself for religious
discipline

Inday - a term of endearment for a woman

Ma-ayong gabi-i - Good evening in Cebuano, a Pilipino
                        language

Narra - a Philippine hardwood

Oracion - a prayer

Pasyon - Passion play as performed in the Philippines

Santa Maria, napuno ka sa gracia - Hail Mary, full of grace!

Susmariosep - a contraction of "Jesus, Mary and Joseph"

The Lenten practice of reenacting Jesus Christ's Passion on the
Cross involving actual crucifixion is still observed today in the
Philippines.

Translations

Page 3

Matam-is nga Hesus,
tungud sa pagtubus Mo sa Kalibutan
nagpasakit Ka sa Krus
Nangamuyo kami Kanimo,
nga tungud sa Imong mapa-it uyamut nga
mga kasakit,
luwason Mo and kalag ni Eulalia, sa mga
kasakitan nga giantus niya,
ug papahulayon Mo sa Imong himaya, nga
walay katapusan.[1]

Sweet Jesus
Savior of the world,
by suffering on the cross,
We ask of you,
because you have suffered the most
profound pain,
To save the soul of Eulalia from all the pain
that she has suffered
and let her rest in your glory without end.

Page 4

LALING:
(Faintly.) Kinsa na? (Who is it?)

CLARITA:
Si Clarita.

LALING:
(Trying to sit up.) Clarita?

CLARITA:

Ni-a ming tanan. Giampo-an ka namo, Ma. (We're all here, Ma. We're praying for you.)

LALING:
Ha-in ka, anak? (Where are you, child?)

> (CLARITA walks over to the
> window and pulls the shades up a
> little. Soft light streams into the
> room.)

LALING:
Kalu-oy sa Dios. (God have mercy.)

.

CLARITA:
(Hushing her.) Pahuway, Ma. (Rest, Ma.)

LALING:
Ma-o na kani? (Making the sign of the cross. Praying.) Matam-is nga Hesus,
tungud sa pagtubus Mo sa Kalibutan... (She begins to cry.)
Nahadlok ko, Inday...Nahadlok ko...ayaw ko ug baya-i. (Is this it? Sweet Jesus, because you have saved the world from sin-- I'm so scared, Inday. I'm scared. Don't leave me!)

CLARITA:
Kahibalo ko, Nay. Ni-a Siya karon. Gihigugma ka niya. Dili gyud ka biya-an. I know, Ma. He's here. He loves you. He'll never leave you.

Page 5

CLARITA:
Ginoo, dili ako angay nga mokalawat Kanimo, apan ipamulong lamang ug mamaayo ako. Ang lawas ni Cristo.

Lord, I am not worthy that thou should come under my roof,
Say but the word and my soul shall be healed.

Page 37
LALING:
Buot ni Pilato buhian si Jesus,
ug busa misulti siya pagusab
ngadto sa mga tawo.
Apan misinggit sila pagtubag kaniya
Ilansang siya sa Krus! Ilansang --

Pilate wanted to free Jesus
So he asked the crowd again
But they cried out,
Crucify him! Crucify him!

81

DADONG:
Where's my rolodex. I didn't pack it, did I? Where is it? (Rifling through the drawers.) Is it here? Where did I put it? (He begins to cry.) Where the fuck is my rolodex? I can't lose that rolodex. (He is weeping now.) I never told her how I loved her... how grateful I was... when I lost Nena, I realized she – you – were the only family I had left... All these years, I was

never there for her… and yet when I needed her, she came, and you, and how it was this that made me want to sing… Forgive me, Inday. Forgive me. Dios mio! Wa gyud nako kasulti-i. Magpasalamat ako. Pagkamatay ni Nena, siya ang bugtong igso-on uyamut ang nahabilin sa kalibutan… pagka walay kasingkasing ang akong pagbakho… (I never got to say it… I never got to thank her. When Nena died, I realized she and you were all I had in the world…My sorrow is heartless.)

> (He sinks to his knees, his face in his hands.)

DADONG:
Pasayloa ko, Inday. Pasayloa ko. Kadako sa akong sa…(Forigve me, Inday. Forgive me. My sin is mortal.)

CLARITA:
(Helping him up.)Unsay imong sa, Tio? (What is your sin, Tio?)

DADONG:
Laling, pasayloa ako. (Forgive me, Laling.)

CLARITA:
Nakahibaw siya, Tio. Naminaw siya karon. (She knows. She hears you.)

DADONG:
Way bili ang akong pagkaPilipino. Ang dakong gracia sa akong mismong atubangan. Ang bugtong ko nga igso-on Kadako sa akong sala. Pilipino lang gihapon ang akong kalag… (There's

no value to my being a Filipino. I have been blessed and there has been grace right in front of my eyes. And I didn't see it. I didn't know…) My soul is still Filipino. Everything else is just Macy's…

Page 87

There is no translation for the dialogue in Cebuano (a Filipino language). It is the playwright's intention to create a brief moment of incomprehension among audience members who do not speak the language, a device the playwright is using to illustrate the gap that exists between the two cultures.

STATE WITHOUT GRACE

by

Linda Faigao-Hall

STATE WITHOUT GRACE

Premiered in 1984 at Pan Asian Theater Company
In New York City.

Cast of Characters:

Celia, Filipino U.S. immigrant, early 30's

Ponce, a houseboy

Laura, Celia's cousin, 17 years old

Rosa, Celia's aunt, Laura's mother, early 40's

Leon, Celia's uncle, Rosa's husband, Laura's father, late 40's

Nene, Celia's youngest cousin, Laura's younger sister, 7 years old

Lola, (Pilipino term for "grandmother"), the clan's matriarch, late 60's

Elise, CELIA's cousin, Laura's and Nene's older sister, early 20's

Notes: In the Philippines, designated terms of respect are attached to an older person's first name. In this play, CELIA is addressed as <u>Ate</u> (<u>A-te</u>) CELIA by LAURA, NENE, and ELISE who are much younger than she is. Aunts and uncles are addressed as <u>Tia</u> and <u>Tio</u>. The grandmother is addressed and <u>Lola</u> by all members of the family.

The ritual of the kissing of the hand is also of paramount importance. Younger members of the family kiss the hands of the elders as a sign of respect, filial devotion and good grace.

Inday (In-day) A term of endearment.

Time: May, 1978

Place: Cebu City, Philippines

(Two clearly delineated acting spaces. Down Center is a dining room that also serves as a living room. There is a window that opens into a garden, lush and very green. There are 2 doors at Stage Right and Left; one leads to the kitchen and the other to the women's bedrooms. There is a general area used for exits and entrances into the house as well as a corridor leading to other rooms within the house. There should also be easy access between the living room and Lola's bedroom, UC. The latter has a shrine of Christian icons festooned with garlands of flowers, a typical feature in Filipino households. On one wall is a veritable collection of family prints. There is a large window. Unless stated in the text, acting space is left dark except when action is taking place in it. There will also be a need for an empty space for Act Two, Scene One and Act Three Scene One.)

Act One
Scene One

(Late afternoon. The dining room. These are remains of a dinner on the table. PONCE, the houseboy, is seen coming and going taking the food away. There are snacks on the table. ROSA, CELIA, LAURA and NENE are heard saying goodbye offstage.

(ROSA will then come in to make garlands
of fresh flowers from a basin of water. The
finished garlands are in a basket. LAURA
and NENE follow to go through packages
from a big brown box. CELIA comes in
last.)

CELIA: (taking her shoes off.) And that's just half the clan.

ROSA: They were all sorry Mark didn't come with you. What a
pity… It's not everyday we get to meet an American son-in-law.

LAURA: (Showing NENE a box.) Look, Nene. It's for you.

NENE: (Opens it.) Shoes!

ROSA: Put them on for the Flores! Go on.

(NENE rushes out.)

CELIA: No big deal. I told you Mark wasn't able to take time off
from work.

ROSA: But you said he was an artist.

CELIA: He is.

LEON: Rosa, in the States, artists work. It's called commercial
art.

ROSA: Really? So how come he can't make a living on it. The
poor girl's been married four years and they still can't raise a
family.

CELIA: Well, you know sometimes it's good to wait. Just in case
it doesn't work.

ROSA: That's why you have them. In case it doesn't work. I'm sure it's Mark's idea… people over there wait so long. Here, all it takes is nine months after the wedding.

LEON: (Laughing) Not even that long. Remember Marilyn? Oswaldo, her husband?

LAURA: He's old enough to be her grandfather!

ROSA: So? He's a manager at McDonald's.

CELIA: What?

ROSA: McDonald's. We passed by this morning. Next to Shaky's Pizza, remember? On Mango Avenue?

CELIA: How could I miss it? I thought I was in Paramus.

LAURA: (Tearing open a package.) Cadbury's!

ROSA: Save it for the reunion!

LAURA: Eighty people fighting over six bars.

CELIA: Eighty?

LAURA: It's being catered, Ate. Club Filipino is doing it!

CELIA: But Lola always held the reunion in April. Why is she holding it in May?

ROSA: Because you came. She's changed it for you. This is the first time in ten years we're all together.

CELIA: I was looking forward to a quiet, restful visit. Just us. Lola. Elise. (Pacing.) Where are they, anyway? We've been waiting since noon.

ROSA: It's Flores de Mayo. Have you forgotten how hectic it gets?

CELIA: Even then. My first visit and she's in church.

LAURA: (Popping a piece of chocolate into her mouth. To PONCE.) Ponce, get me the scissors.(No response from PONCE.) Ponce, the scissors!

ROSA: You forget this is all very sudden.

LAURA: Ma, Ponce's acting deaf again.

(PONCE leaves in a huff.)

CELIA: A month's notice shouldn't be much of a surprise. (Flipping another page) Mrs. Gandiongco... my Algebra teacher...

LEON: The christening in April... See? I was the godfather.

CELIA: Good grief. She's still having babies?

LEON: That's the last one. She finally had a girl. You know how they always wanted a girl.

LAURA: After nine boys.

CELIA: Sounds awful.

ROSA: It's better than nothing.

CELIA: All right...all right... I get the hint. (Turning to the pictures again.) Isn't that Anita?

ROSA: Poor woman... You know her husband beats her up.

CELIA: Really? That's horrible!

ROSA: I know … She stays the night with us when he's in one of his moods. We do what we can for her…

CELIA: My god, why doesn't she leave him?

ROSA: (Amazed.) What's the matter with you? They're married.

CELIA: Oh, excuse me. (Flipping another page.) That's the best portrait of Papa.

LEON: Yes… that's right… that was the last one… just before he died…

CELIA: (Flipping the next page.) Though this is my favorite… When he won the Poetry Contest.

ROSA: Does Mark know your father was a brilliant poet?

LEON: So if he was so brilliant, why did he stop writing?

ROSA: Because my brother was a better man that that. He was a father and a husband. He knew he couldn't make a living from writing so he promptly gave it up.

CELIA: That's not the way it happened.

ROSA: Oh?

CELIA: Lola asked him to give it up. That's why. To run a farm. A farm!

ROSA: Don't use that tone of voice. That business built this house, put you through school and sent you to the States.

(CELIA finally closes the album with a snap.)

LEON: (To ROSA.) You don't give up, do you? The poor girl's not been home a day and you're at it already.

CELIA: I feel as if I've never left.

LEON: (Picking up the album again and flipping a page.) Look. You liked this one, too, didn't you?

CELIA: Yes… Mama… in silk…

ROSA: So lovely… I remember the day she posed for this one… She was the reigning queen at the Feast of San Rogue and my brother was asked to give the tribute. I knew when he set eyes on her he'd never marry anyone else.

LAURA: A storybook romance!

CELIA: Didn't last long, did it. Poor Mama. I bet Papa never forgave her for dying in childbirth.

ROSA: What a blasphemous thing to say.

CELIA: (Laughing.) Well, I guess when you gotta go, you got to go.

ROSA: He loved her deeply.

CELIA: So?

ROSA: That's why he never married again.

CELIA: He should've.

ROSA: Celia. (To LEON, shocked.) Listen to her. What is she saying?

(PONCE comes back in with the scissors.)

LAURA: But I want the one in the sewing box!

PONCE: You didn't tell me that.

LAURA: Where are your glasses, anyway? That's why you never find anything. You're blind as a bat.

(PONCE leaves again.)

ROSA: I suppose American men are different. Lola says over there, the man needs a woman when he's just starting out. Then another when he's successful. Then another when he's retired.

LEON: Not a bad idea!

ROSA: Watch your mouth. But here, a woman is for all the times. I tell you. Filipino marriages are better.

LEON: They are?

ROSA: Because we know how to suffer. After the honeymoon, and the romance, it's perseverance that counts.

CELIA: Exactly. Like purgatory.

LEON: Nah. With a taste of heaven now and then, eh, Rosa?

ROSA: More then than now, believe me!

LAURA: Yuck.

(PONCE comes back, bespectacled, with the scissors and hands them to LAURA.)

PONCE: (Muttering to himself.) Ponce this... Ponce that...

LAURA: (Opening a package with excited frenzy. She gasps. It's a handbag.) Oh, it's for me! Wow, you got it! (Rushing to CELIA to give her a hug.) Thank you, Ate. (Skipping over to ROSA and thrusting the bag up to her face.) Look, Ma, an Oscar de la Renta! Just what I asked for!

ROSA: Dios mio, you'd think it was made in heaven.

(LAURA goes back to the box.)

LAURA: Wranglers! Who gets these?

CELIA: It's for you, Ponce. I hope it fits. You were such a little thing when I left.

(PONCE runs off with them.)

ROSA: Uy that Ponce. Lola's been good to him. She kept him when his mother died. What a good cook she was, too. You know Lola pays him 150 pesos a month! No other houseboy gets that much.

LAURA: Why didn't you get Cacharel, Ate?

CELIA: Cacharel? What's that?

LAURA: (Laughing.) They're French Jeans. You never heard of Cacharel? Where have you been?

CELIA: Oh, just the Lower Eastside.

LAURA: The lower eastside? Where's that?

CELIA: You never heard of the Lower Eastside?

LAURA: Estee Lauder! (Picking up a box of cosmetics.)

CELIA: I thought you said Lola would be home soon.

ROSA: She'll be here any minute now.

CELIA: You sure she's not playing games with me.

ROSA: What do you mean playing games?

CELIA: I think it's odd she isn't here yet. Everybody was at the airport.

ROSA: (Guardedly.) Well, what do you expect? Every Marasigan who's left for American comes back for a visit after a year! Two years at the most.

CELIA: I write frequently.

ROSA: Oh, yes. That you do. Every letter, a revelation.

CELIA: What do you mean?

ROSA: I don't know… it's all mixed up. In my day, one got married, had children and settled down.

CELIA: (Impatiently, holding herself in check.) We can't afford children, Tia.

ROSA: Don't worry about money. Money comes to children. You'll manage.

LAURA: You don't understand, Ma. In the States, it's not enough to just manage. Americans are big on the quality of life. (To CELIA.) I'm taking Contemporary American Culture 201 this term.

CELIA: (Sitting down.) Oh my God, it's worse than I thought. (With effort at lightness, to LAURA.) Maybe I should get the first plane back to New York. I wish Lola would get here soon… you're all making me nervous.

LEON: Relax, Inday. She and Elise are on a special novena to St. Jude.

CELIA: She and Elise? In my day that was Lola's idea of imposing penance. What's Elise been up to?

> (Along silence. LEON, ROSA and LAURA exchange glances. The moment is broken by NENE who comes in, dressed in white with a halo of flowers in her hair.)

LEON: (Breaking the silence.) There she is! (Hugging her.) That's my baby. You look just like an angel. What's this, have you lost your tongue?

> (CELIA stands transfixed, staring at NENE.)

LEON: Have you thanked Ate Celia for your new shoes? Let me see them.

NENE: (Raising one foot.) Thank you, Ate Celia.

ROSA: Looks perfect on you. Turn around. (NENE does slowly.) Remember the white dress?

CELIA: How could I forget? It was too big on me.

ROSA: Well, it fits her just right. (Beckons NENE to come forward.) Though she wanted to be an angel this year, poor thing. (To CELIA.) Do the honors, Celia.

CELIA: (Moving away.) Me? I don't think you want me, Tia.

ROSA: (To NENE.) Go on child. Ponce doesn't have the whole day.

CELIA: (Aggressively, staggering back.) No, please. Let Tio Leon do it!

> (The family, a little taken back watches her in puzzlement.)

ROSA: What's the matter? Have you forgotten already?

> (NENE walks over to CELIA. CELIA hesitates. The family watches. A long pause. CELIA hesitantly walks over to the basin and dips her hand into it, picking up a handful of flowers which she drops into NENE's basket. CELIA then turns to go.)

NENE: (Following close behind.) It's not enough, Ate.

ROSA: (To CELIA.) Don't you remember those days? Your Lola used to do the blessing. Go on! Do it right!

CELIA: Oh, all right. (Yields.) A breath of jasmine over the adelfas, then a spring or two of <u>champacas</u> around the sides. And in the center, a rosal. When you walk down the aisle, drop all of the flowers except this one. This, you offer at the Virgin's feet.

NENE: why?

CELIA: Has no one ever told you about the rosal?

NENE: (Giggling.) No, Ate Celia.

CELIA: They say that the rosal was a star that dropped from the sky and fell on a leaf. That's why you offer it last. Because it comes straight from heaven...

NENE: Why don't you come with me, Ate?

CELIA: I can't.

NENE: Why not?

CELIA: Because I'm not a child anymore. Flores de Mayo is only for children.

ROSA: Go on. Do the blessing, Celia. She doesn't have much time.

CELIA: No. Please. (To ROSA.) You do it, Tia.

ROSA: Come, Nene. (NENE kneels in front of ROSA.) Are you in state of grace?

NENE: Yes, Ma.

ROSA: When was your last confession?

NENE: This morning.

ROSA: God bless you.

> (NENE kisses her hand. NENE proceeds to
> kiss everyone's hand, as each one gives her
> a petition.)

ROSA: Pray for your father that he may have patience.

LAURA: Pray for Ate Elise that she may be humble.

CELIA: (pause.) Pray for all of us. (Groping for words, embarrassed.) So our sins be forgiven. That's right. That always covers a lot of ground, doesn't it?

LEON: (patting her on the head.) Why don't you just enjoy yourself, Nene?

(They all laugh. LEON picks up a
newspaper. NENE exits..)

LEON: I wouldn't take the job of saint if they offered me eternal
life.

ROSA: That's why St. Jude doesn't give you any contracts.
You're always making fun.

LEON: Why, did he personally tell you that? You've got a
hotline? You know it's got nothing to do with him. It's got
everything to do with that devil in Malacanang. (Ruffling the
paper.) Look at that. Pacifico Seares won the contract for San
Miguel. I know my bid was lower than his. I tell you, his cronies
get everything!

ROSA: (Lowering her voice.) Shh! You want to get arrested, too?

LEON: Fifty years old and I'm out of a job. I may as well be in
prison.

ROSA: You will be if you don't stop talking like that. And
besides, you should be grateful Lola's asked the children to stay
here until you get the next one.

LEON: Our house is empty without them.

LAURA: I like it here, Pa. I have my own room.

ROSA: No problem, Leon. Business is good for Lola this year.

LEON: With the current price of copra? How does she do it?

(PONCE disrupts the scene by coming in
with the telephone. He is wearing the
Wranglers.)

PONCE: Phone call for you, Laura.

LAURA: (Taking it.) Hello...hi, Tessie. (Brightening up.) Yes, she's here. You know what, I got my Oscar de la Renta. (A long pause, then throwing ROSA a meaningful glance.) I see... well, I'm sure it's nothing ... no... she hasn't been dancing as far as we know... with her troupe... really? No, you must be mistaken...Yes...I know you mean well... What? (Angry.) What's so funny? In the first place it's none of your business. That's right! Same to you! (Slams the phone down.)

LAURA: I knew it! I knew it, Ma! I told you you'll have to tie her to the bed post!

ROSA: What's happened?

LAURA: She's dancing with those weirdos again!

ROSA: What?

LAURA: That's what she said.

ROSA: Leon, I thought you said they were in church.

LEON: That was this morning. Rosa, take it easy now.

ROSA: Take it easy? What do you mean take it easy? Well, she's at it again. Why don't you do something, dios mio!

LAURA: Jazz. Modern Dance. Ballet. The Joffrey was here last year. That was nice. But no. She has to do Ifugao. (To CELIA.) Oh, Ate. My own sister! Last week, during Founder's Day she brought a whole group of natives to dance in the Faculty Homecoming. And the women – they don't wear tops! I didn't go to school for a week!

CELIA: (Laughing.) I see ethnic isn't chic yet. Maybe she ought to wait a couple more years.

ROSA: That's not the point, Celia. We were always proud of her research. (Faltering.) It's just that –

LAURA: It's just that that was only the beginning. And not the worst part of it.

CELIA: (In mock desperation.) Oh God, there's more?

ROSA: (Near tears.) She actually fell in love with one of them.

CELIA; Oh… I see now. (Laughing a little.) Though I'm not sure about the G-strings.

ROSA: Thank God, he's civilized! He lives in an apartment!

CELIA: He does?

LEON: (Impatiently.) He's an ethnographer.

CELIA: An ethnographer. Now that sounds like something the family would be impressed with!

LAURA: A savage headhunter?

CELIA: Come now. Even I know the custom is extinct.

LAURA: But it's in the blood, Ate.

ROSA: He's a pagan. And he refuses to convert. Elise talked about how she'd live with his people in the mountains someday.

LAURA: You know she has to have a baby first before she can marry. They have houses up there just for that purpose. It's disgusting!

LEON: That's enough, both of you!

CELIA: And what does Elise have to say about all this?

LEON: It doesn't matter. Lola will never let her go.

CELIA: Lola! Ah, ha. I knew the old girl was behind it. (Catching surprised looks.) Sorry. It's been awhile. I just got home… Takes time, you know…

ROSA: Elise can't defy Lola's wishes. Elise knows what will happen to her if she does.

CELIA: What?

LAURA: Lola says defiance is a sign of pride. And as you know, pride brings about a fall from grace.

CELIA: (Looking at LAURA with amazement.) Oh, my god. You got them, too. The same lessons, word for word…

ROSA: But it's not just pride, Laura. There's disrespect for elders, rejection of one's faith.

LAURA: Remember Cousin Norma She went out with this married man she met in Manila? Lola's never forgiven her for that. Now that she herself is married, she can't have any children. She's had blackberries boiled in a pig's blood. Crawled on all fours eating burnt corn. It's devil's work! But it seems even his potions don't do any good.

CELIA: You've even got the gruesome details!

LEON: (To ROSA.) You've been talking too much again.

ROSA: (To LEON.) She needs to know these things. It's true, Leon. Something bad always happens.

CELIA: Really?

ROSA: (Missing CELIA's tone.) Really. And the only way out of it is through suffering.

CELIA: (Snapping back.) Not if you go to therapy.

ROSA: Therapy? What therapy?

LAURA: (In awe.) A support system!

ROSA: What?

LAURA: When a culture reaches a highly industrialized stage of development, traditional family and kinship ties break down and are replaced by support systems like- -

ROSA: (Cutting her off.) Dr. Hwang does some kind of therapy at the mental asylum. Is this what you're talking about?

CELIA: No. this is what you get so you don't end up there.

ROSA: (To LAURA.) Go and tell her to get back here before Lola comes home.

LAURA: No, I won't.

ROSA: Laura, do as I say!

LAURA: No, I won't, Ma. You know she doesn't give a damn!

       (In the confusion, no one notices that the
       door has opened and LOLA stands framed
       against the doorway.)

LEON: Laura!

LAURA: It's your fault, Pa. You let her do anything she wants. It's your fault!

ROSA: You speak to your father this way? (To LEON.) It has come to this.

LAURA: (To anger.) I won't. I won't do it.

LEON: I'll go get her.

CELIA: This is crazy! (Pause.) I'll go.

ROSA: You?

CELIA: Why not? She sounds intriguing, unless of course good old Lola objects!

LOLA: Good Evening.

> (A long pause as they all turn towards LOLA. An uneasy quiet descends on all of them. LOLA comes forward, a small woman, her hair pulled pack in a bun, stark white against her brown face. She wears the traditional Filipino dress that old generation women wear in the country, the saya and panuelo. There is nothing superfluous about her; her movements are spare and sometimes she could look stern, sometimes gentle. But it's when she is quiet that she commands the most respect. There is mastery in her silence. Everybody comes forward to kiss her hand; LEON first, then ROSA.)

LOLA: You will stay for the prayers tonight.

ROSA: Yes, <u>Nay.</u>

> (LAURA is next, from whom LOLA
> withdraws her hand.)

LOLA: I heard your outburst. Apologize.

> (LAURA keeps silence.)

LOLA: We're all waiting, Laura.

LAURA: (Bursting into tears.) I'm sorry.

> (LOLA then gives her hand. LAURA kisses
> it. CELIA comes next. CELIA, too, bends
> down to take her hand, but LOLA pulls her
> hand away, and runs her hand through
> CELIA's hair instead.)

LOLA: (To ROSA.) Give her the flowers. (To CELIA.) Come
with me to my room. We will talk there.

> (ROSA picks up the basket of flowers, gives
> it to CELIA who takes it. LOLA leaves.
> CELIA throws everybody a backward
> glance as she follows LOLA to the door.)

FADEOUT

Scene Two

> (Lights dim on stage except in LOLA's
> bedroom. LOLA is found seated on a
> rocking chair in front of the altar.)

> (The door opens. CELIA comes in. She
> places the basket on the floor.)

LOLA: Are you comfortable?

CELIA: Everything is just as I remember it. Lola- - -

LOLA: Yes?

CELIA: I didn't mean the way it sounded downstairs. I'm sorry.

LOLA: I understand. You've been away a long time.

CELIA: And I'm here for only a short time. I don't want to get involved. Really... I was just kidding.

LOLA: it's not important. So what have you done since you arrived?

CELIA: I've seen a little of the city.

LOLA: And what do you think of it?

CELIA: It's wonderful! It's good to be home. Except, of course, some things have changed... It's very... sad. We passed by that old house in Sanciangko. They're tearing it down.

LOLA: It is falling to pieces. And the young must find a place to build.

CELIA: An Exxon gas station.

LOLA: A bank, a garage, parking lot, it doesn't matter. It's only form. What is important are the things that stay.

CELIA: And which ones are those?

LOLA: Give yourself time to discover them again.

(She picks up the basket of flowers and sets it in front of the altar. She begins to place a garland on an icon.)

Lola: Every morning without fail, you came to place the flowers on the Virgin…

> (LOLA picks up another garland and offers
> it to CELIA. There is a beat. Then CELIA
> comes forward and places it on theVirgin.
> In her carelessness, the statue topples over.)

CELIA: (Picking it up, righting it. Glibly, with a laugh.) As you can see, I'm out of practice.

(She moves away, turning her back. She stands at the window, looking out.)

ELIA: Anyway Flores de mayo is only for children.

LOLA: Is it?

CELIA: Isn't it?

LOLA: (Joining her at the window.)You used to stand right here at this window smelling the champacas…Your father would be sitting at his desk, writing his poetry… The rosal is in bloom. Can you see them from here?

CELIA: I can smell them!

LOLA: And the Camias, see? They're ready to bloom any minute… Flores de Mayo… I knew you'd come home in May. Your favorite month.

LOLA: Early Saturday mornings, you'd march off to church, your basket spilling with Adelfas. Look… They're still there. Though the white ones are new. We planted those five years ago. And the dahlias, wait till you see the dahlias!

CELIA: (Drawn now.) I remember... all of it... the smell of Jasmine. And my father, at this desk... his voice, like a singing...

> (The sounds of the evening come through: insects, bullfrogs, cicadas. There are the shimmer of leaves, shadows of trees.)

CELIA: And every night without fail, this man passing by, strumming his guitar...Papa and I timed our nighttimes by his songs. We'd hear his music from a distance until it would come to a peak beneath this window. And the music would fade out again, dying slowly. Papa used to weave countless stories about this man. What he looked like... where he came from... where he was going... what made him play such sad songs...

LOLA: I'm only sorry your husband isn't here.

> (The spell breaks.)

LOLA: No plans for a child this year, Celia?

CELIA: No. We've decided to concentrate on his art. I mean, for awhile.

LOLA: It's very important to him then? This art?

CELIA: (Quickly.) For me, too.

> (CELIA walks over to stand in front of the wall of photographs. She surveys the collection.)

CELIA: At home, we have a wall just like this one. Except these are faces he picks up everywhere, anywhere. That's what he does, you know. He paints faces. (Looking up at the wall of

297

photographs.) He brings them home the way other people bring stray cats. Father's picture. That one. Taken a year before he died. (Pause.) Mark did that one of Papa. He said he had dead eyes... that's what he said. My father had dead eyes. Long before anyone knew he was dying, Mark saw it. That's his genius. He sees glimpses at a hair's breath and he'd capture them. (Pause.) May I kiss your hand now, Lola?

> (LOLA stand up, moves away, towards the altar and lights the candles.)

LOLA: You've heard about our problem with Elise.

CELIA: I suppose so. Although I haven't heard Elise's side.

LOLA: I'm sure you will. I trust you will handle the situation well. You are, after all, here now in my house. And in this house you will do only what is right for all of us.

CELIA: And what may I ask is right for all of you?

LOLA: That she give up this madness so order may be Resorted.

CELIA: I meant it, Lola. I'd rather not get involved. You do what you need to do.

LOLA: Very well then. But I want your word. Promise me you will not get involved.

CELIA: I promise.

LOLA: Good. At eight o'clock, we start Tiempo para Familia. You will lead the prayers tonight.

CELIA: May I be excused? I'm rather tired, Lola.

LOLA: I understand. Tomorrow then?

CELIA: No. I guess not. For this, I need time. It's been awhile.

LOLA: You will have it.

> (CELIA comes forward. She makes a
> motion to kiss LOLA's hand. LOLA moves
> away.)

CELIA: Lola... I already told you I'm staying out of it.

LOLA: Are you sure there aren't other things you need to tell me?

CELIA: What other things could be?

LOLA: Only you would know that.

CELIA: What do you mean by that? I haven't done anything wrong.

LOLA: I didn't say you've done anything wrong. Go and ask Elise to come home. I need to be soothed.

> (CELIA then walks out of the room. Lights
> are still up in LOLA's bedroom after CELIA
> leaves. LOLA is seen placing the rest of the
> garlands on the icons.)

FADEOUT

Act Two

Scene One

(An open space. There is a native basket, UR. ELISE is seen in denims, bending over her sneakers tying them. She is slim, lithe and graceful. There is a dancer's quality to all her movements. She must also be very intense, like coiled wire. CELIA appears DL. ELISE sees her immediately. ELISE rushes towards CELIA, catching her in an embrace.)

ELISE: But how did you know I was here?

CELIA: It's a small world. (Looking her over, laughing with her.) Let's see now … twenty-one?

ELISE: I was eleven when you left.

CELIA: I should feel so old!

ELISE: Oh, Ate, you haven't changed. You don't look a day older.

CELIA: That's what everybody seems to think!

ELISE: We had a 'tech' rehearsal that's why I couldn't go to the airport. You just missed the troupe.

CELIA: They thought you were in church. With Lola.

ELISE: (Quickly, in a rush.) But I was! Then I told her I had to go to the library. I did go, I mean...

CELIA: (Holding up her hand.) I understand.

ELISE: I'm sure they've filled you in on the details.

CELIA: I'm sure you can give them to me better than they can.

ELISE; Oh, Ate. I knew you'd say that.

CELIA: Well, you can come home again ... speaking of home, we better go, Elise.

ELISE: Yes, of course. As I said I was just leaving. (Not moving.)

CELIA: (Restless.) Shall we?

ELISE: Was Mama angry?

CELIA: A little.

ELISE: And Lola?

CELIA: You know she never gets angry. She just stands there pushing all your buttons.

ELISE: I'm so glad you're home … I've been so alone. And then when I heard you were coming … the one person in the world who'd understand.

CELIA: Well, I don't really know too much about it, Elise. I mean, I'm not sure if I should get involved …

ELISE: But you'll understand. I know you will. I went up to Banawe to do my research. I lived there for a couple of months. The whole culture entranced me. Sometimes I wonder: what if the Spaniards and the Americans didn't come when we were too young? What if we were given time to ourselves. Free to be whoever we were, free to grow, create our own distinction. It's so magnificent up there, Celia. For thousands of years our ancestors have lived in those mountains and fashioned rice terraces out of them by hand.

CELIA: We learned that in the fourth grade.

ELISE: Awiyao said if the terraces were brought end to end they would circle half the globe.

CELIA: That, they didn't say.

ELISE: They didn't tell us a lot of things. That on moonlit nights, if you stand on a peak and look down, they gleam in the dark like coils of molten silver. That at sunrise, they turn to gold and the world spirals into fire. That it's quiet there. No sound expect for the wind. And nothing else but the sky overhead and the mountain under your feet, everything flowing into each other, ceaselessly, no end, no beginning. It's almost paradise.

(ELISE walks over to the basket UR and opens it. The action is strikingly reminiscent of LAURA's business with the American gifts in the brown box. Only this is a native basket. She takes from it an elaborate headdress, a magnificent piece of beadwork. ELISE puts the costumes on as she describes them so that by the end of this speech, she has transformed herself in front of our eyes.)

ELISE: The dancers wear these. Each bead stands for a word. Next to each other, they tell a story. The colors hold the feelings. This is for joy...ecstasy...sorrow. The whole piece, a life. (Picks up a tapestry of brilliant colors.) They say the weaver waits until the patterns come to her in her dreams. (Picks up a necklace.) From the root of the narra... they say if you wear it long enough, it bleeds.

CELIA: Elise... you look magnificent. (Pause.) This is very important to you, isn't it?

ELISE: Did they tell you about Awiyao? Even I didn't count on that. That's when they really came down hard.

CELIA: The proverbial love at first sight, Elise?

ELISE: Like a shock of recognition. Like finding home at last.

CELIA: (A pause.) One of those...

ELISE: (Starts to cry.)But it's no use. Oh, Ate Celia, I make everyone unhappy. And why? Because I'm in love with this man? It was an accident!

CELIA: But you have to be happy, too.

ELISE: Yes, yes. I should be. But I'm afraid.

CELIA: Of what?

ELISE: You know what it is they say. If you do something wrong, then something bad always happens to you.

CELIA: Oh, God, here we go again.

ELISE: Listen. Three years ago, Ate Norma came to see Lola. I remember the day well. A hot Friday afternoon in April. It was Lent. The talk then was that she was living with this married man who had abandoned his own family for her. She and Lola stayed in that room upstairs, talking. No one knows what they said to each other. All we know and remember is that when Ate Norma left, she was in tears. And for a whole year after that, Lola wore black. Ate Norma's never been in the house since. I came across her last year. Ate, she can't have any children! For the rest of my life, I will never forget the look in that face. There was sorrow ... tremendous sorrow...

CELIA: (Angry.) Tremendous crap, you mean! Goddam it, they really get you, don't they. Elise, it's ridiculous! It's nothing but a superstition. Like Flores de Mayo. We don't go around throwing flowers at statues anymore do we?

ELISE: (Drawing back, shocked.) Ate!

CELIA: Blame it on the Americans. They're not such a bad lot. They taught me some things.

ELISE: (To herself.) Oh, to be able to breathe... not to be afraid. Not to be so torn.

CELIA: You've got it right. (Triumphantly.) In fact, there's more to me than meets the eye.

ELISE: What do you mean?

CELIA: Mark and I are getting a divorce!

(A beat.)

ELISE: Ate Celia! But why? I thought you were happy?

CELIA: It happens to the best of us. People drift apart. Such things happen. No big deal.

ELISE: And it's really over?

CELIA: Yes. It's just a matter of time.

ELISE: And no One knows? And you didn't tell Lola?

CELIA: Of course, I wanted to tell her. I wanted to tell all of you. But you know how it is... Look, keep it a secret, okay? Between you and me?

ELISE: But of course, if you want me to. But how about Lola? She hasn't changed, Ate... She feels these things.

CELIA: (Triumphantly.) Well, she didn't!

ELISE: Oh, Ate Celia, how brave you are!

CELIA: That's right. And remember this, Elise, no matter how you live your life, you can choose to skip over the pain. Look at me. No tears.

ELISE: And look at you. How do you do it? What is it like, Ate, to be really free? (Takes out a packet of letters from the basket.)

CELIA: (Picking them up.) My letters!

ELISE: (Laughing.) I keep them here with the costumes. Birthday cards. Christmas. The shortest notes!

CELIA: (Picking up a letter, reading.) The commune in Perry Street!

ELISE: Did you really live with fifteen couples?

CELIA: Sure for about three weeks. I couldn't handle it. It got too public. (They both laugh.) There was this Marxist who I discovered had been using my toothbrush all along. That was the day I found out how bourgeois I was! He eventually left for Cuba. I guess he liked the commune so much he decided to be a communist.
(They giggle. They read snatches of the letters, their reading weaving into each other.)

ELISE: Woodstock …

CELIA: ... Oh, that travel agency spot on Madison Avenue ...There were so distraught when I gave that up...

ELISE: To go back to school! (Mimicking ROSA.) Teaching English to Negroes! (They both laugh. Goes back to the letters.) Connecticut.

CELIA: Rhode Island ...

ELISE: Washington, D.C ... I know all these by heart ...

CELIA: Struggling graduate student backpacking through America ...

ELISE: They couldn't understand why you'd do that. Lola was ready to send you on a first class tour! They held a devotion to St. Jude for you – throughout your whole trip – did you know that? They were afraid you'd get lost. Or worse!

CELIA: So that's why nothing very exciting happened to me.

ELISE: (Picking up another card, reading.) "I'm getting married tomorrow –"

CELIA: (Taking it from her.) Let me see that ... (Reads it quietly, then drops it among the others.)

ELISE: Oh, what trouble that was! When we got the letter, you'd been married two weeks! Brazen!

CELIA: I had my reasons. Tia Rosa would have arrived in a minute and dragged us to church.

ELISE: Well, you know they never considered you married. Living in sin, yes.

CELIA: Almost sounds exotic.

ELISE: That's really why Lola moved the reunion to May. She thought Mark was coming with you. She was planning to marry you here.

CELIA: Oh, Jesus. (She starts to laugh.) Mark will never know what he missed.

ELISE: Pagan. That's how they call it.

CELIA: Not quite. The judge who married us was from Iowa and had come to New York to be a Zen Buddhist.

ELISE: (Gathering the letters in her hand and putting them away.) And I have treasured these years. When things get difficult, I'd take them out and read then to myself, over and over. Someday I too will take flight … And when I do, I will dance forever! (Pause.) Look at me. I can't even take a step without falling. But you'll help me, wont you? You're the only friend I've got , Ate. My other friends aren't here.

(CELIA keeps silence.)

ELISE: You must meet some of them when we're in Banawe. They're holding a healing dance next month. Come with me so you can witness it.

CELIA: A healing dance?

ELISE: In Banawe before a marriage can be accepted by the tribe, the man and the women have to live together. In a year's time, if she is with a child, then marriage rites are performed.

CELIA: And if the woman is not with child?

ELISE: Then they dance that she may be healed.

CELIA: And if it doesn't work?

ELISE: To the Ifugaos, that is the worst fate that can befall a woman. There is nothing to do. One simply lives with it.

CELIA: And if the woman chooses not to have a child?

ELISE: It is unheard of. As in most primitive cultures, fertility is a sign of grace.

(A long pause.)

CELIA: There's something to be said for contemporary culture. (Pause.) We have to go. Lola needs her soothing.

ELISE: (Taking CELIA's hand.) Ate, I'm so glad you're home. (Pause.) The right thing. What is it for you?

CELIA: That which makes you happy.

ELISE: I knew you'd say that! (Addressing someone overhead, offstage.) May we take it from the top?

> (A few beats and then music spills into the space. Slowly, tentatively ELISE begins to dance. Then both she and the music gather momentum, passion, power. The music rises to a peak. Then offstage, commotion. Shouts. It is PONCE. He comes into the light, walks into Center stage, waving his arms.)

PONCE: Stop! Stop! (The music fades out. To ELISE and CELIA.) Lola wants you home. Now.

FADEOUT

Act Two

Scene Two

(Livingroom. Same evening. The family is watching television.)

LEON: She's still our daughter, remember that.

ROSA: Then ask her to act like one.

LEON: Can't you see she's trying. She promised she'll quit after this semester.

ROSA: She told us that last year.

LEON: So some things take time. So we take it day by day. We wait.

ROSA: Wait for what? Maybe one day, she'll just leave and go. We never know, do we?

LEON: No, we don't.

ROSA: And if she does run away, what are you going to do about it/

LEON: What can we do about it? (Desperate.) There's nothing we can do.

ROSA: What do you mean by that, Leon? (To LAURA.) What does he mean, Laura?

LAURA: Ma! I'm watching TV!

LEON: Enough! I warn you. When the girls come, no hysterics!

LAURA: (Adjusting the volume. Loud disco music.) I can't hear anything.

> (The door opens. ELISE and CELIA come in. ELISE goes over to LEON and kisses his hand. She moves over to ROSA who pulls her hand away. ELISE stands awkwardly for a moment.)

LEON: You must be hungry. Laura, ask Ponce to set the table for Elise.

ELISE: I already ate, Pa.

LEON: (Trying to dissipate the tension.) Did you hear? Your Nang Senyang is coming, too! And Marilyn is bringing the twins!

ELISE: Lola told me this morning, Pa. And is Tia Nena really naming the baby after me?

LAURA: That's because she doesn't know any better!

CELIA: (Pulling her down next to her on the couch.) Laura, what's on TV?

LAURA: It's Disco Fever. Look. The Filipino version of the Village people.

ROSA: (To ELISE.) Don't keep your Lola waiting.

> (ELISE leaves.)

> (A few moments, later, ELISE is seen coming into LOLA's bedroom. She gives LOLA a kiss and wordlessly, as in a ritual among countless rituals in this house, ELISE takes LOLA's hair down. The mass

of silver spills down her back. ELISE starts to comb it; no word is spoken, and the rhythm is lyrical and gentle. This scene is played as the rest of the family sit before the TV set downstairs. Downstairs PONCE enters, sans spectacles, bringing a tray of glasses, snacks, etc. NENE comes in with him, kissing everybody's hands.)

ROSA: (Kissing her.) So how was the Flores, Nene?

LAURA: Come, Nene. It's your favorite group, see? (Showing her some dance steps.) Show mama what I taught you yesterday.

(NENE shows some disco steps. ROSA and LEON join in.)

LEON: Celia, do the honors.

(CELIA pours the drinks.)

ROSA: (Taking a sip.) Are you sure this is all right?

LEON: I asked permission. The old girl bends a little during special occasions!

ROSA: What "old girl?"

CELIA: Cheers!

(They all take their glasses and take cautious sips.)

LAURA: Yuck. (Puts it aside.) Where's the coke? (Turning towards the door.) Ponce!

PONCE: What now?

LEON: Never mind, Ponce. (To LAURA.) Laura, behave yourself! (To ROSA.) The longer she stays here the more spoiled she becomes.

ROSA: Laura, that's enough. Ponce, stay and watch TV with us.

PONCE: (Beaming.) Thank you, Manang.

> (PONCE sits in front of the set and puts on his spectacles. LAURA and NENE continue dancing. PONCE watches and then finally rises to the occasion does some rather intricate steps.)

CELIA: I should take this guy home with me.

ROSA: He's never around Friday evenings. He's always going to the disco!

> (Upstairs, the soothing continues.)

LOLA: Your hands are trembling, Elise.

ELISE: It's the excitement, Lola. It's so good to see Ate Celia home.

LOLA: You have talked with her? Keep your hands on my brow, child. There … that feels good. And what did you talk about?

ELISE: Letters. We talked about her old letters.

LOLA: And you enjoyed yourselves?

ELISE: Yes. She's always been my favorite cousin.

LOLA: She looks a little thin. Rather pale, don't you think.

ELISE: I didn't notice.

LOLA: It may be that she has changed. She may have forgotten many things. This is to be expected, of course. Ten years is a long time.

ELISE: Yes, it is, Lola.

LOLA: I trust you will make this reunion pleasant, Elise? (Pause.) For all of us?

ELISE: One last dance. For Celia. That's all I ask.

LOLA: And after that?

ELISE: Then after that, the right thing. I will do the right thing. (She turns away, fighting hard not to cry.)

LOLA: (Gently, very gently.) And what is that, Elise?

ELISE: The right thing never hurts someone else.

LOLA: (Noticing the struggle.) Stay awhile longer, child. Come.

> (ELISE yields to the moment of silence and LOLA'S small dark hands. She lays her head on LOLA'S lap. LOLA runs her fingers through ELISE's hair.)

LOLA: We've all been busy these past few days. You and I haven't had a chance to be quiet together...

> (Lights comes through the window, its silver sheen streaming into the room, curving their sharp –edged figures from out of the evening shadows. Downstairs in the living room.)

ROSA: Uy, it's eight o' clock.

(There's a collective groan.)

LAURA: Five more minutes, Ma!

ROSE: Don't be silly. (To LEON.) Remember. You have a long day tomorrow. The bidding starts at nine, you know.

LEON: Why don't I just tape these prayers? And all you have to do, Laura, is turn on every night.

PONCE: What a good idea, Manong!

ROSA: Don't be foolish

(They file out of the room except CELIA and LAURA.)

LAURA: Are you coming, Ate?

CELIA: No.

(LAURA exits. The family is seen in a few moments going into LOLA's bedroom. They all kneel. Downstairs, CELIA walks back to her seat. She is finally an irrevocably alone. She turns off the set and slumps on the seat. She stares at the empty screen for a while. Then gently, faintly at first, strains of guitar music can be heard from the distance. CELIA looks up, catching the sound. She runs to the window. As of old, she leans out, listening, her body taut; the music falls softly, slowly, plaintive and pure, then cascading into full sorrow directly beneath the window, it reaches its peak as the sound of the family prayer comes up, mingling with the evening.)

Dios te salve Maria
Llena eres de gracia
El senor es contigo
Bendita tu eres
Entre todas las mujeres
Bendito es el fruto
De tu vientre Jesus.
Santa Maria…

FADEOUT

Act Three

Scene One

(A week later. ROSA and LAURA are knocking on CELIA's bedroom door, both in a nervous state of excitement.)

CELIA: (Offstage.) Who? What is it?

ROSA: Elise, where is she?

CELIA: What happened?

LAURA: She's gone, Ate Celia! Lola's got the note!

CELIA: What? Hold on a minute.

ROSA: You know anything about this? Her bed hasn't been slept in!

CELIA: (Coming out of the room, in the process of getting dressed in a hurry.) You don't say rise and shine around here, do you? What are you talking about?

ROSA: She's gone! What did she say last night? (To LAURA.) Call up Leon and ask him to come over immediately. And tell Ponce to get the car ready. Maybe she's still in the university. Quick!

> (LAURA leaves in a hurry. ROSA is
> wringing her hands, pacing the floor,
> throwing accusing glances at CELIA)

ROSA: I worry about your Lola. All this confusion is taking its toll on her. Last night, all she did was stay in her room.

CELIA: In the States, we call it "laying the guilt trip." Remember it well. It's very handy around here.

ROSA: (Angrily.) That's enough of this talk! What is the matter with you, Celia? Didn't she ask you not to get involved?

(CELIA remains silent.)

ROSA: Lola will soon be asking for you. What will you tell her?

CELIA: That I saw her dance last night, and she was beautiful.

> (Lights dim in LOLA's bedroom. She
> stands framed against the window.)

ROSA: It had all been settled. Before you came.

CELIA: You never asked Elise about it.

ROSA: She was asked to give it up. And she was going to.

CELIA: (Desperately.) Why, Tia? Don't you think Elise has the right to her own decisions?

ROSA: Is that all you've learned living in that country?

CELIA: (Defiantly.) It's enough.

ROSA: This pagan isn't one of us. Can't you understand this simple fact?

CELIA: You're not marrying him, she is.

ROSA: Well, we don't see it that way.

CELIA: You mean the "old girl" doesn't see it that way.

ROSA: (Grabbing her arm.) I've had enough of this impertinence! Show some respect! She raised you, Celia.

CELIA: And don't I know it!

ROSA: Ten years in America and what have they done to you? How can you forget so much so soon. We can't talk to you anymore. It's you're on your own all the time now. And if that's true, why have you come home, Celia?

> (There is a knock on the door. PONCE comes in agitated.)

PONCE: Inday Celia, Lola wants to see you now.

> (ROSA nods and gestures for him to leave. He exits.)

CELIA: For this. Goddamit, I should have done this a long time ago.

ROSA: Before you go, remember. When everybody needed her, she was always there. She still is. I don't care what you've learned or what you've seen in the States, but if you don't know what it takes to be able to hold a family together like she does, then you haven't learned much.

CELIA: Oh, yes, I have.

ROSA: What? What?

> (CELIA leaves Full lights on LOLA's bedroom. CELIA comes in. LOLA's fragile figure is framed against the morning light.

But today, we see the side that glints with a
hard, cold edge.)

LOLA: What do you know about this? (Handing CELIA a note.)

CELIA: We came home together last night. She came up here to
her room, and I went down to mine.

LOLA: What did she say to you?

CELIA: She was quiet the whole evening…after the dance.

LOLA: And you were of course telling her how magnificent she
was?

CELIA: She was! You should have been there. You would have
been proud of her.

LOLA: And you think I'm not?

CELIA: Nobody seems to be, at least from what I've seen and
heard around here…

LOLA: And you, as always, think you're the only one who can
feel these things?

CELIA: I wouldn't be so presumptuous.

LOLA: (Snaps her fingers.) Then you will find her for me.

CELIA: What?

LOLA: Find her for me.

CELIA: Why can't you leave her alone now? It seems she's made a decision.

LOLA: Has she made a decision?

CELIA: Well, she's gone, isn't she? Isn't this what the note is saying? (Reading it.) "I know that you will forgive me someday..."

LOLA: I've read it. You don't need to read it again. (Pause.) Find her for me.

CELIA: Why me? Why don't you send Ponce? He's man enough for the job. He can give her a blow on the head and carry her home.

LOLA: No. Not to bring her the choice. Isn't this one of your American lessons? I know you have been teaching it well.

CELIA: I don't know what you mean.

LOLA: You promised not to get involved.

CELIA: I tried not to!

LOLA: Well then?

CELIA: But I was wrong. It's my business, too. Unfinished business. Yours and mine.

LOLA: I warn you. You better be ready to finish it.

CELIA: I have been ready for a long time. I look at Elise and she reminds me of what it was like.

LOLA: And what was it like?

CELIA: I couldn't breathe! It suffocated me. This air is unhealthy, Lola. It can kill a soul. It almost killed mine.

LOLA: I never denied you anything reasonable. I've always been fair or have you forgotten this, too?

CELIA: When why can't you let Elise go?

LOLA: I have my reasons.

CELIA: Because he's a pagan, is that it?

LOLA: No. That was never my reason.

CELIA: (Taken aback.) No?

LOLA: Everybody has her own. Rosa has hers. Laura, too.

CELIA: And what's yours?

LOLA: In this house, one doesn't ask such things. One merely trusts that I am right.

CELIA: Lola, you're not God!

LOLA: Celia!

CELIA: And I suppose you still think you were right about my father, too.

LOLA: You still blame me for what happened to him?

CELIA: Yes, you. All those years. Taking care of business…One after another…

LOLA: And you were the only one who saw what he really was, that's what you thought, wasn't it?

CELIA: Family obligations…isn't that what they're called? Duties? Roles to play—

LOLA: You know nothing of these matters…

CELIA: But I remember everything. He taught at the University. He used to take me to class and I would sit in the back with the rest of his students. I still hear the sound of that voice, and the words—many words—like a singing… then what did you do? You asked him to come and take over a business?

LOLA: Your father had to take over.

CELIA: And when my father died, who took over? Don't do that. It won't work anymore. I spent ten years of my life trying to forget those sad eyes and those soft words. It won't work anymore.

LOLA: And what good came out of all that forgetting?

CELIA: I have my own life.

LOLA: And this country you have escaped to where you can live your life. What has it taught you?

CELIA: That Elise has the right to choose.

LOLA: And you consider your life a good example? Ten years ago, you came asking to be let go. You said you wanted to find yourself.

CELIA: (Faintly. Softly.) I came to you to ask about Elise, not to talk about myself.

LOLA: I thought you said this was your business! Unfinished business! Well then let's finish it now. But first let's begin with you.

CELIA: (Takes a step backward) I don't have anything to do with it.

LOLA: Let me be the judge of that.

CELIA: What are you talking about?

LOLA: Have you forgotten? I can still spot a lie no matter how well you hide it.

CELIA: I have nothing to hide!

LOLA: Ten years you have no need of us. Why now?

CELIA: I wanted to come home for a visit.

LOLA: I've seen your need to kiss my hand, and yet you pretend otherwise.

CELIA: That's not true!

LOLA: (Taking the garlands from the icon.) And May was your favorite month. Once you crowned yourself with flowers. Since you came, you haven't touched them once. You don't pray anymore, why not?

CELIA: Flores de Mayo is only for children.

LOLA: A child's faith grows up with her. If it's lost, it isn't lost over nothing. (She flings the garland at her.) How did you lose yourself, Celia?

CELIA: I have nothing to tell you. Nothing!

LOLA: (Flinging her another garland.) Then why do you feel unworthy?

CELIA: I don't feel unworthy.

LOLA: (Fiercely.) Liar!

CELIA: No!

LOLA: (Flinging the rest of the garlands on her. Celia covers her face with her hands.) Liar, liar, liar! And you want me to let

Elise go? There was only one child I let go and that was you. And look at you! (She holds Celia's face up to her in a vise.) Ten years later, you come back to me with an empty womb and a story of a man who can't love you more than he loves himself.

CELIA: But no one has the right to ask that of the other!

LOLA: But he does. Mark does. And you give it. This white man who peered into father's eyes and saw his death. But he can't see it all. How can he? He doesn't know what it meant for your father to give up something of himself for us. For you. You, above all. He loved you more than life itself. That's why he chose the life he lived. How can Mark than see it all?

CELIA: Stop it! Don't go anymore...please. Stop it!

LOLA: (In pursuit.) Why have you come, Celia? What is it you want from me you can't give yourself?

CELIA: Lola, please!

LOLA: Are you in a state of grace?

CELIA: Don't ask me anymore...

LOLA: When was your last confession?

CELIA: Don't ask me anymore!

LOLA: When was your last confession?

CELIA: I don't remember.

LOLA: You have sinned.

CELIA: I have.

LOLA: What sins are these?

CELIA: Pride.

LOLA: What else?

CELIA: Disobedience.

LOLA: Go on.

CELIA: I was pregnant.

LOLA: And then.

CELIA: He said if I had the baby he would leave me.

LOLA: And so.

CELIA: I had to choose.

LOLA: And whom did you choose?

CELIA: Mark. I chose Mark.

> (LOLA's shock is quiet and slow. Then
> gently, she leads CELIA by the hand. LOLA

sits on the chair, and as of old, CELIA lays
her head on LOLA's lap. She is weeping.)

CELIA: They said I woke up weeping, calling your name, asking for your forgivness. Forgive me, Lola.

LOLA: Oh, Celia, my poor child. You don't need my forgiveness. I have never stopped loving you. I have always prayed for you...without fail.

CELIA: Mark and I...I've left him, Lola.

LOLA: Celia...oh my child...you poor child.

CELIA: A mistake. I made a mistake.

LOLA: (Kissing her, holding her close.) It's all right now. Celia. It's all right. (Raising CELIA's face up to her, gently.) Do you see now why I can't let Elise go? I did it once with you and all these years I know it's caused you pain. I put it there.

CELIA: No, I put it there.

LOLA: (Rising from the chair.) Tell her is she doesn't come back, I won't forgive her. Finish the business now, Celia.

(CELIA leaves. LOLA is left alone. She
kneels before the alter and covers her face
with her hands. Lights go up in the living
room, Dr. LEON, LAURA and ROSA are
gathered together. ROSA is dialing the

telephone. LAURA is standing next to her.
Leon is pacing the floor.)

LAURA: That's the last one, Ma. I can't think of anyone else who'd know.

ROSA:

How about that Helene Monteverde? Wasn't she in her dance troupe last semester? (Slams the phone down)

LAURA: I don't know her number, Ma. It's no use. You know where she's gone to.

ROSA: (Picking up the phone again.) I'm calling Police Chief Estrada.

(Leon runs to her side and grabs the telephone and slams it down.)

LEON: No you're not!

ROSA: Then go fetch her yourself!

LAURA: (Whimpering.) Oh please don't fight. Please, please.

(CELIA comes in.)

LEON: And what does Lola have to say?

CELIA: Lola says if she doesn't come back, she won't be forgiven.

LAURA: Big deal! As if Elise gives a damn!

LEON: (To Laura) Laura!

ROSA: What are we going to do? (To LEON.) What are you standing there for? Do something!

LEON: There's nothing I can do! It's Elise's life, after all, not ours.

ROSA: How can you say that? Your own daughter. Don't you care what happens to her?

LEON: I care for her. I love her. But she's old enough to take care of herself. Why don't you leave her alone now?

ROSA: You've gone mad yourself!

LEON: Shut up!

ROSA: (Furiously.) Don't tell me what to do!

> (LEON pushes her away, violently. ROSA staggers back, in shock. LAURA watches in horror; CELIA rushes to ROSA who is sobbing now. A silence descends on all of them, except for ROSA's muffled crying.)

> (Upstairs LOLA is seen rising to her feet, then lighting the candles in the altar. Then

she walks out of the room. A few minutes later, she walks into the livingroom.)

LOLA: (Very gently.) Laura, take your mother home.

LAURA: (Leading ROSA by the hand.) Yes, Lola. Come along, Ma.

LOLA: (To ROSA.) Don't worry. Leon and I will take care of it.

(LAURA, ROSA and CELIA exit.)

LEON: How?

LOLA: (To LEON.) Cancel all arrangements for the reunion.

LEON: Lola, don't be so rash.

LOLA: You are as much to blame for this.

LEON: I love her as much as you do.

LOLA: Your love makes you weak.

LEON: I'm not weak. It's you who can't give in.

LOLA: Oh, but I have!

LEON: I have never seen it.

LOLA: Because you don't understand anything.

LEON: I do. I just can't live by your rules.

LOLA: I have no sons, Leon. And I'm not counting on living forever. Someday this family will need you more than they do now.

LEON: I do my best.

LOLA: It's not good enough.

LEON: Lola, things aren't as simple as they used to be, don't you understand that?

LOLA: They never were, Leon. That's why I do the things I must.

(CELIA comes back in.)

LOLA: Celia, pack the children's things now.

CELIA: What?

LOLA: (To LEON.) Leon, for as long as Elise is in disgrace, you and the rest of the family cannot come into this house again. (To CELIA.) Tell Elise that. And make her choose.

LEON: Oh, no, Lola...don't do this to her...

LOLA: This is the only way.

LEON: There must be another! The poor girl... poor Elise...

CELIA: Lola, do you know her well enough to take this gamble?

LOLA: Elise must know her life is inextricably linked with others and what she does affects all of us.

CELIA: But she may not come back.

LOLA: You don't know her as well as I do.

LEON: (To CELIA.) Tell her for me. Whatever she does, she is forgiven.

LOLA: And tell her for me, if she stays where she is, her family will share the burden of that choice.

LEON: We'll manage! All I want is for her to be happy.

(LOLA turns her back.)

LOLA: So be it.

(LOLA turns to go.)

CELIA: Lola, you don't really mean it, do you?

LOLA: If you have to ask, then you don't know me as well as you think.

(She exits)

CELIA: She doesn't mean it, Tio.

LEON: Poor Elise...find out if she looks well...they say it'd cold up there nights...bring her some warm clothes...it's a long journey, Celia...take care...

(CELIA gives him one last look and then leaves, leaving LEON, as lights)

FADEOUT

Act Three

Scene Two

(A clearing in Banawe. The stage is empty. Celebratory sounds of tribal music are heard, chanting, much laughter

CELIA emerges DR in jeans and sneakers and a sweat shirt. She looks tired. She sits on the ground, UL.

Elise appears from DR also, dressed in the native garb we saw in Scene 2 of Act I. carrying the native basket.)

ELISE: CELIA, are you alright?

CELIA: I thought I'd take a break. I'm exhausted. (Pause.) That's an impressive display. I only wish I understood it.

ELISE: Even I don't understand all of it myself. But they hold a caniao every time they need to. A wedding, or if someone's sick, or during a harvest. The first time Awiyao brought me here, they held one for a young man who was sick from love. They were asking the gods to relieve him of his suffering.

CELIA: Should come in handy someday. What's the occasion now.

ELISE: They're blessing a new rice terrace. Look, you see that old priest, next to Awiyao. The mumbaki. He does the offering.

CELIA: And this god they—you pray to. What's his name?

ELISE: Kabunian. He once destroyed the world because he wasn't pleased with it.

CELIA: Sounds familiar.

ELISE: He's not one of my favorites. (Seizing her hand.) Ate. I'm so glad you made it! Today of all days! It's fate. You see, tonight I am to be initiated into their tribe.

CELIA: So soon? Can't it wait?

ELISE: It's the full moon. The mumbaki says it's the best time. Stay awhile longer. I have so much to tell you.

CELIA: I have so much to tell you, too.

ELISE: What is it?

CELIA: It's everything you said it was. Though getting here was no joke. Ponce's never flown before. He asked me if it could leave him in Manila.

ELISE: The poor man...so what did you do?

CELIA: I told him it was the bus from there on. The problem was I didn't know it would take a whole day.

ELISE: It is treacherous.

CELIA: We took this one- lane dirt road going both ways at once.

ELISE: There's a foot trail a few kilometers from here. Did you take it? It's very beautiful.

CELIA: I was told. But the guide took one look at us and laughed. Said we'd never make it. Actually it's not bad if you don't look down.

ELISE: But you should! Look! The whole world carved into terraces...and every single one of them fashioned by hand. Think of it. As you go up one terrace to the next, you step over a century of time. (Pointing to one direction.) Over there is the point where fire, earth and water merge. It is considered the spot where God lives. Ate, I will be married there someday.

CELIA: A marriage made in heaven. (Pause.) Do you intend to live up here?

ELISE: Awiyao and I have accepted teaching positions in Lagawe. We will teach there but our lives will be rooted here. You helped me do it.

CELIA: That's what I was afraid of. Elise, I didn't reject a whole history.

ELISE: Then I am better than you? Well, so be it. And I reject the future as well.

CELIA: That is a lot, you know.

ELISE: You've seen who we are, and what we've become. Here, I've been given the chance to start from the beginning.

CELIA: And these people are so pure?

ELISE: These people are so pure.

CELIA: Are you sure about that?

ELISE: (Pause.) Ate, what is it?

CELIA: Look, I'm glad there are pizza parlors up here, okay. But you probably have more in common with that—tourist over there. Elise, you're as Ifugqo as I am.

ELISE: Oh, Ate don't disappoint me now.

CELIA: you don't know these people, not for as long as you have to go to the library to find out who they are.

ELISE: The same blood runs in my veins.

CELIA: Mixed in with a lot of others.

ELISE: You forgot the other reason. I'm in love with Awiyao.

CELIA: Are you really? Or do you love what he represents?

ELISE: What's happened to you? What have you come here for?

CELIA: Elise, Lola wants you to come home.

ELISE: The first time you came for me, you said the same thing, too, but you ended up speaking for yourself.

CELIA: I was confused.

ELISE: I see. And Lola has made you see things more clearly.

CELIA: Yes.

ELISE: And what did she say?

CELIA: She insists that you come home. Or she won't forgive you.

ELISE: But I expected that. (Gently, with sadness.) My father? What does he want?

CELIA: He wants you to be happy.

ELISE: I've always known that, too. And you?

CELIA: I'm not here for that.

ELISE: For what then?

CELIA: I feel responsible for your being here.

ELISE: Don't give yourself too much credit. It's still my own choice.

CELIA: Well then I'm here to make sure you understand every choice has a price.

ELISE: I am willing to pay it.

CELIA: Do you know what it is?

ELISE: I know that no matter how they feel bad for me now, they will forgive me someday. Even Lola. I can wait.

CELIA: It's true I went to live in a country that would not remind me of this one. I chose a country that gave me what I wanted. Room.

ELISE: (Taking out CELIA's letters from the basket.) A city with options. I know them by heart. I've kept them here and read them to myself. I was going to give them back to you. Today.

CELIA: (Snatching a couple.) Destroy them! I lied to you, Elise. I left out a couple of things I should have told you from the very beginning.

ELISE: This isn't necessary. I've already decided.

CELIA: It's not a choice if you haven't heard this side of it.

ELISE: And what is that?

CELIA: Sometimes you get what you want and it doesn't work! I said I wanted room. Well, I had so much of it there came a time I couldn't tell if my life was just empty. And choices…I did have them. The whole world was built on them, except no one was there to tell me how to make the right ones…how do you keep the past from your life…forget all the lessons it taught. The doubts came later; I was so confused. Maybe it is true. Maybe when one breaks free, one is punished for it. I'm a child of this country. I can't run away from it no matter how much I want to and pretend to be another's. I can't borrow a culture. I'm either raised in it or it isn't mine. And this is why you will remain a stranger to these people. Even to Awiyao. This is why there may come a time when he will hurt you deeply.

ELISE: But if I do go back, what will I get out of it?

CELIA: Safety. You would be safe!

ELISE: But I don't want a safe life. I want a memorable one!

(Offstage: Aguinaya! Aguinaya!)

ELISE: (Looking towards the sound.) They're calling for me. I'm happy, Ate. Tell them that. (Relieved.) And so this is why you're telling me these things. You're afraid for me. You think I'm not willing to take the risk. But I am. And I can do it, Ate. I'm not afraid.

(Offstage: Aguinaya! Aguinaya!)

ELISE: It's a long ritual. I will last the whole night. Aguinaya...that's the name I will be given...

CELIA: Then do it. Go ahead...do it. Maybe you're braver than I. I had it once, too. There was something to that, too. There was a time nothing could hold me back.

(Offstage, persistent now: Aguinaya! Aguinaya!)

ELISE: I have to go (Taking out a small tapestry from the basket.) When you see Tina Nena, give this to the baby. She's been named after me. (Taking out a bracelet.) Mama loves beads. Look. Woven into the fabric, not on it. And this is horsehair...for Laura and Nene. For good luck. (Giving her the basket.) Take it...

CELIA: Don't look back.

ELISE: What?

CELIA: I said you go on from here, and you don't look back.

ELISE: What does that mean?

CELIA: Elise, you're on your own.

ELISE: I know that.

CELIA: Do you?

ELISE: Ate, what happened?

CELIA: Elise, Lola has cancelled the reunion.

ELISE: (Pause.) Why?

CELIA: I'm sure they'll have one next year.

ELISE: When Tio Dado was sick, they held it. When Ate Norma left with that man, they held it. It's not because of me, is it?

CELIA: And what if it is?

ELISE: Lola wouldn't do this. (Pause.) Is Papa all right?

CELIA: Yes.

ELISE: Mama?

CELIA: Yes.

ELISE: Laura? Nene?

CELIA: What does it matter?

ELISE: What have you come to tell me, Ate?

(CELIA remains quiet.)

(Offstage: Aguinaya! Aguinaya!)

ELISE: (Seizing CELIA's hand.) Tell me! I told you I'm not afraid!

CELIA: Laura has left the house

ELISE: What?

CELIA: Your father has her away.

ELISE: Why?

CELIA: Lola has asked her to leave.

ELISE: Why?

CELIA: Lola says for as long as you're in disgrace, no one can set foot in her house either. Papa? Mama, too?

ELISE: But this has nothing to do with them!

CELIA: Precisely. So leave it alone. Go!

ELISE: What did Papa say?

CELIA: He says they'll manage.

ELISE: The whole family?

CELIA: Your father forgives you. He wants you to be happy. And they will manage. Go!

(Offstage: Aguinaya!)

ELISE: It's my decision. It's mine. I'd take the risk for me but just for me. (Panic-stricken.) Oh, god, what has she done!

CELIA: She's afraid for you.

ELISE: But I'm not. I can take it. But only for myself. Let me think... I must think... (She starts to cry.) I can't think...

CELIA: It's still up to you. Nothing you know now has to change anything. You're free.

ELISE: Free... so this is free...dear god...

CELIA: What did you think it was? Going on a trip and putting on a costume? There's a price to be paid here, and this is it.

ELISE: This was not what I meant at all!

CELIA: Don't give up so easily.

ELISE: I didn't know. Not this one. This one is different!

CELIA: Don't give it up!

> (ELISE stands center stage, but her head bowed. Offstage, the voices still come, but they are getting fainter, as if from a

distance, until they finally stop. In the silence that follows, ELISE keens, the sound piercing the silence. CELIA watches, transfixed. Then ELISE quietly and with slow grace, takes the headdress off her head. She lays it on her lap. They both wait for the pain to pass. It hangs in the air.

Then ELISE slips the headdress into the basket. She comes across the letters. She looks at them in her hand and with deliberate gesture, she starts tearing them up one by one. Nothing is heard except for the tearing of paper, cutting into the silence. CELIA comes forward, then steps backward. Then turns her back. Then unable to control herself, she rushes to ELISE, seizing them from her.)

CELIA: Don't do this!

(ELISE keeps on tearing them into pieces. CELIA snatches them from her with a cry.)

CELIA: Don't! Don't! They're mine!

ELISE: Don't ever think for once that if I go back, I do so out of weakness. It's you it's you who give up so easily.

FADEOUT

Act Three

Scene Three

(Three weeks later.

The Virgin has taken Center stage in LOLA's bedroom, complete with garlands of flowers and a robe. LOLA sits on her chair at the window, head cocked, watchful. Downstairs, on the floor are piles of clothes, an open suitcase, and various packages. CELIA is seen sorting clothes.

The sound of the Flores de Mayo procession comes up. CELIA rises, goes to the window to watch.

ROSA comes in. She sees CELIA at the window, and stands next to her. CELIA kisses her hand and ROSA kneels down, making the Sign of the Cross as the procession reaches its height. CELIA remains standing. The sound fades out as gently as it came in.)

ROSA: (Rising.) I'm so glad it's the last day of May. Flores de Mayo tires me to the bone. (Pause.) Are they ready?

CELIA: (Sorting through the clothes.) Not yet, Tia. It's quite a lot. It's almost as if she didn't take anything with her.

ROSA: (Picking up a pile of clothes.) Maybe I'll take them to the Mission. (Bursting into tears.) When Lola asked me to come and pick up her clothes, I knew. It's been three weeks. There's no hope for it now…this is it.

CELIA: She really means business. (Pause.) It's okay, Tia. You have other things working for you. Tio Leon got the contract, right?

ROSA: You don't understand. It's more than that.

CELIA: But that's good, isn't it?

ROSA: I suppose so. Well, he's been seeing all these people he never used to associate with… I suppose there's nothing wrong with that…making friends…he says it's time to make deals…you have to make deals… know the right people…maybe he's right. I don't know anymore, Celia. All I know is that Lola's always been good for us. She keeps things in place. Now who knows? The way things are… (Wandering through the room, touching familiar objects.) It's so empty. I can't believe it. We'd be having the reunion right now. Remember how Lola would light up all the room. And the garden…so many dahlias this year, have you noticed? And the music…oh, they used to play it so loud the neighbors ended up dancing, too… and the food…enough to feed a whole barrio…

CELIA: (Trying to distract her.) How long is this project going to last, Tia?

ROSA: What?

CELIA: You know, Tio Leon's contract. How long is it going to last?

ROSA: Three years. Maybe four. It takes almost a year to build a highway from here to Talisay. And that's flat land. This one starts from Camarines del sur all the way up to Lagawe. Half of that is mountainous terrain. He'll need thirty to forty men to cut through the mountains…

CELIA: Did you say Lagawe?

ROSA: They won't need a highway up there. Unless of course they build a dam.

CELIA: You're not serious.

ROSA: I'm not? Westinghouse is in the area right now. There's a rumor they want to build a nuclear power reactor. There's water up there, you know. Leon says if they decide to do it he'd want to be a part of it. Who knows…

CELIA: (Pause) The spot where God lives…poor Elise.

> (There is the sound of voices. LOLA gets
> up. She looks out the window.)

> (In the dining room, the door opens. NENE,
> dressed in white, runs towards ROSA.)

NENE: She was at the Flores, Ma! Waiting for us! Ate Elise! Ate Elise! Ma!

(LEON and LAURA are not too far behind.
PONCE appears from the kitchen area.
There is pandemonium in the household.
ELISE comes in the last. She looks tired; she
has a small overnight case with her. LOLA
appears UL. She moves DC, as ROSA,
LEON, LAURA and NENE come forward
to kiss her hand.)

LOLA: Leon, you may lead the prayer tonight.

(The whole family except ELISE file out.
The family is seen later to enter LOLA's
bedroom. Their scene is done with the least
of movement. LOLA remains hovering in
the background.) CELIA and ELISE don't
speak. ELISE opens her suitcase and starts
taking out her clothes. They come out, one
by one. Then from the suitcase, she takes
out the headdress, the tapestry and the
necklace. She gathers them into a neat pile
and very gently she carries them across the
room. ELISE offers them to CELIA.)

ELISE: Are you going back? If you are then take these with you.
In this house, there is no room for them.

CELIA: What will I do with them?

ELISE: Hang them on the wall. Make conversation. Just don't let
it be forgotten.

CELIA: Elise…

ELISE: (Touching her lightly in the face.) Don't. Don't feel sorry for me.

> (ELISE leaves the room. She comes across LOLA who offers her hand. ELISE does not kiss it. Then ELISE proceeds to exit where she will emerge in LOLA's bedroom, upper level. LOLA walks into the room.)

LOLA: Come with us and let us pray.

CELIA: All is well for you, Lola, isn't it?

LOLA: For all of us.

CELIA: And for Elise, too?

LOLA: It will pass. Elise is young. She'll go on to other things. She'll learn to forget.

CELIA: As for me it's time. I'm going back.

LOLA: I suspected as much.

CELIA: I want to go home.

LOLA: Home? This _is_ your home.

CELIA: Home is where I live, and I live in America now.

LOLA: That doesn't make it a home. You don't belong there.

CELIA: America is full of people who don't belong there. (Pause.) My life is good, Lola. My life was good.

LOLA: And what is there for you now?

CELIA: Possibilities.

LOLA: Possibilities?

CELIA: There are things out there I still need to discover.

LOLA You can always do that here.

CELIA: You don't have room. And I need room. Much more than you could ever give me.

LOLA: I will be afraid for you all over again, but we will live with our choices. Yours and mine.

CELIA: It's good for you, too, Lola. This way you're no longer responsible for me. (She bends down to kiss her hand and just before she brings it to her lips, she lets go.) This time, I'm letting you go.

> (They stare at each other for a few beats, and then LOLA turns around and leaves. She stands Down Center, her back turned. We don't see her weep. Then she exits. In awhile, she is seen going into her bedroom where the whole family rises to kneel. Both spaces remain lit.

(Downstairs, CELIA is seen placing the tapestry, the headdress, the necklace into the suitcase. She snaps it shut. Then she goes to the window to wait for the music. As usual, without fail, he comes tonight, this bringer of music passing by. Lights dim in both rooms as downstairs CELIA's figure is seen silhouetted against the evening light. She stands very still, as if trying to catch every sound, every shadow, every detail of this moment, woven out of music and nightlight and prayer and the smell of wildflower, as if knowing fully well that this moment now would never come to her again.

> Dios te salve Maria
> Llena eres de gracia
> El senor es contigo
> Bendita tu eres
> Entre todas las mujeres
> Bendito es el fruto
> De tu vientre Jesus.
> Santa Maria…

FADEOUT

END OF PLAY

AFTERWORD

ABUNDANT CHARM, A FIERCE HONESTY

By Ian Morgan

Despite having had long and interesting career, Linda Faigao-Hall has not yet, to my mind, been properly acknowledged as a truly individual and exceptional writer. My only thought about why this might be, other than the obvious vagaries of chance, is that Linda's work somehow reminds me of no one else's — which, of course, makes it difficult to classify and for others hard to accept. As you see with the plays in this volume, they are each quite different, and alone or together, they represent a distinctive mélange that you'll see nowhere else. That said, the most characteristic thing about Linda's plays are their excellence: searingly vivid characterizations, muscular writing with (as it were) a sting in its tail, and a way of weaving stories that draw us closer to the people in them.

I am especially glad to see these plays collected, because I have come to know Linda's work in the past six or seven years, and, with the exception of *God, Sex and Blue Water*, these plays are actually new to me. Rather than expound on their substantial virtues, let me say a bit about my experience of Linda's writing, coming to it late as I have. Marcy Arlin of the Immigrants Theatre Project introduced me to Linda when Marcy directed a reading of *God, Sex and Blue Water* as part of a series we co-produced for the Martin E. Segal Center at City University of New York. My reaction was something like: "Wow! What is THIS?" An exploration of Catholic mysteries from the point of view of true believers encountering the secular world? Not something you run into every day on the American stage. Add to that, the author manages to tell a haunting story with great humor, in a way that leaves it open to all kinds of receptions.

I have since worked with Linda on three plays that are not included in this volume, each as interesting as anything in here. A brief description of them will give you a sense of both her persistent themes, and of the variety of her work. Like *God, Sex and Blue Water*, the next play of hers I got to know also dealt with the awkward way that faith and rituals interact with the modern world. That play, entitled *Dying in Boulder*, is about what happens when Jane, a woman dying of cancer, asks her largely secular family to enact an elaborate Buddhist ritual around her death, including an open pyre. She's a white woman with a Filipino Catholic husband who teaches Tai Chi, and their relationship to Buddhism is complicated and is arrived at late, but is no less sincere or earnest for that. Again while there is a great deal of humor gleaned from the culture clash around the religious practices; nothing is ultimately belittled or dismissed (as "New Age," say). Rather, faced with the specificity of the rituals, each character struggles with how to make sense of the way they lead their life. Linda's play is a fascinating journey for an audience to take, because we are constantly questioning where we stand in relation to these rituals, our own rituals, and to our own culture versus partially understood ones — all of that while we watch the family in Linda's play, that is itself in between cultures, try to find its bearings.

Other threads in Linda's writing are seen in her one-act play *Sparrow*, which I directed a few years ago in New York. In this play, a Filipina woman who has lived in New York for ten years returns to the Philippines and arranges a meeting with her best friend from high school, who had promised to join her in New York but who never came, and with whom she had lost contact. When the two women meet, it turns out that the friend had fallen in with a revolutionary (or perhaps terrorist) organization, and is now herself in danger. As with *A Female Heart* in this volume, *Sparrow* centers on some of the extremes of life in the Philippines, and contrasts them baldly with constraints of life in urban America. It's taut storytelling with a horrifying background, and yet the basis for it is decidedly emotional: it's about relationships and lives torn apart by distance and political commitment. *A Female Heart* has the same heartbreaking quality to it, as it reveals in a rhythmic array of scenes and brief communications (it's got quite an original structure) how the best of intentions by all concerned have led to the total betrayal of the lives of this family. As with the treatment of terrorism in *Sparrow*, *A Female Heart* zeroes in on the personal — the effects on the hearts of individuals — as it deals with topics like mail-order marriages and unequal treatment of AIDS. And the characters are always totally individual.

Lastly I'll mention a new play, *Lay of the Land*, which is perhaps very much in the vein of *Woman from the Other Side of the World*. Both works present seriocomic slices-of-life set in New York. In *Lay of the Land*, a young Filipina woman, not long since arrived in the U.S., tries to rent an apartment in the East Village from an American gallery owner. It's 1986, and the moment is charged in two ways: it's when the bubble of the downtown '80s art scene is about to burst, and it's in fact the day that the Philippine dictator Ferdinand Marcos was forced out of power. The depiction of a counter-culture art scene being consumed by venture capital is pointed and funny, and again the contrast with the political horrors left behind makes these feel all the more like open wounds. This story does what many of Linda's plays do: it makes us see anew the absurdity and hypocrisy in the American way of life, and question how much we really understand about it. But it is not from a place of aloof criticism; her characters accept that there is much to value, or even envy, in Western culture, and often find themselves choosing life in America or the Philippines. However, they are left with the pain that comes from being unsure of what the choice means. Even in its somewhat comic mode, we see that pain in both *Woman from the Other Side of the World* and in her earlier play *State Without Grace*, both family plays in which the family is in a state of confusion about their place in the world.

It's interesting to note, actually, that Linda has a real way with family plays; in fact, all of the plays in this volume would qualify. I think this is because she is, like the best dramatists, always interested in seeing a subject both close in, and from many sides. Families, with their built-in conflicts and complex histories, are good ways to frame her stark and original observations, and they allow her to get right to the heart of the matter. There is an echo of what the South African playwright Athol Fugard does in his own pointed family plays, as well; Fugard, like Linda, is interested in unusual family configurations, often ones created by the pressures of cultures in conflict. And Linda, like Fugard, is an artist who wants to talk in a big way about the world, but through how people actually lead their lives. In addition to abundant charm, a fierce honesty is evident on every page of Linda's work. Is there any better quality when it comes to the theater?

NOTES ON CONTRIBUTORS

LUIS H. FRANCIA is a poet, journalist and nonfiction writer. His poetry books include *The Arctic Archipelago and Other Poems* and *Museum of Absences*. He is the author of *Memories of Overdevelopment: Reviews and Essays of Two Decades*; the editor of *Brown River, White Ocean: An Anthology of Twentieth Century Philippine Literature in English*; and co-editor, with Eric Gamalinda, of *Flippin': Filipinos on America*, and of *Vestiges of War: The Philippine-American War and the Aftermath of an Imperial Dream, 1899-1999*, with Angel Velasco Shaw. His memoir *Eye of the Fish: A Personal Archipelago* (2001) won both the 2002 PEN Center Open Book and the 2002 Asian American Writers literary awards. *The Beauty of Ghosts, poetry for the theater*, premiered in 2007. Born and raised in Manila, Francia has written for *The Village Voice*, the *Nation*, and other periodicals. He writes a monthly online column, "The Artist Abroad," for Manila's *Daily Inquirer*. He teaches Philippine-American Literature at Hunter College and Tagalog Language and Culture at New York University. He most recently wrote *A History of the Philippines: From Indios Bravos to Filipinos* (2010), published by Overlook Press.

IAN MORGAN is the Associate Artistic Director of The New Group where he has been developing and directing work since 1999 as well as running The New Group (naked) second stage series and the New Group/New Works play development program. He also supervises and directs Life Stories, the New Group ensemble for New York City high school students. For The New Group, he has directed *Critical Darling* by Barry Levey, *A Spalding Gray Matter* by Michael Brandt, and the Drama Desk-nominated *The Accomplices* by Bernard Weinraub. Recent productions also include *Progress* by Matei Visniec (Immigrants

Theatre Project at HERE); *Ham Lake* by Nat Bennett and Sam Rosen, and *The Toad Poems* by Gerald Locklin and George Carroll (both at the Soho Playhouse); *Ethnic Cleansing Day* by Brett Neveu (The Production Company at the Kraine); *Missing Time* by Michael Brandt (Breedingground at CSV); and the *24 Hour Plays* at the Lucille Lortel and the American Airlines Theatre on Broadway. He has also directed and workshopped new work at the Atlantic, Center Stage, the O'Neill, the Public, Rattlestick, New York Theater Workshop, New Dramatists, and Ensemble Studio Theatre. Ian previously worked as a director and dramaturg in Minneapolis, where he was a literary manager at The Playwrights' Center.

PLAYWRIGHT'S BIOGRAPHY

Playwright LINDA FAIGAO-HALL was born and raised in the Philippines and was already a published playwright and fiction writer there when she immigrated to the United States in the early '70's. Her late husband of 26 years was Terence G. Hall, and their son, Justin, has just completed his undergraduate degree in International Relations, History and Political Science (First Honors) at Trinity College, Dublin, Ireland. Shes divides her time between Dublin and New York City.

Faigao-Hall's most recent production was *God, Sex and Blue Water* at the Lion Theater in Theater Row 42nd Street under the aegis of Living Image Arts (LIA) in 2009. It was first given a barebones production by the distinguished Lark Play Development Center. *God, Sex and Blue Water* was the second play by Faigao-Hall produced by LIA. In 2008 LIA produced *Sparrow* as part of an evening of three-one act plays called *Coming Home* at the same Off-Broadway Lion Theater. Another one-act play, *The A –Word*, appeared in an evening of short works, *Snapshots*, in August 2007 at the Samuel Beckett Theater in Theater Row presented by Diverse City Theater Company. The play appeared in Smith and Kraus' inaugural publication of *The Best Ten-Minute Plays of 2008*, which featured a scene from Faigao-Hall's play on the book's cover.

Her full-length play, *The Female Heart*, was a sold-out hit in June 2007 at the first Asian American Theater Festival; the play originally premiered as a co-production with Ensemble Studio Theater and Diverse City Theater Company in 2005. Her play *Woman From the Other Side of the World* was produced by Asian-American Repertory Theater in San Diego, Calif.; InterAct Theater in Sacramento, Calif.; East West Players in Los Angeles; Ma-Yi Theater in New York City; and most recently (November

2009) in Al-Khobar, Saudi Arabia.

A full-length play commissioned by The Working Theater, *Walking Iron*, was the recipient of a National Endowment of the Arts award. *State Without Grace*, her first play to be produced in the United States, was presented by Pan Asian Repertory Theater in New York City and by Asian-American Theater Company in San Francisco and was followed by a Northeast college tour in Arlington, Virginia; Washington, D.C; Tufts University; Rutgers University; Syracuse University and Cornell University.

Other produced plays by Faigao-Hall include *Salad Days and Other Stories*, produced by Ma-Yi Theater Company; *Pusong Babae* (the original version of *The Female Heart*); *Duet*; and *The Interview*, all of which were developed and produced by Find Your Voice, Inc. (formerly Starfish Theatreworks Inc.) at the Clark Studio Theater at Lincoln Center Plaza. Her current full-length play, *Dying in Boulder*, was read this June 2010 at the Ensemble Studio Theater with Laila Robbins in the lead role and was directed by Ian Morgan, Artistic Associate Director of the New Group, where Faigao-Hall is currently developing her recent work-in-progress, *Lay of the Land*.

Faigao-Hall has a Master of Arts in English Literature from New York University where she continued her doctoral studies in Educational Theater. She studied Medieval Theater at Bretton Hall College, Wakefield, England. She currently teaches English at the College of New Rochelle and runs the Writing Center at Mercy College.

She remains an active supporter of the pioneering Cornelio Faigao Writer's Workshop for fiction, drama and poetry in Cebu City, Philippines, now in its 26th year, and named after her father (a poet, writer and journalist who died in 1959). The annual workshop has been instrumental in the development and subsequent renaissance of writing in Cebuano and other Visayan languages in the Philippines.

NoPassport

NoPassport is a Pan-American theatre alliance & press devoted to live, virtual and print action, advocacy and change toward the fostering of cross-cultural diversity in the arts with an emphasis on the embrace of the hemispheric spirit in US Latina/o and Latin-American theatre-making.

NoPassport Press' Dreaming the Americas Series and Theatre & Performance PlayTexts Series promotes new writing for the stage, texts on theory and practice and theatrical translations.
www.nopassport.org

Series Editors:

Randy Gener, Mead K. Hunter, Jorge Huerta, Otis Ramsey-Zoe, Stephen Squibb, Caridad Svich (founding editor)

Advisory Board:

Daniel Banks, Amparo Garcia-Crow, Maria M. Delgado, Elana Greenfield, Christina Marin, Antonio Ocampo Guzman, Sarah Cameron Sunde, Saviana Stanescu, Tamara Underiner, Patricia Ybarra